QUONSETT

QUONSETT

James F. Murphy, Jr.

Rawson Associates Publishers, Inc., New York

Library of Congress Cataloging in Publication Data

Murphy, James F.
  Quonsett.

  I. Title.
PZ4.M9784Qo 1978   [PS3563.U737]   813'.5'4
77–92074
ISBN 0–89256–050–9

*To Edward L. Hannibal, who possesses that
rare quality—loyalty, and who had more
confidence in me than I had in myself*

Acknowledgments

My thanks to William Sangster for his technical assistance and to Debra Sangster for her clerical help.

QUONSETT

Prologue

In the brooding dark of the high woods, under a canopy of aging oaks, the square, black cube of a van squatted in the cricket-sounding night. Several birds fluttered overhead and disappeared deeper into that inner world of forest and wood. Fish splashed in the deep black pools that periodically turned silver when the moon emerged from behind low-trailing clouds.

The rear door of the van opened slowly into the night and the figure of a man emerged, a boy really. He stood naked under the moon, a flashlight in his hand. He lingered for a long moment and then snapped on the flashlight, smothering the bulb's glow with his hand. He turned then, and played the soft yellow beam on the interior of the van.

There was a clinical cleanliness and sparseness about the van. It was like a room that was waiting, a room in readiness. A white smock hung neatly from a wire clothes hanger. A surgical mask was tied loosely to the hanger. Four white porcelain pans were set a few feet from each other under the long table that unfolded from the center wall panel. The table was covered with white crisp sterilized hospital paper. A long black hose attached to the faucet of the portable sink dripped laconically.

The naked boy switched on the overhead light, which sent an oval of infrared over the table. He opened a drawer to the left of the table and took out a leather case. He spread the case before him, removing the needles from their individual compartments.

Satisfied that they were clean and ready for use, he placed them back into the leather sheath. From the next drawer, he drew out four large scalpels. He checked each one methodically. They were sharp and gleaming clean—sterilized. He was ready.

One

At 1:15 A.M. on the thirtieth of June—a Tuesday—The Pequod wasn't exactly jumping. The guitars had been unplugged and the amplifiers sat hunched in the darkening room as lights winked off and the eighteen to twenty-ones picked their way out to the parking lot. "Party? Party?" A giddy voice broke out of a crowd. "Last call, your place." And the cars jerked out of the lot and squealed on to Main Street.

Urine bounced and danced off the asphalt as two older drunks stumbled and veered off, spraying the bushes that bordered the lot. One man laughed and gulped down an attack of hiccups. He aimed in the direction of The Pequod sign, which made a point of welcoming young singles, and squeezed off another round. "Da dada, dada, da, da. Gotcha, ya mother."

The cop behind the wheel watched from where he was parked in the Mobil station. He played with the idea of going over to them, but shook it off. It was early summer and he didn't have the feel of it yet. It would take a few weeks and the adrenaline would flow quieter and the momentum would give him the common sense that he needed for the job. It was like that every year Eddie began his part-time job as summer cop.

The drunks stumbled back into the all-night light of a store window while zippering their flies. They looked up and down the street and headed along the sidewalk toward town.

He felt the kid's movement beside him. Not much, but a minute sense of movement, an uneasiness.

"No sweat, Jack. They've had a couple. The Pequod doesn't water the drinks. They're ok, though. Once they get a hero sandwich in them to sop it all up, they'll be ok."

"How do you know, Eddie? I mean, I would have cuffed them for drunkenness."

The other cop had a baby face, wine-colored from the season's first sunburn. The jowls had peach fuzz and they shook when he spoke.

"It comes, kid. I'm not too steady myself, tonight. I need a little time, too. I've made some very bad busts the first of the season. Too quick. Just take your time and think before you act. Unless of course it's an emergency."

"You know, Eddie, I appreciate the opportunity. I mean, riding with you and all."

"Well, sir, I ain't exactly Columbo." And he tilted his head while gesturing with the imaginary cigar butt. "But, ya see, sir, who knows, maybe I can tell you a few things that happened to me, so you don't let them happen to you, ok, sir?"

"Ok, great." And the kid laughed and the jowls shook.

"See that porch over there?" Eddie pointed to The Pequod, which was now in complete darkness. "It really jumps around the Fourth of July. They hang over the railings, dance in the parking lot, you know—freaky. My first year, there was a brawl, and I went storming in alone—no backup. See this?" And he tapped the separation in the nose as though the nose had two distinct bones. "Always, my friend, always"—and he emphasized "always" with an extended finger—"call for a backup in a situation like that."

The jowls shook again as the angel face pivoted back and forth in disbelief.

"Broken?"

6

"Oh, very broken."

"What about the guy who threw the punch?"

"It was a deck chair, kid." And Eddie laughed. "I always had a big honk, but you should have seen it the next morning."

"Did they get the guy?"

"Not that I know of. It was a mob scene. The Pequod attracts young kids. Like gooks—they all look alike." The kid shook with laughter.

"Why do you do this, Eddie? I mean, not to get personal, but you seem to like it. Why not full time instead of summers?"

Eddie chewed on a thumbnail and then tore it off and blew it out the window. "Well, I've thought about it a lot. I passed the state cops' exam. One of the last to.

"My, wife, you know, she got scared thinking of me out on a highway at night. So instead I became a schoolteacher —in Boston." He laughed at the irony, "And sometimes it was worse than being on the highway at night. Some of those kids are goddamned tough. You, gonna teach?"

"Sort of. See, I've got this theory." And he turned full around to Eddie. "Social workers get to teach people when they're even more open to teaching. Because life is a classroom, and you really have to know how to balance your budget, how to get good housing, nutrition. Poor people miss so much of the good life . . .

"One year, on the money she saved from newspaper food coupons, my mother got us two weeks at Hampton Beach —my mother and three brothers and a sister and myself. I mean, poor people don't have to be poor. You know what I mean, Eddie?"

He became aware of his rising voice and stopped. He turned full around facing the windshield.

"Sorry, Eddie, I got a little carried away. One prof told me that I was going to be a very disenchanted social

7

worker after six months."

"Fuck him." Eddie said it—talking more to himself, "Don't let anybody talk you out of it. That theory is bulletproof."

"Thanks, Eddie, a lot. That makes me feel good. You being a teacher and all."

"Oscar Eleven, 572." The voice cut through the cruiser like a thin metallic blade.

"Oscar Eleven here."

"Oscar Eleven, a 10–31, corner of Proctor and Marine." The very broken nose sucked in some air as Eddie replaced the receiver.

"Priority call, kid. Accident with injuries. Hang on."

The car fired up, left some loose gravel, pulled on to Main and headed south.

Crossing Main and slipping on to Anchor Road, the cruiser braked on a dime as a van shot out from behind a hidden drive.

"Son of a bitch. Where'd he come from? If I didn't have this call, I'd grab that bastard."

"Vans are big these days," the kid said to the windshield.

"Yeah, big and bold. Seduction wagons, we used to call 'em. Now they're all decorated. That one looked like Niagara Falls. Remember that."

The wheel moved easily in his hands. At times he barely touched it. It had a softness to it. He ran his fingers along the rim delicately, while coaxing more out of it, but always controlling it. Never aggressive, never tightening the grip, but almost teasing along the curve of the road.

He thought of Sandy and their three-year-old daughter, Stacey. He let go of a mind flash of Sandy in tennis whites as the road jumped and humped in front of him. He was cooking now, cranking out the miles, whipping and snapping the horses.

He caught a peripheral of the kid, all bug eyes and jowls

swiveling from speedometer to windshield.

"If you're wondering, we're up to ninety."

The kid white-knuckled the vertical shotgun that sat silently between them.

The front seat, the highway, the trees, were a weird disco as the overhead bar and headlights flashed a freaked-out psychedelic pattern in a wide wig-wag of the road.

At a deep dip, the cruiser did a roller coaster and met the top of the hill in midair.

" 'Streets of San Francisco'?" Eddie yelled.

The kid gritted his teeth and almost ripped the shotgun loose.

The car leveled off as it approached the harbor.

Two Coast Guard cutters hulked like gray ghosts in the moonlight. The ferry boat parking lot was almost deserted and the cruiser's spearing lights found the Do Not Enter sign.

Eddie caught it all because he knew the territory. He banged a right on Marine, in cool control of the vehicle.

He heard the kid say casually, as though commenting on the scenery, "Oh, the drawbridge is up."

He was going sixty-five miles an hour. He jammed his foot heavily on the brakes, feeling a sudden hold and then a giving as the rear brakes deserted him and shot the car into a zigzagging spin. The drawbridge was coming up fast, looming like a black wall, the gears reaching out with steel hands. He handled the wheel roughly now, spinning it around while charging ahead into and through the low picket fence and on into the parking lot adjacent to the bridge. The sudden spin threw the car sideways, but not before its rear end banged into the pedestrian gate. It tore it loose from the cinder block and spiraled it up and over the cruiser and down onto the hood, where it lay, while the car, like a worn-out stallion, galloped and circled, bucked, bent and bowed, until the circle became smaller

9

and the night became still again.

The town was early-summer quiet. A yellow stab of light from Point Quonsett reached from harbor to sound to the offshore islands, spilling over the two figures in its arc. They sat there as though waiting for the curtain call of a bad play; waiting for the applause that never came.

"Are you ok, kid?" The perspiration dripped from Eddie's nose as he reached over to pry the kid's hands from the barrel of the shotgun. "You saved our lives, you know that, don't you? Jack? Jack?"

The easy banter was gone. The sentences were clipped and tense. No slang. No tricks. He heard his own voice. It was hollow and formal. Somewhere between the top of the hill, the circus stunts, the screeching of brakes, and the squealing pain of rubber on asphalt, the easy give-and-take of the June night was lost.

They sat there looking at the wide section of chain-link fence and wooden door of the pedestrian gate that had slammed and embedded itself into the hood of the car. They stared through the interlocking links that were propped in front of them.

Eddie shook his head and looked to the ocean. Then he smoothed out his mustache with thumb and index finger. He inhaled through the nose and blew it out in quick spurts like a weight lifter.

"My grandmother—the Irish one, not the Jewish one—used to say, 'The Lord takes care of fools and drunks.' Well, grandma, I wasn't into the sauce tonight, but I feel like one fucking fool."

They were coming out of it. Slow. But coming out. A foghorn groaned.

"My grandmother, the Jewish one, you know what she would have said?"

"No, what?"

"Now you're going to have to pay for the cruiser, already."

The kid laughed. It was more of a giggle that could have come from the back row of an eighth-grade parochial school in Lawrence or Lowell.

"You think that was bad? Our little accident? Now comes the tough part. Got to call it in."

"What will they say?"

"It's what they'll do. Might take the car away, and I've been the only summer cop on twelve to eight A.M. I'm kind of proud of that."

"What the hell, Eddie, it wasn't your fault."

"Hey, kid, I'm the senior man here. I was careless. I was too fired up getting to the accident."

He grabbed the mike and reported the accident and location in that order.

"Sorry, sergeant," he was saying as the kid opened the door and spread his supper all over the parking lot.

"I'll be right back," the kid gagged.

The backup arrived in two minutes.

"Are you ok, Eddie?" the big black cop was asking when the kid came up from the sound, saltwater fresh now.

"Yeah, Slim. Except for my ego."

"Hey, Eddie, maybe you saved somebody else's ego."

"What d'ya mean?" Eddie turned to Slim. He had been watching the kid.

"No accident corner of Proctor and Marine! Someone jimmied the door on the operations booth and put the lever down."

"Sadistic bastards!" He pounded his fist on the roof of the cruiser.

"No, just Halloween came early this year, 's all."

A second cruiser pulled into the lot. After filling out the accident forms, they switched places with the cop who delivered the cruiser and drove around the buttoned-up town.

"Who would pull a stunt like that, Eddie?" the kid was saying as they doubled back to Main Street.

"Kids, rich kids who learn all that shit in prep school.

They're here for the summer with their parents and have nothing else to do with their time. Probably figured the cop driving the cruiser would have more sense than to come barreling up to the bridge like A. J. Foyt. Sure as shit they watched the whole thing from one of those sliding-glass decks on the sound. I'll bet they'll get more mileage out of this than a Toyota truck. They'll sit around those preppy dorms and jaw off talking about the night they destroyed the Quonsett cruiser."

"What fucking meatballs."

Eddie smiled to himself. The kid was getting into it.

"This is a typical tourist town, Jack. Winter here is like most Cape Cod communities. Zippered-up and quiet. Then, the summer, and four thousand people become thirty thousand: the spoiled, rich kids. The middle-class professionals down on the beaches. The cranberry pickers and vegetable farmers over on the other side of Grand Pond. And hidden behind the oak trees and high hedges smack in the middle of town, with ocean view from the widows' walks," he added in a circus barker's high-pitched patois, "is the quiet, pasty-faced establishment who live on pea soup and saltines and send their kids to any school that has ivy growing out of its ass."

The kid loosened his tie. The cruiser was getting warm. He had closed the windows against a sudden early morning chill.

"Then you have the group rentals, either way out of town, where they are harmless, or on The Hill, where they're not so harmless. Let's get a cup of coffee." And he slapped the kid's knee.

"Sounds great." The kid straightened his tie.

It was 4:00 A.M. and they grabbed coffee and Danish in a breezy shack that teetered on gray pilings on the edge of a wharf to the north of town. The Cove, as dirty as a glass of sin, served the hottest cup of coffee on Cape Cod.

The remainder of the night was quiet except for an occasional car horn and the always present crickets.

They checked the harbor, hit the town—north, south, east, west—and then a make-sure tour of The Hill. Everything was cool at 5:00 A.M.

The Hill hunched out over the ocean like a broad shoulder. The cottages seemed to grow out of the ground. Many of them had been there as long as The Hill itself. They bore the gingerbread trademark of other days, days of elegance when summer people dressed for dinner. The women in long chiffon dresses, picture hats, and parasols, and the men sporting white flannels, boutonnieres, and Malacca walking sticks as they strolled together halfway down the hill to the Ambleside Gardens, where they took their chilled drinks on the wide veranda overlooking the sound, the merry chatter drifting along after them into the high-ceilinged dining room with the oak wainscoting a quarter way up the white plastered walls.

Now, as the cruiser approached The Hill, the sky was dawning pink, trailing white puffs of clouds on invisible strings.

"I think today will be a hot one," Eddie said.

"Yeah, that sky is really beautiful. My girl friend is coming down today. Good beach weather." He tightened his tie again.

Eddie tooled past the old Ambleside Gardens, once an elegant restaurant, now Freddie's. Over the stucco veranda was a Schlitz sign and high over the roof hung a marquee announcing: The King and His Clowns—One Week Only. On past Freddie's, along the back streets and lanes littered with beer bottles and unraked leaves, then sliding by the cracked gingerbread houses, the broken windows, some replaced by plywood, fences without pickets, tilting sun decks strewn with precarious pyramids of beer cans, a jockstrap hung over the entrance of an old house, the place name of

13

the past partially obscured—The Green Glen. They stopped to check the hundred-room guesthouse, The Loft, with its great blue disposal dumpster bursting at the seams, waiting painfully to be emptied.

The Loft was home for two hundred college students who worked the restaurants and the shops for the ten-week summer. Housed and protected by the white-bearded, barrel-bellied Ben Moffit, father confessor to the working college kids—one room, a rope for a fire escape, and a cockroach-crawling bathroom for every twelve kids.

A coed commune with its own sandwich shop, booze, pot, and paired-off accommodations if needed. For Ben Moffit, the kids would give their lives. But all he really required was payment in advance. If any kid needed bail money and could get the call through to him at his home ten miles out of town on September Island, Ben would be standing tall at the Quonsett police station slapping his wallet on the front desk. The ten-percent interest rate was worth it to the kid who had nowhere to turn at the time.

And for those college girls who experienced some lean weeks when the tips weren't coming, Ben Moffit was always there with an opportunity to earn enough money to take care of one full year of board, books, and tuition.

Ben was hardly a respected fixture of the town. He was rather a grim glimpse of Quonsett's possible future. When the old hotel came up for sale, he saw the great potential in an age of displaced youth looking for a freewheeling summer and bought it.

The first thing he did was replace the silent green rocking chairs with blaring rock that reverberated and echoed all along the old streets, sending the ancient residents into deep depression.

He sent brochures with rolling sand dunes and blue ocean to colleges across the country, and by the time the takers had found out that the brochures were less than accurate, it was Labor Day and the kids were heading back to Shakespeare, Accounting II, Tolstoy, Toynbee, and *The Theory of the Leisure Class.*

This was The Hill, now more properly termed The Hole by everyone from the police to the kids themselves. The town officials also used the term—but only in the privacy of their offices.

By 8:00 A.M. they had covered most of the thirty-four square miles that comprised the township of Quonsett.

Eddie dropped Jack Buckley off at the police station parking lot. The kid pointed to a blue 1959 Volkswagen in excellent condition. The June sun was sending flashes off the polished roof and chrome accessories.

"There it is, a real beauty, Eddie. I take very good care of her," he said as he slipped out of the cruiser. "It will be paid for this December."

It was a good first night, Eddie thought. He liked the kid. They got to know each other fast. Had to. What an opener! He decided he would not tell Sandy about the drawbridge incident. He headed home to her and Stacey.

He was dressed like hundreds of other young men who came to Quonsett every summer to work.

His hair was not long, not short, a nondescript brown that furled a bit about the ears and hung to the nape of his neck in a ragged duck's ass. His T-shirt, with the popular Adidas written in red script across the chest, hung outside his Levi's. He was wearing blue and white track shoes, and he could have been thumbing a ride in Aspen, Santa Barbara, Boca Raton, or Stowe. As it was, he was standing under the early morning sun at the edge of Quonsett where the oaks crisscross the highway in a shadowy cathedral setting, more like those spiritual little roads in northern New Hampshire than the scrub pine and brush of Cape Cod.

As he walked along the highway with his back to the traffic, he gestured phlegmatically with his right thumb. Traffic was light until a string of cars came into view. The last of the pack, a blue Volkswagen, pulled over and the driver smiled and said,

"Get in."

The thin one was guarded at first when he saw the sheriff's hat on the seat.

"Hey, that's all right. I'm not going to arrest you. 'Sides, I just got off duty." And the driver flipped the hat over his shoulder into the back seat.

The Volkswagen shifted into gear effortlessly and headed off where the road branches to the ocean.

Two

He was feeling the first twinges of summer so he decided on a leisurely drive home along the shore route. Early morning stiffness joined in all night sleeplessness, and he settled back and allowed the whitewashed houses to mesmerize him. He curved in and around the cobblestone streets, dipping into shadows and then coming into full sunshine.

Although there was an early morning calm, there was also a very optimistic tone in the air. It could be seen and felt in the freshly painted cottages, in the roses that climbed halfway up the weather-shingled guesthouses, the gleaming, spanking new sailfish and catamarans that lay like beached whales on undulating green velvet lawns.

He accepted the salt breeze with appreciation and it stirred him from his laziness. Up ahead he could see Charlie Mendoza, the local news vendor, seventy years young with bushy white hair. He was gesturing and laughing loudly to his neighbor, Billy O'Brien. O'Brien, Quonsett High's football coach, stood in his pajamas looking like a POW.

He belonged in this town. He had only been here three years. There were the four years at U. Mass. directly after Viet Nam. Then a year as a permanent sub in Boston, and the three years at Quonsett High School. Since he had worked here summers, off and on for years, he knew a lot of people. He would live and die in this town. At a time in his life when he needed some permanence against a transitory world he had found it in Quonsett, an old sea-captains' town, incorporated in 1668. A town that prospered from the sea and the China trade, then eased itself into the nineteenth-century whaling adventure and prospered even more.

Now, as Eddie drove past the marina, his head bobbed up and down with the yachts and the dinghies.

The summer, clean and fresh, lay all around him and the tone saturated him. He broke from the village and climbed to the highway, leaving the pinging sound of windy masts ringing behind. Along the shoreline, hungry gulls dipped, banked, rolled and dived in a lazy and systematic primordial precision.

Frank Patterson sat over his half-eaten, freshly baked croissant, stirring his coffee. He was still annoyed at the tardy arrival of Gino's bakery truck. "Goddamn it, when I say I want my croissants at seven thirty A.M., that's when I want them. Tell your boss that for me." His words were still ringing throughout the large house.

The two-day-old *Quonsett Log* stared up at him from the oak serving table at his knees. The headline pleased him and slowly eased him out of his grim-faced, tight-lipped anger. A faint smile replaced the tightness as he read the article. "Warm, humid air is expected and sunny skies will be the rule rather than the exception for most of the summer according to long-range weather forecasts." The smile widened. He thought of all those cars and vans and campers and motorcycles streaming over the bridge. All carrying passengers with money to spend at the beach concessions and bar rooms, the liquor stores, the malls on the rainy days, the shows and clubs, [downtown for the smart set,] and the marinas with their excursion boats and ferries to the islands. There would be violations to be checked, of course. Summer was busy for him. It was no easy task being selectman in a town whose population mushroomed

18

during the hot months. He felt a sense of freedom when he thought of the other two selectmen who would be no bother until the summer was in full swing and almost coming down the other side into late August. They were off vacationing.

He sipped at his coffee and chewed on the still hot croissant with square white teeth. He was an attractive man with curly white hair that was giving way to a slightly balding crown. The sudden baldness only over the past two years bothered him. The gray he accepted because it gave him a certain air of distinction. Many women liked white-maned men. But the baldness he regarded as a disease.

He checked his watch. It was 8:30. He walked around the main body of the house, to kill time. He paused and fondled his objects d'art. This almost always filled him with delight. He was not experiencing that delight this morning, though, as he handled the Revereware which had been commissioned by an ancestor.

The downstairs of the house was white-walled with green hanging plants. Wide glass windows and two skylights allowed the morning sun to color the room gold.

Oriental rugs casually caressed the polished oak floors. There was the quiet mark of abundant opulence in Sargent and Copley portraits and eighteenth-century highboys and lowboys. Tightly strapped teakwood trunks and pre-Revolutionary blanket chests made it a man's room.

Frank Patterson took it all in. It all pleased him. But he would be more pleased after he made the call. Having to make the call unnerved him. It was demeaning and he would make that point. This would be the first and last time this summer that he would debase himself.

It was 8:45. He would not wait any longer. He dialed the private number and a sleepy voice answered.

"Kalmir. Who is it?"

"You sleep late, don't you?"

19

"Oh, Mr. Patterson." The voice on the other end cleared itself. "How are you, sir?" Patterson could almost see the sickly smile crossing the rubbery purple lips. The smile was in the voice. So obviously phony.

"Well, I'm just fine. But I am becoming somewhat apprehensive. The summer looks good. I mean the prospects of a successfully commercial one, but I find that my flowers are late."

"Yes, I know. Simply a technicality. Getting everyone together. You know how it is."

Patterson covered the bald spot with the palm of his hand. It was a gesture that was becoming a habit, although he did not know it.

"When can I expect the florist?"

"How about today?"

"Fine. What time?"

"Four ok?"

"Four is perfect. I will make a point to be home. Please, do not disappoint me. It has been over a month."

"Rest assured, Mr. Patterson, you will be receiving the floral arrangement at four."

"Good. Oh, and one other thing. When will you be having another wet T-shirt contest? I may be in the area checking violations and I just might drop in."

"The Fourth of July weekend looks promising." The voice smiled.

"Thank you, I'll remember that. And you remember something, too. Don't put me into this situation again. There will be no next time." He placed the receiver back on the cradle.

He strode across the room. He felt much better. He did not like matters pressing on his mind like that. He had to meet them head on and solve them. He pushed open the French doors that led to a brick patio. The air was clean with a hint of salt in it. He strolled along the grass to the pond that looked landlocked from the opposite banking three hundred yards across. Yes, it was pleasant. It had been for seven generations of Pattersons and it would continue to be for his own progeny. If not his own married sons, then his grandchildren. Other than his obsession for ownership, for possessions, he was rooted in family.

He appraised his yacht, a thirty-four-foot Tartan. A sudden chill came over him. It crossed briefly over his heart and down to his elbows. Money. Money was tight lately. Tighter than usual. The thought of ever having to settle for less threw him into a mild panic and he sat on the dock and tried to regain his composure.

The selectman's post paid $18,500, but he also had all of his investments and his property. His wife was in real estate but not to any great degree. She spent most of her earnings at the club on golf or dinners, clothes, hairdressers, and booze. She was her own person and he had no quarrel with that. In fact, it suited him.

But it was his own lifestyle that was catching up to him. He had the insatiable urge to buy. To have the best collection of art, of china, of antiques, of anything he could get his hands on. If an auctioneer told him it, whatever *it* was, had been sold, he would track the buyer down and double what the selling price had been.

The selectman's job was peanuts, but it was the side adventures and deals that gave him the financial independence he lived for. Kalmir was one of his newer clients and he would make a good one.

Patterson tugged at the docking line and thought of his late afternoon bouquet.

Abruptly, he got up and turned on his heel and walked briskly to the garage. He threw up the overhead doors and revved up the Alfa-Romeo 500. He backed out onto the drive and sticked his way past his neighbors who were already tennised up for a morning on the court.

Let them play *their* games, and I'll play mine, he smiled as he waved to them and then whipped his way out onto Main Street.

He had not troubled to wake his wife because he could tell from the bumping sounds that had come from her room, that she must have been hard into the booze the night before. He could care less. It was a good arrangement, he thought. No scenes, no public demonstrations, and every once in a while she could be quite interesting in bed. It was, he liked to think, a very adult relationship.

As the thought of sex flashed by, he was just passing the newly opened Greek restaurant. He scribbled a memo on his mind pad to drop in sometime soon for dinner, and maybe something else from the firmly built owner. It would not be the first time someone came across for a favor. Liquor licenses were hard to come by these days. The obvious pun on *come* forced his head back into a roar.

The phone shook the night table and Eddie rolled over to make it stop while checking his watch.

"Yeah?"

"Eddie," the voice at the other end said, "Sergeant Boyd. Sorry, did I wake you?"

"Yeah, what can I do for you, sergeant?" He thought of the damaged cruiser and waited for the ass-chewing he knew was coming. "I was just getting up anyway," he lied. It was only 4:00 p.m. and he always slept until 6:30. That gave him his eight.

"You don't happen to know where Jack Buckley went when he got off duty this morning?"

"Where he went? No. I dropped him off at his car. Why?"

"Well, two young guys are here, and they say he didn't come home. They all room together out on the point on shore road."

22

"Maybe he picked up some bird. What the hell are they, dorm mothers? It's only four P.M."

"Yeah, well, that's what I told them. But they insisted it wasn't like him. He's too routine a guy, they said. Very responsible, and his girl friend was coming down from Boston today. She's out in the car now."

"That does seem strange. He seems like a straight kid— very kind, trusting, almost naive. I'm sorry sergeant, all I know is that I left him at eight this morning."

Sandy came into the room and sat on the bed. He pulled her over. She was wearing yellow shorts and a white halter. Her black hair was cut short, and her body glowed from sun and surf. His free hand reached for the halter clasps.

"Well, that's all I know, sergeant. Yes, sir. I'll see you when I come in."

"What was that call all about? Who did you leave at eight this morning?"

"Jack Buckley. The new kid. Never showed up at his house. His roommates reported him missing."

"Isn't that a bit premature? I mean, after all, that's only eight hours. Maybe he slept someplace else, ya know what I mean, Fast Eddie?"

"I know what you mean." His brown eyes flashed. "But this kid is different. He's very straight. Refreshing *these* days."

"You're really serious, Eddie, aren't you?"

"Yeah, I am, the more I think about it."

"Well, forget the shave. I'd better take you while I still have some of your attention." Her lower lip pouted as she straddled his long muscular body, which rose up to meet hers while she began unhooking her halter.

This night was more routine than the night before. Other than handing out two speeding citations, he patrolled north to south of town and back again. Jack Buckley still had not shown up, and Eddie feared for him. He could feel it, there was just something about that kid. He had known guys like Buckley in Nam. They were too good for this world. They were too trusting, and that had turned out to be an extravagant virtue. They didn't come back from patrols. Sometimes they would be found with their throats cut. Very close work. He knew the situation well, because it happened to him once. An old woman, bent over with rheumatism, stumbled up to him asking for food. When he put his M-16 down and reached for his pack, she straightened up and flew at him with a knife as thin as an ice pick, missing him by inches as he rolled away. He managed to kick her in the face, grab his weapon, and empty a magazine clip into her stomach. He never trusted anyone after that. No, the kid would never have come home from Nam.

"I just hope he comes home from Cape Cod," he said to the lonely stretch of highway.

Eddie was the last to arrive. He drove his own car—a neat blue Chevy Impala. He parked it halfway up the hill that led to the dunes. His heart pounded, and he felt tremendous sadness, almost an incapacitating depression that made it difficult for him to walk past the polished Volkswagen that was parked at the top of the hill. He kept hearing Sergeant Boyd's words on the phone.

"Sorry, Eddie, here I am again, but I thought you should know—" And he hesitated. "The Buckley boy—he's been found. He's dead, Eddie."

"Oh, God. How?"

"Eddie, it makes me sick to tell you. His—" And there was a tomblike silence.

"For Christ's sake, sergeant, what the hell is it?"

"His head was gone, Eddie."

Now, as he walked over the rise, he saw the group huddled around the rubber sack near the jetty. About twenty-five people were kept at a respectful distance by two full-time cops. No one was swimming, and the blue-green water lapped serenely at the shoreline.

"A perfect incision," the coroner was saying to Chief Medina. "It's fantastic. I mean, it's unbelievable. A perfect incision between the fifth and sixth cervical vertebrae, and with complete evidence that the central nervous system was severed expertly."

The coroner, a scholarly little man whose bony hands had liver spots the size of nickels, looked out at the ocean, and back at the chief, and then at each of the five cops. Eddie knew him from two fatalities, and had him as a guest speaker at the high school on career day. Now he looked directly at Eddie and nodded.

"His lower extremities are contorted, that's the worst part," the doctor continued.

"What does that mean, Dr. Laris?" Eddie was finding it difficult to speak as he pondered the rubber sack in the lifeless heap on the sand.

"It means, Eddie—" His words were clipped and emphatic. They seemed to soar over heads and lose themselves somewhere in the surf. He spoke louder. "It means he was alive until the end. The lower right extremity was in complete flexion."

"Jesus Christ, help us," one of the cops at the edge of the group whispered. It was a prayer, not a curse, and the group, knowing that, bowed their heads and studied the rubber bag.

Chief Medina broke the silence.

"Who are we looking for, doc? A madman, a sadist?" The chief was wiping the perspiration from his neck and face with a red checkered handkerchief.

"If I had to make a guess, I'd say a doctor or a med student—a goddamned good med student. This job was done with a scalpel. A scalpel!" His voice was too big for his body, and he realized it. He spoke softer. "I mean, gentlemen, that this was a slow, methodical decapitation."

An ambulance arrived, and the sack that contained the remains of the kid were lifted onto a stretcher by two older officers who shrugged off the help of two lean and tanned summer cops. They trudged through the golden sand holding the stretcher at their sides with the help of two hospital attendants who, with quiet efficiency, performed their job as though bulging rubber sacks were commonplace. They gained the top of the hill and disappeared down the other side. The only sounds were the breaking of the morning tide along the three-mile stretch of unbroken beach and the click of the ambulance door. The group broke up into smaller groups and spun off in various directions.

Eddie walked along the shore to a jetty and stepped absently onto the moss-slicked rocks out at the end. He stood staring out to sea. Waves formed, curled, and struck the jetty, throwing water against his pants. He did not seem to notice as his eyes became moist and tears spilled down his face. There was no sob, just the tears. It was all from very deep inside and he remembered his puzzle at over whom it was that Jack Buckley reminded him of. He knew now, as he stood in the swirling wash of the ocean crying for himself.

Chief Joe Medina was a realist. He was shocked and sickened by the death of one of his officers, and probably more so in some ways because the officer was only a summer cop who had not planned on much more action than breaking up a noisy party or handing out parking citations. He had never met the kid, nor seen him in the two weeks he was on the force. Maybe, he thought, he should get to know new employees better. Interview them. Instead of Boyd or Captain Swanson, his chief administrator. And the regulars, too. Play golf with them. Drink with them. But, no. That had not been the game plan. The stipulation, when he was given the job eleven years before, was simple. Be the front man. Cut the ribbons. Speak at the Little League banquets, Kiwanis, Rotary, Knights of Columbus, Masons, Boy Scouts, Cranberry Association, Order of the Rainbow, and every organization that had more than twelve members. "When there is more than one gathered in my name," the irreverent Patterson had told him, "go and speak to the bastards."

And he did. And he did this part of the job well. When a civic dam was about to burst. "No police protection." "Vandalism at the town landing." "Pot smoking on The Hill." "No Stop sign next to the Senior Citizens' Center." He was there to calm, to give succor, to pat old backs reassuringly, and to shake younger hands firmly. He never felt like a lackey or a patsy for those who hired him because he understood the nature of the job when he took it. His name helped, too. He was a token. Not to himself, but to the minority he came from, and they did not always appreciate it. His Portuguese neighbors had dignity and they did not always feel Joe Medina was the leader he could be. And should be. His job was 9:00 A.M. to 5:00 P.M., excluding dinners and speaking engagements, and he seldom wore a uniform.

The outspoken and respected Charlie Mendoza referred to Medina casually and without rancor as "our community's Uncle Tom." Joe laughed at this because he was fortunate enough to know exactly who he was and what he wasn't. PR man, yes. Super-cop, no. Save that for Boyd, who would always be just that and only that: super-cop.

But, as horrible as the kid's death was, there was the very real specter of the coming tourist season that was being thrown into bold relief. The season and the town shared center stage.

Quonsett gritted its teeth every summer, plastered on its

pancake makeup, pulled back the corners of its mouth, east and west, into wide YMCA smiles, rose from the backstage mirror, and greeted the out-of-state folks with bean-supper grins and spread hands—palms up.

Quonsett could do it with just a little effort and some ambivalence, because always up ahead, the day after Labor Day, were the lazy weekends, and blue-green water, and the miles of sandy deserted beach that lay out there in the autumn gold of Indian summer.

The chief wiped his face with a clean linen handkerchief —white this time—and folded it neatly and stuffed it into his pants pocket. He felt penned in and uncomfortable. He was wearing his summer suit because he had to speak at the Golden Age luncheon at 1:00 P.M.

He dialed town hall and asked for Frank Patterson.

He pulled the handkerchief out of his pocket again and began dabbing at his face. He looked down at his gut. It folded over his belt buckle. He made a silent promise to cut down on beer.

"Hello, Joe. What's up?"

"Frank, we've had a homicide. I thought you should know as soon as possible."

"Shit, what lousy timing. The Fourth of July coming. What are the facts? Son of a bitch."

"Frank, it's not just a killing. This is different."

"Yeah, how?"

"It was one of my boys. A summer cop."

"Jesus!"

"Yeah, that's what I said. But even worse, Frank, is the way he was killed."

"Whaddya mean?"

"Somebody cut his head off." And even though it did not seem necessary, he added, "And we can't find the head."

"Jeezuz H. Cheerist!" There was a long whistle and then

28

a pause at the other end.

Joe waited.

"Who knows? How many? Cops?"

"Well, yeah, there were people there when he was found."

"Don't say any more on the phone. Get up here right away. Ok?"

And the phone slammed in the chief's ear.

Bayside Straights was already filling up with preholiday traffic, both car and pedestrian, as the chief drove the unmarked cruiser past the smart sweater shops, antique stores, bric-a-brac, and Charlie Mendoza, who rocked leisurely at his newsstand as though the Fourth were months away instead of two days hence.

There was no telling what the kid's murder would do to the tourist business. He knew what Patterson would say. He would look Joe in the eye, and that cream-skinned face of his would twitch and he'd say, "Goddamn it, Joe, tell them you have no details yet. Just say it's under investigation. Stall until the fuckin Fourth is over."

"But the Log comes out tomorrow and sure as dogs shit on the lawn, there will be a reporter on my ass, or worse, a call from old Mr. Dean himself. What the hell can I tell Old Dean?"

"You can tell him to go fuck himself. You're running the police department. Let him bury himself in that rag of his but you run the fuckin cops. Understand?"

That is exactly how it will be, he thought as he wiped his face with his eighth handkerchief of the day. He knew that was exactly how it would be. He pulled into the assessor's parking space.

And that's how it was.

The silver head of Cyrus Standish Dean bobbed up and down from his sloping shoulders like a two-mile marker in a storm. The blue and white sneakers gave him considerable bounce, as his squat, round-bellied frame continued across Main Street past the duck-feeding pond and through the quacking groups of feathers, which scattered as he bounced along in wrinkled khaki slacks and blue buttoned-down short-sleeved shirt. He had written more than one editorial in an effort to rid the town of these leeches.

Letters poured in attacking his lack of feeling and sensitivity. Those were the obvious ones. The more sophisticated readers, and there were a few in Quonsett, attacked his prose.

But nothing fazed him as he bounced along every morning—hell, high or low water, hurricane, rain, fog, or creeping wet mist. Because he had power. The word. The word in print. No matter how imperfectly and clumsily phrased —no matter how partial to obvious factions.

And so on this morning as he rubber-balled along the sidewalk, crossing the old wooden bridge, he nodded and waved to those who would gain his favor for a wedding blurb or a club outing, a slide show, or a church bazaar.

He passed the law offices that clustered in the new professional building. Thompson and MacNichols, Jackson and Keith, O'Shea and Lane. He drew in his breath at the last. It wasn't enough they were down there on the Irish Riviera on the other side of town during the summer months. Now they were moving in year round.

When he was a boy, the Irish did not come to Quonsett. They were lucky to put two days together for a holiday, and most of them never left the back porch, where they drank away their vacations. Then something happened. Their kids started to go to Holy Cross, Boston College, Fordham, Georgetown—the Loyolas. Then because that wasn't enough, they went on to law school and medical school— doctors, dentists, and teachers with their waterfront houses and their island views and their tanned long-legged sons and daughters.

Someone once asked him years before what he liked about Cape Cod, and his curt, cracked smile reply was, "Down Cape, there ain't no Jews or snow." Christ's sake, while he was thinking Jew, the goddamned Irish moved in.

He enjoyed walking to the paper because he liked being seen and greeted by his fellow citizens. He carried his brown bag lunch and a battered clipboard on which he wrote down random editorial ideas.

The *Log* had been his mother's newspaper, left to her by Dean's father, who died of the flu in 1918. After graduating from Quonsett's Bryant High School in 1937, off he went to the University of Maine, where he majored in journalism. Four frostbitten, bone-jarring winters taught him perseverance. He worked summers and school vacations in a lumber camp and every cent he made went into his college education. His mother was back in Quonsett holding the *Log* together with second mortgages, bailing wire, and glue.

She accepted him as a college graduate when he returned, leather-skinned and raw-boned. She made him managing editor, a position he held without interruption except for World War II. As a first lieutenant at the Battle of the Bulge, he distinguished himself in combat. He never spoke of the war and most people forgot that he was ever in it. He loved capitalism, free enterprise, and the Republican party, and he was an usher at the Memorial Church. He hated welfare, malingerers, draft dodgers, and striking public employees.

His mother died in 1968, but he still carried her name on the masthead of the paper she loved.

His wife was sixty-three, the same age as he. She was a philatelist and a compulsive gardener. Their two daughters, both happily married, lived in town.

The *Log* had survived the Depression, World War II, taxes, journalism codes, and high salaries. The average salary for a reporter was $127.50, take home. His writers were not the cream of newspaper row. But writing was not the raison d'être of the paper. Advertising was. Weekly circulation was fourteen thousand, and all five employees received a twenty-five-dollar gift certificate to Nettle's Department Store each Christmas and a twelve-jar case of cranberry jelly. Cyrus Standish Dean was a man for all seasons.

The ocean was still; postcard perfect, so Mary Flanagan decided to walk to the Anchor restaurant. She could catch the sun and salt spray that she missed while working, sometimes, three shifts. But the money was good and tuition was high. She owed the burser six hundred dollars, but figured she would be ahead about a grand to begin her senior year at Simmons. She was pleased. Things were going well. She had turned the corner on her life. She was sure of that.

She stopped and breathed in the day and the salt. Turning, she noticed the tumbling cascade, and then the several small waterfalls that fell and swirled about in misty splashes on layer upon layer of rocky ledge. The water *was* very realistic, she thought, but the jungle background was a very phony green. Too heavy on the old paint. She knew vans. Her brother had one.

"Do you like it?" He stood by the panel, half leaning into the van.

"I like the waterfall," she smiled. "I don't like the green."

"It's not your favorite color?" His mouth was very sad, and that bothered her. Why so sad on a beautiful day like today?

"I'll paint it over." His mouth relaxed somewhat, barely hinting at a smile.

That's better, she reflected.

"Green's my favorite color. When you're Irish, it has to be."

Two catamarans bobbed in the quiet sea, their red sails limp.

"It's a gorgeous day, isn't it?"

"It certainly is. Too bad you have to work." And he nodded to her navy blue waitress's uniform. She filled out the blouse abundantly, and her long legs, tawny against the blue, made her a very lovely young woman. She palmed shiny black hair back from her forehead.

He did not stare at her. He appeared almost shy, and she liked that. She did not like aggressive males.

"Got to save for college."

"Where do you go?"

"Simmons. Senior year coming up."

"Like it?"

"I love it."

"What's your major? English Lit, I'll bet."

"No, Special Ed. What made you say English Lit?" She cocked her head and the black hair fell across her eyes. She brushed it back again. He lurched away from the van and straightened up. He was taller than she thought. Probably six feet. He tucked the T-shirt in so the Adidas was legible.

"Because you're out here on a lovely morning walking to work—walking to work, for God's sake! Walking to work and drinking all of this in."

He spread his arms out and enclosed the ocean, the purple-colored islands, five miles near, and the blue dome of a cloudless Cape Cod sky.

"Now who sounds like the English major?" Her laugh was throaty. She liked him, he could tell that.

"Hey, I better get going. I'll be late. Tips, you know. Those big fat tips. Oh, Wow!"

"Hey, let me drive you."

"No, I can make it. Daddy said."

"Yeah, I know what daddy said."

"Yeah, what?"

"Never take rides with strangers." He knelt on the ground before her. "Oh, please allow me to drive you. Oh, please." And he looked up into her blue eyes and broke up as he slapped the sidewalk.

"Hey, you're spaced." She hesitated, then checked her watch. "Ok, I guess you're crazy enough to be cool."

"Great." And he loped around to the other side and bowed gracefully while opening the door.

"You know, I generally don't take rides from strangers."

"Strangers?" He looked hurt. "Do I look strange?"

She laughed at how silly she sounded and climbed in.

They were all there. The girl friend standing apart from the others. The three black-haired burly brothers, the blue-eyed sister, and the sparrow of a mother, whose interlocking hands in her lap were silent prayers.

The daughter hugged the mother as the brothers stood behind the bench. Occasionally, the call for a doctor broke the hospital quiet. Boyd was finding it difficult. It was the only time he could remember ever wanting to change places with Chief Medina. For once let Medina be super-cop and he would pass out the cotton candy at the county orphanage. But, he knew, thoughts like those were a waste of time. This was the way the ball game was played. At 6:30 P.M. Medina was umpiring a Little League game and he was telling Mrs. Buckley, "He was a good kid, ma'am, we all liked him. I wish I could say something to make it all right again. I'm sorry you had to come down."

Her lips trembled and moved in silent prayers.

"We tried to tell her to stay home, sergeant, but she wanted to come and take his things back. She didn't want anyone else to touch them."

"We would have taken care of things."

"She wanted to be with him on the ride home," the pretty blue-eyed sister said, and then she broke down. One

34

of the brothers went to her immediately and knelt beside the bench. His thick arms enfolded her and she wept into his neck.

They're close, Boyd thought. Very close. They'll make it. He wished he had brothers and sisters. They could be such a comfort. He thanked God for his wife and the boys. The thought of them home alone frightened him. What if this fucker is after cops or their families? He wanted to move. To ease his way to the door. To be out of there. To be home with his family. Instead he said simply, "We will do anything we can to make things—well—you know—anything."

Dr. Laris came out of a room down the corridor and motioned to him.

Boyd's jump boots resounded off the polished tiles.

"Wayne, the autopsy confirms all I told you on the beach."

"Anything new?" He was twisting the sheriff's hat in his hands.

"Yes, he had been shot with a large dose of Sodium Pentothal. Must have knocked him out almost immediately."

"But you said he was conscious."

"Yes. I know. The shock to his system could have jolted him to consciousness, maybe not for long, but long enough."

Wayne Boyd looked back over his shoulder to the close, mourning group.

"Do they know the circumstances?" Dr. Laris was saying.

"Not the mother or the sister. I told the oldest boy. He said he would handle it."

"Well, the undertaker is downstairs. I'll call him up and release the body. Take them down the back stairs."

"Yeah. Yeah, I guess that would be best."

He watched the cars leave the parking lot. He raised his

hand in a farewell gesture and jumped into his own car. He was not driving the cruiser. Something told him that would be in poor taste. Maybe yes, maybe no. Right now he wasn't sure of anything. Some crazy bastard was on the loose. Patterson, the only voice of official Quonsett, was trying to make like it never happened, Medina was out, and he was sitting in the hospital parking lot trying to figure out what to do next. He thought of doubling up the shifts and putting more men on duty, especially in the less thickly populated areas west and east of town. But then there was the Fourth of July and The Hill, and too much had already been said about the fuckers on The Hill planning a real mob action for the Fourth. Suddenly he felt tired. He wanted to be with Kate and the boys anchored somewhere offshore with fishing poles, and Portuguese bread and a cold six-pack of beer. He switched on the ignition and headed back to police headquarters.

Three

Eddie sat hunched over in a captain's chair on the deck that faced into the dark shadows of pine that stood as sharp as black pencils in front of him. The pine bordered the nine-hole golf course, and he generally took great delight in musing on the fact that he, Eddie Singer, late of her majesty's jarheads, owned, along with Alcott Savings and Loan, a house that abutted a golf course. "Only in America," his father parroted Harry Golden more than once. "Only in America, Eddie."

But tonight, on the eve of the Fourth of July, he did not see the pine, nor catch its sharp aroma as the wind changed and stirred the leaves in the mulch pile. He lurched forward, straining his ears. The wind rustled again and he leaped from his chair and jumped off the deck. He stood in the shadows, listening, while his eyes formed crow's feet at the temples. Sweat broke out across his forehead. I must be wacked out, for Christ's sake, he thought. He walked a little way into the woods and froze as a startled rabbit flashed by and disappeared into the thicket. I'll have to get a hold of myself. He did not laugh at the old joke. Instead, he stood in the dark looking back at his house washed in yellow light.

Sandy stood at the stove doing something with the spatula she held poised in her right hand. She looked good from where he stood. Her blouse fit into her shorts, tightly emphasizing her breasts. Her long, tawny legs curved subtley from thigh to calf, indenting to the slim ankles.

She had a habit of locking her right hip and extending her left foot. Her spatula-free hand rested on her buttocks. She always stood like that when she was preoccupied.

He had the urge to go in, let his hands search her body, and then take her to bed and make love to her all night, and forget where he was, and where he had to go. His conscious mind told him that Jack Buckley's killer was long gone. On his way west or north. But not here. Not Quonsett. It had been a bad break. It happened. But it was over. That was his conscious mind. But stuck back there behind the ears was the thought that the killer was right here in his backyard, and as soon as Eddie left for the station, the killer would strike Sandy and Stacey. The killer hated cops, ex-marines, mongrels who were half-Jewish–half-Irish, English teachers, mill-town kids who made good and had a beautiful wife, a child, and a house on a Cape Cod golf course. His shirt was soaking. He unbuttoned it and wiped the perspiration from his chest. In Nam he had felt this way. He had been on patrol, lying by a stream waiting for Viet Cong he knew were coming through. He lay there most of the night drowning in his own sweat. His mind triphammered and banged out a hundred paranoid fantasies. His mother and father were dead—in a car crash—one of his sisters had cancer, the other was going to die in childbirth. The Viet Cong could see him. They were waiting for him to crack. They were watching the sweat run down his chest. They knew his flak jacket was unzipped. They had a thousand automatic rifles on him ready to blow him apart. They were behind him, beside him, on top of him. He thought his head would explode. The night turned gray, and then pink, and he picked up his tired, soaking body and joined the rest of the patrol and returned to base camp for breakfast. Charlie never showed up. That had been his first night, his perspiring baptism of nonfire.

Sandy called to him from the deck and her voice broke

him out of it. He wiped the wet from his forehead and neck with the back of his hand.

"Eddie, are you out there?"

"Over here, honey." And he walked out into the light of the moon.

"You had me worried. What are you looking for, lost golf balls, for God's sake?" She laughed and handed him the glass of iced tea.

"C'mon, Eddie, it's leveling time. You haven't been right all night. I'm sorry if I had to go to my mother's, but with daddy out of town at that sales convention—well, damnit, you know my mother."

"No, kid, it's not that. It's a lot of things." He had no intention of getting into Nam. That was bullshit talk. He saved that for a couple of vets like himself. Once or twice a year they got bombed and bullshitted. When it was all over and the head began clearing, he was always sufficiently embarrassed to let the whole service thing lie. But that fucking killer had brought it all back. He wished he had a bayonet. He would take great pleasure in hacking away at that son of a bitch. And that precisely was his problem. The kill thing, the deep down, gut throb to kill, was returning and he hated it. The kid had been so pure and simple. The way Eddie used to be. If only he could tell Sandy all of it. But it would just sound phony. So all he said was, "Thanks," and he sipped the tea.

"What did Sergeant Boyd say about the wake?" She sat on the edge of the deck. Crickets were doing their nocturnal thing.

"Boyd said everybody was busted up. He must have been a hell of a kid. Real quality. He would have made a difference somewhere."

"Eddie, maybe you ought to give up this police stuff."

"Why do you say that? I mean, out of nowhere. Just like that."

39

"It's not just like that. I've been thinking about it. Because it's, well, it's just that it's too much like the marines. Guns and conflicts and fights. You're a teacher, Eddie. I mean, you got to decide—sometime."

"Hey, look, it's thirty-five hundred a summer. That's a hell of a chunk off the mortgage."

"Honey, what difference does it make if we pay off the mortgage in twenty years or twenty-five?" Her voice was urgent, insistent.

"No difference, I guess. Besides it really isn't the money."

"Yes, I know. I was just hoping *you* would say it."

"It's the excitement. There's something about it. When I get into that cruiser, my whole body is pumping blood."

"It's the goddamn marines. That's what's pumping." Her voice rose. "Eddie, you had it tough. But you survived. Jesus. Didn't you learn anything?"

"Like what? What was I supposed to learn?"

"To live out the rest of your life in relative quiet."

He sipped from the glass, his eyes studying her. She was beautiful, he thought. The tip of her nose had the touch of the moon on it.

He smiled.

"What are you smiling at?" She cocked her head in one direction and then the other.

He got up and went to her. He stretched his hands out and pulled her up from the edge of the deck. She came into him. She fit so perfectly, he thought.

He kissed her warmly on the mouth. "How about a quickie."

"It would be a quickie. You have just five minutes to get out of here." He pretended to pout and then kissed her on both cheeks. Her face was still warm from cooking. "See ya."

"See ya."

On the way out, he grabbed another T-shirt and a uni-

40

form shirt from a laundry basket. He was halfway to the car when he ran back, pausing in the doorway of Stacey's room. Her little tanned body was partially covered by the white sheet as she slept in a world of teddy bears and rabbits and saltwater taffy. Hers was a soft-as-fur world.

Sandy came and put her arm around his waist. "You're one in a million, Eddie Singer."

He looked down at her. His eyes were very serious. "You know something, Mrs. Singer? You're absolutely correct." He picked her up and held her against the door. "Oh, wouldn't I like to, though."

She slapped his rear end. "Get the hell out of here, you egotist."

She watched him pull the car out of the garage. "Be careful tonight, Eddie. Watch out for the weirdos. Especially on The Hill. The Fourth is always so scary. And maybe that—oh, God, that maniac is up there."

But most of it was lost to the roar of the engine.

As he drove into town, he settled back against the leather seat. The night was warm but not sticky. There would be a breeze later on that would curl in from the islands and soothe the town while cooling down the trouble spots. Hot nights were action nights. He cruised past the bird sanctuary and the state wildlife reservation. The town had everything. Beaches and birds and ducks and gulls. Playgrounds, golf courses, good schools, bike paths, theaters, restaurants —and peace. There was the constant problem of The Hill during the summer months and the blatant disregard for the residents. Business as usual and the residents of The Hill had a goddamned good case because they were the ones getting the business.

But now even more than by the usual summer harassment, that peace was disturbed by the brutal murder of Jack Buckley. When this story broke, and it was bound to, even though he had heard around the station that Patterson wanted the story sat on . . . "When this story breaks," he sighed, "this town is going to feel it."

He could not figure out how word of the murder could be kept quiet. The people on the beach that morning, they would get the word out. And the cops, what the hell, they're human, they tell their wives. Kids hear it. But the official word. That was the thing. Patterson could tell the Log to keep it quiet and they would, just like that. Cyrus Dean might be eccentric, but he was no dope.

"The world really does come down to money, doesn't it, Edward, my son?" he said to the black strip of tree-lined highway. "Life really is the big buck, and it's business at all costs. Business as usual."

Maybe at that moment he was just a little proud to be a schoolteacher. It had never been the big buck, just pay the mortgage and eat. That's really what it was all about. Clothes, food, shelter, and family. "Heavy, Eddie. Fucking heavy."

Wayne Boyd held firmly on to the steering wheel with his left hand while crossing over his right to button the left cuff. It was not like him to come out half dressed. At forty-four, he was formed. He had certain habits—black coffee and toast before going on midnight to eight, a spoonful of honey three times a day, a four-mile jog three times a week, winter or summer, and on and on until sometimes his wife thought he was living by a chart.

He drove east along the highway that ducked in under the crisscross oaks and then he glided into town.

The town was shiny with cars all along Main Street. The bars were emptying out onto the street, while the walls bulged from overflows. He reminded himself to take a spot check later, on overcrowding.

The night was carnival and it was only the beginning. Up

ahead he saw five Rent-a-Cops standing in a group, backs against the doors of a closed shop. They looked as though they were waiting for a shell to land and maybe if they stayed together it wouldn't go off.

Still, he could not blame them. They were summer cops like Jack Buckley. He knew what was running through their minds. Everybody had a theory. Already he had begun going through the records. Rent-a-Cops who had been fired over the last ten years. Guys with a grudge. Or it could have been guys turned down for permanent duty. That aspect he was still working on. Christ, you have to start somewhere, he had told the captain. The captain had agreed.

He thought about breaking up the group T session and said, "Fuck it. Let the poor bastards hold each other's joints."

He knew that fear. The fear of being alone and in danger. Korea was not that long ago and would never be that long ago.

He pulled into the station parking lot.

The scene inside the station was a repeat of Main Street. The older cops stood in hushed corners with their coffee cups, and cigarettes. The phones rang off the cradles. The news was spreading.

Eddie talked to Frenchie the Bondsman, who leaned against the water cooler.

"Ya see, Eddie, this killer, at least my theory, this killer is out for kicks. He's a doctor who's lost his license to practice. So he has to keep that knife workin. See?"

"Let's forget it, Frenchie, everybody has a theory. Who knows? Who the Christ knows?"

"You're a college man, Singer, you know everything. Who do you think he is?" The voice was biting. Eddie shot a puzzled look at Rick Pierce and said nothing.

"Hey, Singer, I asked you a question."

Eddie ran his tongue along his lips. "Yeah, I heard you, Pierce."

"Well, then why the fuck don't you answer when someone asks you a question? Is that how you run your little red schoolhouse?"

Eddie turned his back and walked to the dispatcher where he ripped the yellow sheet of LEAPS information from the teletype.

He came back out to the desk to hear Pierce, "Fuckin teachers, not enough they got a tit for ten months out of the year, they got to take a job away from someone who needs it."

"Pierce, cool it, you're beginning to bother me. If you're sweating it out, maybe Sergeant Boyd can give you a job hosing down the cruisers until the streets are safe again."

Pierce was on him with a right lead to the head that spun Eddie around enough so that his countering left hook caught Pierce halfway through his followthrough. Two more hooks and a right slammed Pierce against the Coke machine.

"Knock the shit off. Knock it off." Boyd filled the doorway.

Pierce straightened as Eddie backed off. "What is this shit? What is it? Singer?"

"Nothing, sergeant. It was personal."

"Personal? Well, if it's so fucking personal why don't you go out and find an empty beach. Not the main lobby of the police station. Anymore shit like that and I'll suspend both of you for a week.

"Understand, Singer?"

"Yes, sir."

"Pierce?"

"Yes, sir."

"And the rest of you, look alive, for Christ's sake. You've got a job to do."

"Sergeant?" a short, red-headed cop offered cautiously.

"What is it, Dunn?"

"The captain wanted to see you as soon as you got in."

"The captain? What the hell is he doing here at this time."

"I dunno, he's been here since morning."

Boyd hustled along the corridor to the open door of Captain Swanson's office.

"Evening, captain, what can I do for you?"

Swanson was slate thin with a gray perplexed face. He had long bony hands that held up file cards.

"I've been over records that you wouldn't believe, Wayne. That pile there? It has the name of every cop-hater in town. And you know something that I didn't know even after thirty-two years on the job?"

"No, what?" Boyd grabbed a folding chair, turned it around and straddled it.

"There are a lot of people who really hate cops."

"You don't say."

They both laughed. Boyd liked the soft-spoken Swanson. He was a good administrator.

Now he placed the folders on his desk and squared them together neatly.

"Tomorrow we start to trace these. There are twenty-seven men in these folders. Their ages range from sixty-five to seventeen. I thought maybe the sixty-five-year-old might be too weak and then I remembered Luchesi, the special cop we call in on emergencies. He's sixty-two, and I wouldn't want to tangle with him."

"I thought the medical examiner said the killer would have to be a doctor or a med student. At least someone with some expertise."

"He did. Several of these men are fishermen. Pretty good at slicing up fish."

"And the rest."

"Who said we're looking for one man. Our medical man could be doing a favor for someone. Anyway, we give everything a shot."

"Whatever you say, captain. You have been known to be right in the past—once or twice," he added slowly.

"Thanks. Oh, and, Wayne, I don't want to push it, but your men are on edge. I can feel it all over the station. This can be a busy night."

"I'll talk to them. That all?"

"Yeah, I'm going home, my bones are rubbing against each other."

"Night, captain."

Wayne Boyd sat straddling the chair. He broke open a new pack of cigarettes and stuck one between his lips. He lit it and brought the smoke deep. There was a half hour before change of shift. He sat alone, thinking.

While Wayne Boyd inhaled the smoke of his cigarette, Joe Medina squashed his out in the seashell ashtray. He finished off his eighth bourbon and water before he answered the man sitting next to him. He had to talk in a roar to be heard, but because of the nature of his message he did not want the whole table to hear him. He had put off most of them during the night even after he addressed them and they threw questions at the dais. They, of course, were the Fraternal Order of the Mariner, most of whom owned their own fishing boats or worked for someone in the Order who did.

But the man was insistent. He kept tugging at Medina's sleeve. Medina acknowledged the drink someone sent over from the bar and he cupped his hand over the man's ear. "Let's get out of here. It's too goddamned noisy." They grabbed their drinks and pushed through the drinking, lurching crowd out to the side porch off the hall.

The air was clear and free of cigarette smoke and Joe blew his nose. "That goddamned smoke doesn't help my cold," he said to the man. His eyes were smarting.

"So what gives, Joe?" the man was saying as Joe continued blowing his nose.

"What gives is simple, Mr. Dean. Frank wants to keep the cover on this thing. And he is really pleased with you and the paper. I mean, just skimming the surface about the death of a summer cop. If that decapitation thing ever hit the papers, this town would go crackers."

Joe enjoyed using British expressions. He had served in Hanover, Germany, attached to British security during the fifties.

"Yes, I know. Frank and I talked and I agree. I hated to kill the story, but we are all in business. Where do we go from here? What do you think, Joe?"

"My theory is simple. Some pothead came through town, met the kid, jabbed him unconscious, did the decapitation, left him on the beach, and is somewhere west of Chicago by now."

"Where's the head?"

"Cranberry bog. It'll turn up. Some poor bastard will find it during harvest season. Probably have a coronary."

Dean's red, soft-skinned face broke open in a grin. "That would be a shocker. Son of a bitch, can you imagine!"

They both shook with laughter and finished their drinks.

"One thing, though, are you going to print anything more?"

"Not unless I have to. I'll keep it quiet until I have to do something. We've got a hell of a lot of advertising to attract before this summer's over."

Chief Medina smiled. Frank will be satisfied, he thought.

"Let me buy you a drink, Mr. Dean."

"Well, it's getting late. Just a light one."

At 9:00 that night, long before Boyd, Eddie, and the midnight shift had even thought about arriving at the station, and about the time Joe Medina was flawlessly fielding questions from the floor from tanked-up brothers of the Order of the Mariner, Douglas Peters walked, barefoot and barebacked, through the leaves and high grass of the woods which housed him.

His mind was keen and alive. His nerve endings fused and sparked in a kinetic energy that spurred him into an exhilarating jog through the immensely thick and hoary growth. He could not restrain himself. The high he was experiencing carried him through the tree-lined paths, down the pine-scented hill, and in a flat, racing dive into fresh unspoiled waters of his own hollowed-out pool. He broke the silver surface of the water and lay on his back staring up at the sky. The only intrusion on his private world was the sound of whizzing and hissing Fourth of July eve traffic, a mile below his woods.

He drifted and floated in a soothing, timeless world. The pain in his head and neck that he had been experiencing diminished in the purgatorial waters. He felt good about the cop. It had been his first time, but it was not unlike the exploratory surgery he had performed in med school. Quite similar, in fact, and the jerking body had not affected him. An intense paroxysmal, involuntary muscular contraction, he smiled remembering his pathology lectures. It had been disappointing at first when he thought he had a full-time police officer caught in his web. He wanted the first to be a townie. But as the cop had unfolded his summer part-time police status, Peters began to look at it in another light. He could kill a cop, who was only working because of an influx of tourists anyway. And after all, it was the tourism that must suffer, that had to suffer. "And will suffer," he formed the words to the few clouds that momentarily obscured the moon.

Driving into Quonsett, he had been beset by conflicting feelings. Quonsett was the scene of some of his happiest memories. Laconic and never-ending days and nights of pure and natural joys were very much a part of him. The fishing, the swimming, the long walks through surf and sand with his father by his side. He submerged, leaving the image of his father back on the black surface of the water to trail away with the clouds. Thoughts of his father served only to unnerve him, to drive him into deep depression, where he could not think straight. And tonight he must be very alert.

He surfaced to new thoughts. They were the other-side-of-the-moon thoughts. The thoughts that hurt him but drove him on to carry out a plan which most people would have thought impossible—the closing down of a town. The closing down of an entire fucking town. The thought and the absolute awe he felt in such a plan and his ability to carry it out overwhelmed him. He stroked to shore. Stiff and ancient vines served as a ladder. He pulled himself up on the grassy bank. He could not prolong it any longer. He raced back to the van and wiped himself dry, threw on a shirt and a dry pair of cut-down Levi's and slowly pulled the van out from the overhang of foliage that obscured it from the eyes of the casual observer. He had no real protection from the more curious observer. That, he had weeks ago decided, was his delicate balance. He would take the chance and toe that line.

He eased the van onto the narrow dirt path. Branches scratched and clawed against the windows and sides like grasping hands mysteriously holding the van back. He inched the van forward through the slapping, screeching growth until he was out onto the rutted path. The van slipped easily down the hill now. There was more growth at the entrance. He looked both ways through the interweaving patterns of branch and brush. No lights appeared from oncoming traffic, and he jammed the accelerator and tore out of the woods. He drove parallel to the highway on a fifty-yard stretch of soft shoulder and then he was into the festive traffic along with the rest of them. He was just another van. Just another dude out for the Fourth of July action.

He allowed the flow of traffic to carry him into town. Most of the packed, horn-blowing cars were headed past the fireworks display at Mariner World and on to The Hill. The fireworks would be for the next night. But fireworks did not interest him as the streets and alleys and houses began to film memories. His mind was being flooded with those memories that only included his father, his mother, and himself. There were not too many friends and playmates in those days. He had been, then, as he was now, pretty much of a loner. A slow but steady pounding began in his heart as streets, decks, backyards, and sloping roofs became familiar.

He did not want to see it. He had consciously planned not to see it. But it was too late, as the van's headlights picked it out of the night. It stood square and Victorian with peaked roof not as plain as a tepee-shaped roof because of its scalloped curlicue designs, but sharply pyramid-shaped. He remembered every line of the house because he had been so happy there. The columns, chair rails, dentrils, and every crenelation that was notched discriminately into the old structure. It was still painted white with black shutters. His Halloween house, he had called it once when they spent a long October week there. But then it was just he and his mother. His father was gone by then. Even that had been a good time. Not as it had been with his father. But his mother had taken him each day up to town for lunch to one of the year-round restaurants—The Whaler's, The Delft Room, or The Wisset Inn —and they had enjoyed the food and the day. Frequently, during that week, a man appeared at their table and insisted on paying their check. Doug did not like the man. He had not liked the man the first time he had seen him, a few years before. It happened on a day he had come home from The Fish Shack early. He had rowed across the harbor and cut through the backyards to his own house. He had been carrying four lobsters he had caught in his trap—a surprise for dinner for his mother and father. He would hide them in the three-room guesthouse to the rear of the main house. But when he had opened the door and run the water into his bucket he heard a noise—a creaking noise like the springs of the old bed rocking in a rhythmic pattern. When he shut off the faucet, the noise stopped. He went to the bedroom door and asked who was in there. His mother came quickly to the door wearing her robe, which seemed odd at that time of day. "Get out of here. Get the hell out of here now. What do you mean by spying on me? Get out." And she slammed the door of the room shut in his face. He had stood in front of the door for a minute. The blood leaving his face and the sobs beginning. He ran up the hill and into the house, where he washed the tears away. As he was wiping his face he could see from the bathroom window, a man coming out of the guesthouse and then disappearing down the back path.

His mother had joined him soon after explaining that she was sorry for yelling at him. She kissed him and everything was happy again. They had the lobster and then went out for ice cream.

But he never forgot the man. Although he was ten or eleven at the time, the figure of that man coming out of the guesthouse and that same man at the restaurant haunted him. It seemed the man's appearance came shortly before the death of his father. That man was responsible for the void, the absolute loneliness that replaced what his father had meant to him.

Later, of course, when he was older and could understand, he constantly dug away at his grandmother for answers to a child's question. He finally had pieced it all together.

He was out of the van now, walking down that same slope of hill to the guesthouse. It was too dark to see inside, but it appeared to be a catchall—a storage house.

He turned, gazing up at the lighted bay windows and turrets, remembering the irregularly shaped rooms and high ceilings.

"What do you want? Hey, you, what are you doing there?"

The voice knifed through the darkness. His heart leaped, he felt for his leather case.

"I'm, I'm sorry, sir, don't be alarmed, I used to live here, summers," he added, as he approached the barking voice.

He met the man, elderly and stoop-shouldered, halfway up the hill. The man looked down at him.

He repeated, "I used to live here. I was just a little sentimental as I drove by. So I decided to roam around. Not very smart. I should have told you first. I'm sorry."

The old man eased off. "Oh, that's ok, son. I know the feeling. We're retired down here, but when I go back up to Boston on business I always nip out to West Roxbury to see the old house. It's nice to see young people are sentimental. Would you like to come in?"

"Gee, I appreciate it, but maybe another time. I'm parked in a tow-away zone. I better move my van."

"Suit yourself. Come by anytime."

They walked out of the yard to the street. He did not appreciate the old man's being able to identify him. The van was parked under a streetlight.

"That your van?"

"Uh, yeah."

"That's quite a picture. You paint that?"

"Uh, no. I bought it that way."

The old man was getting him panicky. Maybe he would take the old man now. He felt for the leather case and his hand passed over the razor sharp scalpel.

A door opened and a figure appeared in the light of the door frame. "Dad, is that you?"

"Yes, Fred. Just talking to a young man here. Used to live in the house."

"Well, sir, I best be getting along. Thanks for the offer to come in. I'm leaving for California tomorrow, but when I come back maybe I'll take you up on it."

He hopped into the van and backed down onto Main Street. His head was throbbing and a sharp pain ran along his neck. He tried to palm the pain away.

"That was too close, too close. There are too many people here." And he drove back along the route he had come to a less populated section of town.

"Why did I tell the old bastard I used to live there? Goddamn it. I lost my fucking cool—" He screamed it out. His anger was fiery and intense. "One stupid move could blow it forever. This is my only chance to get even, for all of it. For all of it," he bellowed. He gritted his teeth until his jaws hurt. He needed a joint to quiet him down. Two miles out of town, he pulled over and turned on. The calm came quickly and his head did not hurt anymore. "I'll take care of things—the old man—anybody I have to." He giggled in a giddy fashion. His body felt ticklish. He began laughing uncontrollably. "Shit, but I feel good." Up ahead a camper pulled off the highway and choked and sputtered into a rest area.

He dug into the joint and sat back against the leather cushions, allowing his entire body to luxuriate in the numbed warmth he felt.

Four

Freddie's and the other drinking spots were fairly well policed until last call. Then the bikes and cars roared down The Hill and tore along Ocean Drive spiraling off into the lanes and back streets of The Hill's compact little village. Horns blared and obscenities filled the air, winches rattled and banged as illegally parked cars in private drives or on resident's well-manicured lawns were hoisted to the rear of tow trucks that added to the midnight din as they groaned off into the night. The park adjacent to the ocean was a haven for the drunks who puked their guts onto the infield. Some stumbled up the embankment to sleep off the pot or the booze. Some made love openly. The park was a public urinal.

Most nights, a few passes by the park, and the cops cleared the area by 2:00 A.M. Tonight, however, it was different. It was the Fourth of July and Sergeant Wayne Boyd felt it in the tips of his fingers. He smelled it in the salt air. There was a tension in the town all along Main Street.

He was not surprised when the calls began coming in from the residents of The Hill. "Urinating on my lawn" . . . "Broken window from a beer bottle" . . . "A fight in my front yard" . . . "People copulating against my car" . . . The calls came quick and fierce.

By 1:30 A.M. the switchboard in police headquarters was a Christmas tree. The Hill, according to all reports, was no longer a festering wound. The cancer had spread and the patient was living on borrowed time.

Sergeant Boyd called his men together. At six-foot-one and with military rigidity, he spoke in a deep and efficient voice.

"Gentlemen, we go. No panic. Do your jobs. Do not lose your cool. The Park, at this moment, seems to be home for eight hundred drunks. We all know there is a small chance we have a crazy with a scalpel out there. We all are feeling a bit jumpy. Control yourselves. Calm yourselves. This is a Fourth like every other Fourth. Eddie, you're in Oscar Five with me."

The wide wooden porch of The Loft bulged with refugees from the park. Some hung out of second-story windows. Catcalling, jeering, and spitting, as the cruisers like sheep dogs nosed people into the already bulging cottages.

Sergeant Wayne Boyd stepped from his car. He had already directed his officers, "If there is any concentration of commotion from one house, one dwelling, I don't give a shit if it's a phone booth, we all, I repeat, we all hit that dwelling."

He picked his way through the crowds, staring straight ahead. A drunk threw a right hand at him. Boyd caught the fist in his hand, twisted the man around, and sent him crashing into the trunk of the cruiser.

Wayne jumped back as a television set crashed at his feet. He looked up at the open window of The Loft. He wasn't crazy about the Moffit's children's army—they caused more trouble than they were worth—at least to the police force—they were worth a lot to the merchants and to Moffit. His temper flared. He forgot his own instructions to keep cool, calm, etcetera.

"We hit that fucker now," he shouted.

Twenty-five officers burst on to the porch. The front door was ripped off the hinges and kids screamed and shrieked as they sprang for the rear exits.

55

Boyd was the first to arrive on the second-floor landing.

"Everyone of you. Out of those goddamned rooms or I'll drag you out by your pubic hairs."

When he emerged from The Loft, The Hill was wall-to-wall skin. He stood on the porch and looked at them. They continued their jeering and he stood erect and rigid, looking straight into them. He never moved. His shoulders were square and his jaw was firm. He did not smoke. He did not scratch. He did not flinch. There was no movement from his chest. It seemed he was not breathing.

The chanting became less audible until it died slowly and gradually. But it died. He looked down at them one more time, and said softly, almost conversationally, in a resonant bass voice.

"Everyone of you fuckers, find a home. Now!"

"Fuck you, pig." A skinny voice from across the street yelled out.

"I will personally shove a pistol up your ass and pull the trigger, fucker. Now find a bed and wet it. I'm not shitting you people." If there were a crazy at least he'd go back to his hole—or to the station.

Sergeant Wayne Boyd headed back to the station, but not before he drove by Anchor Road and flashed his searchlight on the secure saltbox house sitting in a grove of oak trees. A light snapped in the kitchen. He drove on past. He felt better. The kids were sleeping. Good. Everything A-OK. The boys would need a good night's sleep if they were going clamming today. Today! He checked his watch. The illuminated dial said 3:10 A.M.

Eddie sat watching it all. He knew the routine. Boyd never let a night go by without checking his house. It was a ritual, just as much as the cigarette he would now have on the ride back to the station. Eddie said nothing. He knew if Boyd wanted to say something he would. He didn't.

The parking lot of the police station was jammed with cruisers from surrounding Cape towns. Across from the station adjacent to the high school football field tow trucks shuttled back and forth depositing their dangling prey and then banged off into the night prowling for more.

Boyd stepped out of the cruiser and Eddie followed him up the steps of the station.

He headed directly for his office while lighting a cigarette. The oak paneled hall gleamed and shone from the maintenance he insisted on. He clicked open the door of his office.

One folder was on his desk. Sterling-silver pen-and-pencil set gleamed. The blackboard was erased and clean. He carefully folded up the empty pack of Marlboros and dropped it into the wicker wastebasket. A small sweat stain had formed under his right armpit. He wouldn't like that if he knew, Eddie thought as he watched Boyd go to the window. A hint of dawn ever so slightly pinked over the Cumberland Farms store.

Eddie was beginning to feel awkward. He folded his arms. He coughed once. He wished he hadn't given up smoking. It would be even more awkward to ask for one now. He coughed again.

Boyd turned from the window. His eyes were set back deep in his head. They were blue, cold blue.

"Eddie," he said, "tonight I want you to take the desk."

"The desk, sergeant?"

"That's what the man said, Eddie. The desk."

"But, sergeant—"

Boyd did not let him finish.

"For a minute tonight, you lost it, Eddie. The cool."

"Yeah, I know. Rick pissed me off."

"It's no good, Eddie. That could have cost us. I know how you feel, but if we lose our cool the whole town will panic."

57

"I know. I know." Eddie licked his lips, he nodded and said it again, softly. "I know."

Boyd went to the file cabinet with the folder. He found the place and slipped the folder in. He closed the cabinet. His back was to Eddie. "That's all, for now, Eddie."

Eddie cleared his throat as Boyd went back to the desk and sat down.

"Eddie, remember this. We all liked the kid. He was good to have around. Uncomplicated and happy. Lousy cop, maybe, but a good kid."

Eddie began to form words, but they wouldn't come.

"Ok, Eddie. Dismissed."

Eddie waited for a long minute and then he made a half-military right turn and was gone.

"Now I'm going to get that fucking selectman out of his four-fucking poster and show him his town.

As smooth as the operation on The Hill had been, there was little doubt among the officers on duty at the station that there would be an early morning onslaught. Those few walking the downtown beat were almost forgotten by the station. They were the lost souls hanging tough through another night. The pure violence and head splitting on The Hill would have been a welcome change. No specters. No elusive shadows to follow. No footsteps down darkened alleys. Just the pure violence of splitting someone's skull or smashing a stick through bone. But they were out there checking doors on Main Street wondering if the next door might be their last. Wondering where he was. If he was still in town or long gone.

Sitting at his high stool, the dispatcher fielded the phone with a golden glove. The calls filtered through the static urgently.

"272 Oscar Twelve—bringing in five."

58

"Right, 10-4."

"272 Oscar Five—five comin in."

"272 Oscar Nine—four en route."

"272 Oscar Nine—set five places for breakfast."

"272 Oscar Twelve—got six stuffed in my trunk," and then the snicker being cut off by the dispatcher.

Boyd called in for the school bus backup.

"Send three school buses to the park. There might be a hundred head of cattle by the time they get here."

Seldom were the buses used like this. Only during a catastrophe, a hurricane, flood evacuation, or a tornado. But tonight was a small catastrophe, and the cops stood among the glass and turned-over cars trying to prod the drunks into some kind of human corral on the infield of the ball park.

The bus rolled past the station to the side entrance, where five officers held over from the day shift stood with folded arms waiting for their new quarry.

They stood ashen-faced and red-eyed, vaguely recalling the great Fourth of July blast they left back there with their booze and grass and broads on The Hill overlooking the serene and blue ocean. They were as yet unaware of the lurking danger, but they could sense that the cops were tense, unusually brutal. The new kids figured they were pigs, just like all the other pigs. The kids who were regulars or townies were surprised by their abuse. Usually the cops were more laid back—more in control. The tension was contagious and the kids caught the disease.

The buses unloaded and a steady stream lined up from the door through the cruiser pit right on through to Officer Delgrado's desk. Delgrado sold used cars in the winter and his fast banter got him through some tight situations and it would get him through this holiday.

"Name, please." He said it slowly, sleepily.

"Fuck you, pigman."

Delgrado did not look up. "Throw him in solitary. Strip him and throw him in." It was quick. Black and white.

One of the cops standing in the doorway grabbed the kid and spun him around and out the door. The kid spit on the cop, who wiped it slowly from his shirt front.

As they disappeared around the communal cell block, the kid let out a shriek.

And on it went, droning into the dawn until one hundred and twenty-seven were glued and stuck to each other in a cell thirty feet long and twenty feet wide.

Now, when the booze and the highs began wearing off, the daylight realization of the cell took over.

Restless sleepers bunched up on the piss wet floors, the shaking sobs from the first-weekend-away-from-home kids and the dry heaves from the novice drinkers turned cell to nightmare and snakepit.

Upstairs, Eddie sat hunched over the dispatcher's desk. His eyes had large black quarters under them. The phone rang irregularly. Its persistence of the early part of the night gave way to a lazy and intermittent interlude. The town was, for the most part, sleeping.

"Excuse me, Eddie?"

Eddie looked up slowly, rubbing the sleep out of his eyes. His eyes were penetrating brown buttons now. They came alive.

"Yes?" It was formal, brusque.

"Eddie, I'm sorry about tonight. You were right. I was on edge." The right hand played with the badge on his chest. "I think everybody's on edge. Everybody I look at, I think . . . maybe. You know? I was an asshole."

Eddie stared at him for a long minute, hanging him. He did that with Sandy sometimes. It was wrong. It was righteous. He caught himself staring. The silence was becoming awkward. He had better break it. His straight white teeth broke into a wide smile.

"Forget it Rick. I'm on edge, too. You're right. We all are.

The sun was coming up orange over the sound. The view from left to right as far as one could see was ocean. Aqua ocean, broken by the occasional lapping and curling of the white caps against the jetties, and the screech of a hungry herring gull. This was *the* Cape. The early morning calm Cape. This was what was shut up inside him, and he shared it with few people. His wife on occasion, and his boys when he and the two of them would be drifting out there, leisurely fingering their lines checking for a bite.

He looked out over the sound. His right foot rested on the white board fence that separated The Hill from the ocean below. His pistol sent off lights. It was a Smith & Wesson .357 magnum with an eagle on the stalk. The polished jump boots glistened and the pleated blue shirt fit tightly into the waist; clean and fresh from his locker after the lingering shower. He had the look of airborne. But he was not airborne. He was infantry all the way. And at forty-four, he looked as though he could soldier all day and night.

Out of a grubby, sparse, flea-bitten town in Arizona—Bend of Two Rivers—an Indian town; he left for the army and Korea in 1951. The service had been good to him. He ate often if not always well. He found acceptance among non-Indians. He was never sure if it was his mother's whiteness or his strength that brought him quick respect. He was reserved but watchful. After several successful fire fights and night patrols in the Kumwa Valley, he was promoted to sergeant at the age of nineteen.

After two years of dull duty in charge of security at a Nike site on the Cape, he took his discharge and married Kate Fornesi, a dark-skinned Cape Verdean whom he met while she was waitressing at a restaurant near the site.

Kate's father, who later died of a heart attack, convinced Boyd police work was secure, safe, and rewarding. And not a bad way to live, especially if you could live in the quiet, peaceful Cape Cod town of Quonsett.

Wayne liked the town. It seemed a good place to raise a family and, after all, it was Kate's hometown and whatever made her happy made him happy.

Kate's father was a police sergeant in the Quonsett force. He did explain a vital point to Boyd one night while they were stuffing quahogs.

"Kid," the leathery-skinned man had said, "the cops can be a good life. You and Kate can get your own house —they're cheap now. But it won't be long before the Cape will grow. You'll be on the ground floor. There is one thing, though. You'll never go beyond sergeant."

"Why's that?"

"Because you're not a townie. Cape's funny like that. But you can make enough on side jobs. I'm not pressuring you, kid. But, let's face it, it would be nice to have you and Kate around."

The Cape had other compensations other than advancement, so he stayed. Kate bore two sons, Brian, twelve, and Mike, eleven. Life was good.

As he looked across at the islands, he sucked in the morning. He could taste the salt as the morning rolled in with the tide from the opposite shore.

The Hill was quiet but the refuse of the mob was everywhere. A car screeched to a stop behind him. He knew it was Patterson without even turning around.

"What the hell is the big idea of getting me out of the sack at this hour?" Patterson yelled at his back.

Boyd lingered, looking at the stretch of ocean front, and sighed and said, "Maybe it's about time you began to look around at the *whole* town."

"Who the hell do you think you're talking to, sergeant?"

"The chairman of the board of selectmen. That's the point, isn't it? That's why I called you and not Monsignor Gillespie."

"Don't wise-ass me."

"Hey, look, *Mister* Patterson, I'm not wise-assin anybody. I just want you to know—we had a near massacre on our hands last night. And this time the Indian almost lost. My boys are getting anxious. They're overreacting and I can't blame them, for Christ's sake. That crazy bastard can be hiding behind every hedge or cottage with a goddamned machete."

"Your job is simple, sergeant. Your job, as I see it, is to make sure they do not overreact. Now, let's get it over with. I haven't had my breakfast yet." Patterson moistened his lips thinking of his croissant. "Show me your Battle of the Little Big Horn." The grin was half sneer and the derision was not lost on Boyd.

They got into the cruiser and Boyd jerked away screeching rubber. Patterson's head jolted forward. "Hey, for Christ's sake, go easy."

"Sorry, I must have jumped the accelerator."

"Yeah, well go easy. That rubber costs money, you know."

"I'm happy to see you are budget-conscious, *Mister* Patterson."

"I said before, sergeant, don't wise-ass me or you *will* see a sizable budget cut."

They cruised by a van that was drying off from the early morning mist. The driver stood beside the waterfall mural and casually waved at them. Boyd nodded and leveled off into the backalleys and closes that abutted The Loft. "That fucker almost burned down last night. You can see where someone set those wooden swings on fire."

It was all there, the smashed windows, an overturned car lying half in and half out of a hedge.

"Get a tow truck for that baby. Call Symmington, he's good."

Boyd called it in. He made a turn and passed The Loft on the other side.

"Something else is bothering me, *Mister* Patterson."

"Yeah. What's that, *sergeant?*"

"This."

And he tossed the folder over to him. "What is it?" Patterson's voice was scratchy and at 5:30 A.M. it was husky from sleep.

Boyd did not like Patterson and Patterson did not like him. It was tidy and neat. Neither made a pretense.

"What am I supposed to do with this? The Buckley kid was murdered. What else is there to say?"

"How come you put the lid on it? Every cop on the force has got one hollow-point bullet in the chamber and the safety off."

"Well, you just tell your boys to cool it. I just want to get this Fourth of July over."

"How did you keep the papers quiet."

Mysterious Death of Summer Police Officer Under Investigation

Boyd had the brief account from Friday's *Log* cut out and placed alongside the coroner's report in the folder.

"Old Mr. Dean and I go back a long way. A hell of a lot longer than you newcomers." And he looked right through Boyd. "We know what's good for this town. Why get people riled up, for Christ's sake. Some nut comes in and does his thing and he's gone. Let some other state worry about him."

"Yeah, and in the meantime every cop in town has got his hand hooked over his piece." His own hand palmed for his pistol for emphasis. The feel of the eagle sent a warm shock through him.

"C'mon, get me back to my car. I've seen enough of this. It's the same every summer."

"Does it have to be?" He knew he sounded righteous. Patterson picked him up immediately.

"You sound like one of those red-necks from the Quonsett Improvement Association."

"I'm asking you, does it have to be?"

"Look, Boyd, you run tin soldiers through their maneuvers. That's what you're paid for and that's what they're paid for."

"What happened up here could have been a lot worse— a lot worse. We could have had some people killed up here."

"But you didn't, because you did your job. What do you want, a medal? Look, day after Labor Day, I'll hand out medals on the steps of town hall. Maybe the police association can get you a merit raise." His voice was sardonic.

"You're not even listening to me, are you? I had just about every available officer on The Hill last night. The rest of the town was bare-assed for police coverage."

"We got through it, didn't we!"

"Yeah, we got through it. Now we got to get through the Buckley thing."

"You have any ideas?" Patterson's tone was soft, not prodding. Quizzical.

"Yeah, I have some ideas. I think we have a psychopath on our hands. Mainly, because there seems to be no *apparent* motive here. I don't think we have the operation to handle this case alone. I'm going to request we call in the county—the DA's office."

"Are you crazy? Call in the DA's office and you open a can of worms. That killer has been here and gone. We cool it and it's all forgotten in a week. We bring in outsiders and we kiss the summer season good-bye."

"Is that all you think about? Tourists?"

"You bet your finger-lickin ass. And when you and the boys in blue are looking for a raise next year, you'll be goddamned happy that's all I do think about. It's a fact of life, face it. So you put those ideas out of your head. But just to be sure, I'll acquaint Medina with your scheme. He still runs the department. And I still run him."

Boyd pulled up to the Alfa-Romeo that hugged the curb along the skyline drive of clear ocean view.

Patterson reached for the door handle and then let it go and turned to face Boyd. "You don't forget that, sergeant. I run your chief. That means I run you."

"You don't scare me, Patterson." The indentation of high cheekbones brought the Plains Indian resemblance into focus. "I know a few things about you."

"No shit." He spit it back at Boyd. "No shit. Well, what do you know?"

"I know about your love of flowers. Especially bouquets."

Patterson had been in the arena too long. He had been pushed, punched, and accused, but he always came out of a barrel of shit dripping ice cream. He was seldom caught off guard. The nature of his lifestyle had taught him always to be prepared.

"You bet your ass I like flowers. Maybe I'll send *you* a bouquet for retirement. Now, I'm telling you," and the voice turned soft again, "you just watch your own ass or you'll be lucky to have special assignments at supermarkets. I'll see your butt behind an eight to five desk. And when you can't keep up with all the paper work, I'll get you for inefficiency. So don't fuck with me. I was on top before you got here and I'll be on top when you're long gone." He opened the door and stepped out. He allowed the door to click quietly behind him. He had made his point. He looked like a poster portrait of a New England senator as he craned his long neck back into the cruiser.

66

"You just do what you're paid to do and leave the Quonsett citizenry to me."

"What about the year-round residents of The Hill?"

"Screw 'em, there aren't enough to worry about." And he slammed the cruiser door and shuffled off to his car.

Boyd was not shitting himself. He could feel the vice. If Patterson didn't screw him, Medina would. Those two were a tight little island.

"Oscar Five—372," the dispatcher broke in.

"Oscar Five."

"Sarge, could you 10–19 immediately?"

"Be back in half an hour. Going to grab a coffee. 10-4."

"Oscar Five—372."

"Oscar Five." He was tired and his voice reflected it.

"Wayne, this is Medina, forget the coffee and get back here. On the double." He turned the cruiser around.

At the station, he wheeled down the ramp and leaned on the horn. The overhanging doors shot up and he came to a rocking stop at the farther doors.

"Gas it up and wash it down, Billy. Something tells me I'm gonna be using it again."

He took the door to the back stairs. He did not want to see the bulging cells now. He had had enough of The Hill and its freaked-out humanity for one night. He would visit them after coffee. Besides, the chief was flying about something.

When he entered the conference room from the back stairs, he knew there was an emergency.

"Oh, Sergeant Boyd. This is Mr. Fred Palton." And Medina gestured to a round-faced, forty-year-old man sitting at the table. The man scarcely acknowledged Boyd's presence. He just tapped a book of matches nervously against the tabletop.

"What's the problem, chief?"

The chief closed one of the doors that had remained open, but not before Boyd could see three children sitting near the dispatcher. One was crying. A boy of about seven.

With the door closed, the chief said, "Mr. Palton, would you please tell the sergeant what happened?" And he added softly, gently, "He's my best man. He will be able to help, I'm sure."

The round face looked up. The eyes were red, bloodshot, and puffy from lack of sleep and crying.

"Well, like I told Chief Medina." His speech was jerky. His voice broke and he began to cry.

"Take it easy, sir. Have someone send some coffee in, chief."

"I'll get it." And Medina left them.

"I'm—I'm ok now, sergeant. It's the kids. I keep thinking of the kids."

Boyd sat on the edge of the table and lit a cigarette. He took the book of matches that the man held out abstractedly.

"Want to try it again, Mr. Palton?"

The man took a deep breath and began again. "We come from New York, Elmira. And we came down to the Cape for two weeks. I couldn't get off work until late yesterday. But everything was packed. The camper, everything. I ate a sandwich while driving. I didn't want to waste any time. I wanted to get here. And look what it got me."

Boyd thought the man was going to break down again. But after another gulp of air he continued. "We made good time. We didn't hit any bad traffic until Route 28, then it was bumper to bumper. By the time I got into Quonsett, the gas tank was empty. I finally ran out on the shore road. It was almost midnight, and it was pitch dark. We were still five miles from the trailer park. I told my wife. Oh, God, my wife." And he brushed away tears with

68

rough red hands. His voice quivered as Medina returned with the coffee.

"Here," the chief said. "It will warm you up."

The man drank the coffee while gripping the cup with both hands.

"Don't worry about the kids, Mr. Palton. They're having doughnuts and milk."

"Thank you."

"What did you tell your wife, sir?"

"I told her to stay in the camper. Not to get out. I would be back as soon as I got some gas. But the kids said they heard a noise outside and she thought it was me. So she went outside to check. The next thing they heard a scream and a car drive off. When I came back an hour later, they were hysterical. We waited, hoping there was some mistake. When it got light enough, I found a phone and called the police."

"This car, did the children see it? Could they identify it?"

"No," Medina said, "but they said it made the noise of a truck or another camper, sergeant. I asked them and at first they had noticed nothing, but then they thought it did not sound like an ordinary car." Medina was stirring his coffee with a pencil. "Could have been a van. There are a lot of them around these days."

"All we can do now is wait, Mr. Palton. Sergeant, I'm going to drive Mr. Palton and his children back to the camper."

"Ok, chief."

When they left, Boyd smashed his fist against the door.

The rope tightened more. A middle-aged woman taken from a camper. Almost in full view of her children. The anxiety crept up his back. He did not want to believe what his instincts told him. He felt helpless. He was the top cop and he had no help. The chief was great at getting coffee and driving victims' husbands back to trailer parks. But what the hell kind of help was Boyd getting? If he called in the county on his own, Medina could get him for insubordination. And how Patterson would pounce on that. Medina would weakly agree that that was up to the chief and, "You leave me no alternative, Wayne, because you have taken it upon yourself to run this department, and we just can't have that."

Why was his mind racing like this? The woman could turn up. It could be a prank. Maybe someone knew the camper and was just enjoying a sick, practical joke—

But at that hour? An out-of-state license plate? He knew without doubt or reservation that the chances of the woman's being safely returned were out of the question.

He wondered how Patterson would handle this. No longer was it a self-contained situation of a summer cop. The missing woman was a tourist, and you don't shut up tourists. Maybe Patterson would have to turn around. Maybe the county *would* be called in.

The poodle raced along the beach, darting and splashing into the surf, and rolling over in the sand. The sun was eight-o'clock high over a clear ocean. The man walked leisurely along, chuckling at the playful antics of his dog.

The man stopped to relight his pipe and to look out at a passing trawler. As he waved to the fishermen, he heard the dog whine and then bark fiercely. The dog would approach something and then backtrack whining and barking.

"François, stop that, stop that at once." The man yelled at the dog as he took the leash from his pocket and approached the place where the dog was scratching at the sand.

"Stop that at once," he repeated, and then he turned white, his heart felt heavy and he thought he was about to faint.

Sitting up in the sand was a woman, fully dressed, propped against the sea wall a few yards beyond the edge of the beach where the tide ended. She was staring directly out to sea and her face was death white. Her skirt was tucked up to her thighs, and as he stared at her in disbelief, he could see that her right leg was missing.

He held her two hands in his. There was something so special about her. So delicate and sweet that he wanted to possess her.

"I like you, Doug. But I've noticed—" She did not finish.

"You've noticed what?"

"Well." She looked away at the ocean. "Well, you seem preoccupied. You seem as though you're far away, that you really don't care if you're with me or not—not always, just sometimes."

"That isn't true, Mary. That isn't true at all." His voice rose. He tried to keep it from a shout.

"Ok, ok, Doug, don't get so excited."

"But that's just the problem, Mary. I tell myself that I shouldn't enjoy being with you so much. I almost convince myself that you're just like any number of girls. But I know that's not true. I know you're special and that's what frustrates me."

"But, why?"

He always parked down by the harbor. Her father wasn't crazy about young men with vans. The last two weeks had been very special for them both—quiet, meditative. A kind of spiritual intimacy. And he needed that kind of intimacy more than physical closeness.

"Because I have—things—things to do, and I don't want any obstacles."

"Well, I'm hardly an obstacle," she giggled, and her eyes danced. "Don't be so serious, silly. We're not making any lifetime commitment. We're just having a good time. Or at least I am."

His mouth broke into a grin. "Yeah, I guess you're right. Why am I getting so upset?"

"As for the things you have to do, now. What are they?" Her voice was soothing, like a mother to an injured child.

"Oh, nothing, I guess. Some direction in my life. A future."

"First things, first." And she leaned over and kissed his cheek. "Now, I've got to get going. Four o'clock ok?" And she flashed him a smile, jumped to the curb, waved and was off.

He watched her until she disappeared into the Employees Only entrance. He knew he wanted her. His heart thumped when he thought of entering her. He felt himself getting hard. His hand reached for his fly and then with a great, frustrated smash he banged his fist against the dashboard.

"I hate her. I hate her." He spat the words out in a venomous stream. "Women fuck everything up. Everything is going along fine and some woman—some woman you really trust fucks everything up. Well, she's not going to ruin my plans."

He forced himself to put Mary out of his mind because the desire to lay her was coming back. He held his head tightly, trying to concentrate on something else.

He began to recreate and fashion the previous night's scene in minute detail and the thought of Mary receded to a dull, then silent, cave in his mind.

The scene unfolded and he began to glory in it.

He had seen the camper run out of gas and the man trudge off down the black strip of road. At first he had decided to go to The Hill, where he knew all hell was about to break loose. He could easily pick up some stoned dude or girl and drive around for a while before the killing. But

72

seeing this opportunity, he could not pass it up.

She had come out of the camper when he banged on the side of it. He came up from behind and grabbed her. Unfortunately, she screamed once before he plunged the needle into her. She was lying unconscious on the portable table in the van in a matter of seconds.

He drove around until he heard her move. He parked the van and put on his surgical gown and mask and climbed into the back.

She was groggy, and he gave her a cup of water from the cooler.

He kept her fully clothed, but pushed her skirt up to the thighs.

She was coming out of it, and she struggled, but her arms were locked into steel braces at the table's sides.

"Please don't. Please don't rape me," she rasped. He had laughed at that.

He reached for his scalpel and made a small incision at the thick section of thigh where her underpants ended. He used the elastic seam of the underpants as a guide and began the cutting process around the thigh. Her eyes bugged out of her head as she began the long, anguished screaming. He did not want to etherize her until he absolutely had to—at that time when her screaming was too loud and prolonged.

The leg was half separated from the trunk when her shaking and convulsed body slipped into unconsciousness. He tried to revive her by slapping her face. He wanted her to see it. To know what a sharp blade could do. The wet stinging sensation of the cut. He had lived with the thought of it for too many years.

"What do you think my father felt when he ripped his own throat open. Well, feel it, feel it. Like others will feel it." He pulled her limp body up by her hair and pushed her face forward. "Look at it. Look at and feel it. See it.

Do you see it? Do you see the blood the way my father saw it? Do you? Take that to your grave with you. Nothing will stop me." She groaned and her eyes rolled around in her head like large marbles. The dull, reddish overhead light revealed she was in the second stage of shock. He separated the leg from the body.

He cleaned and inspected the wound. He neatly tied up the arteries and wrapped the leg up in a day-old copy of the *Log*. The *Log* stared up at him circled by the overhead light. The *Log*. The thought of Mr. Cyrus Standish Dean and the hate that name and that paper summoned up in him. Dean, who held no regard for the reputation of good people. His father was murdered by Dean's words. Dean's words in that newspaper. Tears came, as he continued wrapping the leg. It would make good eating for the fish. He looked at the woman. She lay silent except for an occasional twitch. She would die before the night was over. And of special significance to his plan was the fact that she was a tourist. Would they still come in their cars packed with kids and bikes? Would the campers still squat in the grassy fields next to the ocean?

He took the black hose from the sink and cleaned the table and the floor, directing the blood into porcelain containers. His med school mind dictated cleanliness and sterility.

When he was finished, he drove to the beach, where he left her in the sand. He was careful to walk in the surf, and double back to his van.

In some respects he had enjoyed the young cop more, because of the complete shock and terror the cop had shown and because the daylight had sent flashes off the blade into the dazed cop's eyes. But, for overall impact, he knew a tourist's murder would do more to accelerate his plan than anyone else's.

He spun around the corner of The Hill. Oceanfront

greeted him. Sea from shore to horizon with race horse waves washing along miles of beach, their great white manes flashing in the sun. And on the beach itself, sprawled and curled, were the bodies of the young and athletic: spry, lean, lithe, the bath towels and the Sudden Tan, the Bain de Soleil, the six-packs, the radios, and always the swimmers. They dove through breaking waves and stroked out beyond the markers only to be whistled back by the long-legged lifeguard.

He watched them play summer grab-ass in the sand.

"Have a party, you bastards. Who knows? One of you might be next." He laughed as he parked along the harbor front.

He sat back in the van and pulled a curtain shut on each side with only a straight windshield view of the harbor and a square weather-beaten clapboard restaurant and fish store with a take-out window for clams and french fries. He reached under the seat and pulled out a tin box. He grabbed a joint and lit it, careful not to lose anything. His lean cheekbones became leaner as he sucked in the smoke. He kept it down and his stomach pulled it in, but not before lungs and chest tightened and then at the last moment gave way. His attention was on the restaurant and he could see himself as a small boy of eight rowing up to the wooden ladder that was still there. He saw his father leaning down, tawny, sun-washed, reaching for him and then hugging him as they walked off to the fish store.

Tears dimmed his vision and almost washed out the memory of those glorious summers of just him, his dad, and mother.

How many sun-bleached summers had there been? He counted them on his long white fingers.

"Four, five." And he switched to the other hand while he sucked in the smoke.

"Seven, seven of the happiest summers of my life." He

wiped the tears away with the knuckles of his right hand. He tried to remember the station wagon his father had. It was a Morris Minor and it had "The Fish Shack" on the front door panels, which always made him proud when they drove down Main Street. Because it was their place, their very own business that they were advertising.

The Fish Shack opened every summer right after Memorial Day. His father would come down alone, and when school got out, Doug and his mother would join the father until Labor Day. From the very first, it was a success. The best clams on the Cape with the finest view, the posters had said.

At night, after closing time, he would sit with his mother and father and listen to the waves lapping against the pilings and he would smell the oil from the boats or the gas or the saltbitten night air. When August rolled in on damp nighttime fogs, he would huddle between the two of them and—when he was younger—fall asleep against them. Sleepily, he would feel his father's strong arms pick him up and bundle him off to the car.

No one could have had better parents. It wasn't that he was spoiled. It was just that he belonged with them. They did everything together and went everywhere. His father had finally sold everything in New Rochelle—the house and the small diner—and moved to the Cape for "the great escape," he had called it.

Now he could not make out The Fish Shack at all. The tears were too much. It was as though he were looking through a rainswept windshield.

He punched out the joint and lay across the seat sobbing until he thought he would choke. He sat up abruptly and pinched the tears free from his eyes with thumb and index finger. He sat breathing deeply for several minutes until the breath came normally and without the periodic jerking that had accompanied the sobs.

"I will personally rape this town where it hurts. Where it fucking-A hurts them—in their pocketbooks."

He took great delight in remembering the story of the little town of Tesno only twenty miles north of Quonsett. For years it prospered as a booming tourist haven. Everybody had a piece of the action until one night in the early fifties when the murder of a Boston secretary turned everything around.

She had met someone at a dance and had gone off with him, but not before introducing him simply as Hank to some of her friends. Her naked and mutilated body was found in a cranberry bog the next morning. Hank was not found and the case was unsolved and finally dropped after years of investigation.

Tesno became a ghost town and lingered in his memory as a ghost town. On his way into Quonsett, he had traversed the highway and dipped down into the cluster of cheap bars, rotting buildings, pool halls, one adult movie house, and a Mister Dairy. Even the water that lapped in against the corroded and decaying wharves was murky and fetid. The only boats that tied up did so out of necessity, for gas or food or booze, and then they were off for the clean waters on the other side of the bay.

Tesno was a high-poverty area now and the murder of the Boston secretary did it. And all you had to do if you didn't believe it was to check *The Boston Globe*, which ran a story on Tesno entitled "The Death of a Town." He had checked it.

It was ironic. He had seen it the week he left Boston Medical for lack of funds. He had been having coffee at Hayes Bickford's in Cambridge while checking the "Wanteds." There it was, right directly in front of him, screaming into his face. All he had to do was change the name of the town in his mind.

The Death of a Town—Quonsett. His heart had

pounded with excitement and his mind exploded with the hows. How would he do it? How would he bring that town to its knees?

It had been a thought constantly gnawing away at him since that terrible summer of 1966. He turned fourteen that summer and the world was a bright and glorious place to be. Every day would find him working behind the counter of The Fish Shack with his father and mother, or exchanging the easy banter with the fishermen who dumped their catches in wriggling, shiny mounds in the basins under the Shack. Business was getting better everyday and his plan to be a doctor—a surgeon—was a pleasant one to think about. They had made the permanent move to Quonsett, and Doug liked the idea because he already knew so many of the townies he would be going to school with.

And then it all collapsed like those sand castles he used to fashion on Quonsett town beach. He would cup his hands firmly but cautiously around the Norman towers, dig cavernous passageways beneath the main keep, pat down the walls and soak them with seawater and place a multicolored flag stiffly in the sand of the main tower. He would step back and admire his creation and then run off for a quick swim, and when he returned his castle was a waterhole and the flag was floating on the waves.

The tone seemed to change. It was little things at first. His father did not seem to have as much time for him because he was always working. There were discussions between mother and father about money. Then the discussions became bitter shouting matches and many times the father would not come home at all. Doug would find the rumpled cot and cigarette butts the next day when he would be sweeping out the back room of the Shack. There were fewer rides uptown and there were continual schemes for borrowing money.

One night Doug's mother had cried that she could save the business and she would do it anyway she could. But the father was too drunk to hear her or care. Doug had watched it all from the shadows of the staircase and his heart twisted in knotted fear and sorrow. It was all so unlike his parents. It had all happened so fast, just when everything was going so well. The business had been good one day, and the next day everything turned gray, then black.

He had been visiting family friends in Boston when the call came. He was told nothing except that his father had had an accident.

When he returned to the house in Quonsett after a silent journey from Boston, it was his mother standing in the doorway of the breezeway who told him what he really already had suspected.

He flew into her arms and they clung to each other for an eternity as she kept sobbing and screaming.

"They killed him. They killed him."

His father had cut his own throat with a paring knife. He was found lying down in the fresh fish tank by Doug's mother. The insensitive Log reported it colorfully in its usually folksy way by stating "The tank was a red tide."

The funeral was on the Cape because, as his mother told him many times, the Cape had been a happy place for Doug's father. And at first Doug thought the same, but as the weeks passed and the mother began to clean up family matters, Doug's attitude changed. "The Cape destroyed my father. It was responsible for his death. Especially this town." He knew he did not know all the facts, but the facts would be there and he would find them out.

His mother did not sell the house immediately. It was as though selling it, giving it up, made the father's death absolute. And as long as they held on to the house, they held on to the father. And there was the strong presence of that man. That first autumn, they came back on weekends until late October to visit the grave.

Finally, and very quickly, the house was sold and they went back to New York to live. They never came back. Until Doug came back now. During the years of growing into maturity, he heard bits and pieces from his mother. Especially when she was drinking. She would scream how she had tried to help. How he had misunderstood. How he hadn't understood. The drinking nights were torture for him at first, but after a while he waited for her to drink and then she would screech it all out.

Her drinking became worse until she had to be hospitalized. One night as he sat in the starched white room of the hospital, she raved. The man had made promises. Promises that were never kept. It was not until weeks after the suicide that she realized the man was responsible for everything.

Two days later she lapsed into a coma and died. Doug did not cry. He simply remembered.

All his mother left him was $1,200 and a scrapbook of clippings that told in detail why his father had killed himself.

ILLEGAL WEIGHING PROCEDURE BRINGS PROFITS FOR FISH SHACK—DOUGLAS PETERS SR. DENIES

was the most damaging headline in the *Log*.

According to Doug's mother, the father denied right up until the last. He had maintained he was set up by Ray Daren, who was his assistant manager. The fishermen and the town argued that Daren could get nothing out of a setup like that. The profits wouldn't be his. They would be Doug Peters's.

On the day of the inspection, Peters pleaded that there had to be a mistake. Why would he be so stupid as to rig the weights when he knew inspection for him was long overdue. All the inspector offered, and later the town, was "They all say that."

A week later The Fish Shack was closed for failing to stay within the limitations of a right to sell. Douglas Peters killed himself as the final closing notice was being printed in the press room of *The Quonsett Log*. Peters left a brief note for his son asking the son to forgive him and to love him as he had loved his son, and please to continue in his plan to be a doctor.

The ensuing years were difficult. Doug managed to excel in high school and be accepted at Cornell. He lived with his mother's maiden aunt, who helped him with love and as much schooling costs as she could, but when she died in his third year of med school, Doug just could not go on. He loved her as a surrogate mother, and at her death the bitter years came crashing in on him. The cutthroat competition of med school and the complete alienation and scars of youth were fanned into a flame of hate at her death.

He was holding the scalpel now as he calmly looked across the narrow harbor to The Fish Shack. Of course, the name had been changed several years ago. The yellow quarterboard on the leeward side of the weather-shingled shack said simply, *Patterson's*.

At her mooring, *The Molly O'* bobbed up and down like a cork. She was anchored at the near side of the harbor alongside the slip that was the old Fish Shack's private wharf. The police cruiser drove slowly past the wharf and parked in Patrons' Parking Only. Wayne Boyd got out and approached the takeout window.

"Two medium clams and one order of onion rings to go," he told the blond girl whose hair was tightly held in by a hairnet.

She gave him a number and he sauntered over to the pilings that rose out of the oily slick of the harbor. He rested the right jump boot on a piling and looked out to Mariner Land. The ferry was coming through the channel, and its passengers waved to the landlubbers in that timeless and ancient ritual of the sea. It always amused him to see yachtsmen, ferry passengers, and the like raise their hands in a salute to their fellow man on shore. Once they stepped on terra firma, they shoved that same hand up your ass, he thought.

The crew of *The Molly O'* jumped from the trawler and went off in separate directions. He watched them greet wives, children, and girl friends. A few minutes after the last car left the parking lot, a huge, well-built man wearing a sweat shirt with sleeves cut off at the shoulders jumped onto the pier. He had the beginnings of a beard and his biceps had very prominent veins running down the arm. He ordered a cheeseburger and coffee from the girl with the hairnet, then walked over to where Wayne Boyd was balancing his foot on the piling.

"Great day," he said to no one.

"How many days you been out?"

"Five."

"Where?"

"Georges Banks. Good haul."

The girl called, "Number thirty-six."

"Hey, that's me. See ya. Five minutes or so. Same place?"

"Fine," the muscular one said.

Wayne Boyd left and grabbed his order. He handed it through the open window to Swanson, who took an onion ring.

"I thought you didn't like onion rings, you bastard," he said slipping behind the wheel. He drove off a mile up the road and down a quiet lane and parked by an old boathouse. The red paint was peeling and there was an air of disuse about the place.

They dug into their clams until a Ford pickup truck arrived and the driver got out. He was chewing something vigorously and washing it down with a Styrofoam cup of hot coffee.

"Hi ya, Boyd, Swanson."

"How ya doin', Chester!"

Chester Bridges was still wearing his hip boots and he smelled of fish.

"Some of the guys are fuckin pissed, Swanson. You investigating them and all."

"Yeah, well, they're all clean, nothing for them to be excited about. Everybody's clean," he said with disgust.

"I know, but like they said, 'Shit, what kinda country is this, ya can't even hate fuckin cops no more!' "

"But they can, Chester." Boyd was grinning, showing a mouthful of full-bellied clams. "It's just that a cop-killer brings out the best in us."

"Or the fuckin worst."

"Or the fuckin worst," Boyd mimicked. "C'mon, Chester, what have you got? I got your message this morning. Must have been three or three-thirty. You bastards stay up all night?"

"Betcherass, if the fuckin fish are bitin."

"Well, Boyd, it may not be nothin, but we got a new guy on board who can fillet fish like a fuckin doctor."

"What's that prove? That's probably why he got the job."

"Yeah, yeah, I know, but he really looks like he enjoys it. So I start talking to him, right?"

"Right! How old is he? What's he look like? Where's he from?"

"Hey. Chrise sake, one question at a time." He finished the coffee, crushed the cup in his greasy bearlike paw, and threw it into the back of the pickup.

"He's about twenty-eight. Got a medium built. Dark

83

curly hair. Name's Cormier, Pete Cormier."

"Anything else?"

"Well, I'm curious about this guy."

Swanson swallowed a clam the wrong way and began a spasm of choking coughs until Boyd smacked him hard on the back.

"Jesus. Take care of that guy, Boyd."

"Go on, Chester. Why curious?"

"Well, we were sitting around last night having a couple of pops. About ten o'clock. And the talk turns to this cop who was murdered. Nobody seemed to know too much. Some guys were surprised about the cop's head missin. So naturally everybody has a theory. You know, the one most of the guys figured on?"

"No, what?"

"Cop-hater." He smiled when he said it.

"Figures. Go on."

"Well, this kid, says somethin about the killer usin Sodium Pentothal. Now, I thought that was funny that he would know that. Because I didn't know that."

Boyd's eyes became large as Chester continued. "In fact, I still don't know it. Is that true, Boyd?"

"It doesn't matter, Chester. Where does this guy live?"

"I dunno. I asked him. He said he sleeps around."

"Ok, Chester, thanks. Thanks a lot. You've been a big help. Keep in touch with yourself."

"Yeah, see ya Boyd. Captain." And he tipped the peak of his soiled bleacher's cap that said Red Sox World Series 1975.

"Ok, let's check out this Cormier. And save me a god-damned onion ring. I thought you didn't like them."

"They grow on you." Swanson laughed.

At 4:10 P.M. Mary came out of the restaurant and waved. She said something to a short stout blond girl who looked over at the van and then waved good-by to Mary.

He was hoping the blond did not see him as he pretended to be occupied with something on the floor of the cab. When he straightened up the girl was gone and Mary was climbing in.

"Hi, did I keep you long?" She didn't wait for an answer. "Where shall we go? Look. Onion rings, clams, the ones with swollen bellies. They look pregnant, don't they! Let's find a nice quiet spot and have a long cool swim. Doug? What do you say?"

"Huh?"

"Say, are you listening to me? I've got a picnic lunch here. The boss was going to throw it all out. Can you imagine? And clams at those prices."

"I'm sorry, Mary. I was preoccupied." And he grabbed a handful of golden clams, still hot from the oven.

"Good, huh? Have some tartar sauce."

"Mary, who was that girl you were talking to?"

"You mean Liz? The waitress?"

"Yeah."

"Liz Thorne, she goes to Simmons with me. She got me the job. She's great. What a sense of humor. Why, do you think you know her?"

"Uh, no. I was just curious."

"I told her you were my friend. My special friend." And she moved closer to him. "She loved your van."

"Did you tell her my name?" He said it in an offhand manner.

"No, well just Doug. Why? Are you wanted in ten states or something?" She crinkled her nose and looked up at him.

He forced a smile.

"I just wondered what you called me, you know, if you ever mentioned me to other people. Doug, Dougie, Pete, Mr. Peters?" How many people out there know me. How many. He had to find out. As difficult as it was he kept the crooked smile. He had to know. But he had to be casual.

"Well, as a matter of fact, you may be angry, but I really haven't mentioned you to anyone except Liz. She's the only one I talk to at the restaurant. My family is going in all directions and there's no time on the job. God, that guy Perkins who owns it is a slave driver. Jesus." She reached out and squeezed his hand.

"Maybe that's why I like being with you, Doug. We're both loners, I guess. You'd say you were a loner, wouldn't you?"

"I guess so. Yes. That's safe to say. You have a family at least. I have no one."

"No one?" Her smile was ingenuous.

"Well, almost no one." He felt warm inside. That was nice, he thought. "You're a very sincere girl, Mary. You have a lot of goodness in you. That's rare these days."

I feel good, and kind of safe with you. Even more so, it seems, sitting here in the van, high up and away from everybody else. Sort of away from time and place."

"Are you sure you're not an English major? That has to be Emily Dickinson talking." He wanted to get off it now, his mind was getting soggy and soft. He was feeling something inside that he had not felt before—ever. He did not want to feel this way. He must close off all valves that let emotion flow. Sex. That was all right. He needed that. But involvement. That he did not need.

"Here, special summer friend. Have some clams."

He left the main road and ducked the van in and out of sun shadows until they came to an abandoned windmill. He low-geared the van through the high grass until they stopped by the white sand of an almost deserted beach. A few sailboats, their sheets puffed and billowing, dipped and rose several hundred feet from shore.

A hundred yards to their left, three middle-aged day-trippers fished off the jetties for flounder. They were wearing too much gear to be pros. Otherwise, the beach, the sand, the surf, and the sun belonged to them.

"Doug, I never knew this place was here. Look, that old windmill, I've seen it on a thousand postcards. How did you find it?"

"I found it. I've found a lot of hidden and secret places in this town. Maybe some night I'll give you a tour of my secret places. Would you like that?"

"Yes, I guess so?" Her answer was more of a question. "Why does it have to be at night? You're strange."

"Smile when you say that, Mary." He broke it off quickly and added, "Hey, I just remembered, what are you going to do for a bathing suit? You can't go in with your uniform on. Unless you want to pretend we're in Truro, and do the skinny."

She jumped from the van and raced to the top of the sandy hill. She yelled over her shoulder, "Never mind Truro." And she began slipping out of her uniform, letting it fall to the sand.

"Violà!" She stood there wearing a maillot swimsuit with sea-blue stripes. Her chest swelled, accentuating sharp cleavage.

"Well, I'll be ripped."

"Last one in is a fried clam." And she raced to the surf, diving into a whitecap just as it curled for its break.

He was glued to the spot for a moment and then he raced after her. She had come up on the other side of the wave. Her black hair was shining in the sun, giving her the look of some Tahitian beauty.

He stroked easily and strong after her. When he reached her, she was lying on her back, the rays of the sun full force on her face.

He treaded water beside her. He wanted to pull her into him. His heart thumped. He had not had that feeling, that deep-seated emotion, for a long time. He let the urge pass and said simply, "You're very beautiful out here."

"Just out here?" And she caught him full force in the face as she chopped and slapped at the water until they were both enveloped by the egg-white foam.

He felt immense joy and pleasure in being with her. The urge came back and this time he did not fight it. He surfaced, dived and swam underwater in several directions until his face was level with her long well-tapered legs. Her legs were sinewy in the green shadows under water and he wrapped his left arm around them while running his right hand up and along her buttocks. He broke for the surface with both arms around her waist.

"Well, Moby Dick! Or are you an octopus?"

"Do you mind?"

"No."

He put both arms around her and brought her into him. He kissed her long, but soft. He raised her body out of the water and eased her on her back. Her legs opening and closing around his waist. They floated that way in the timeless afternoon until she said, her voice husky with sex, "Why don't we go in?"

He reluctantly released his hold of her and she stroked for shore.

Pulling herself up out of the water, she jogged to her tote bag and took out a towel. Her body shivered more from their watery intimacy than the swim.

He joined her on the blanket she had spread, but not before he squeezed the water from his cut-down Levi's.

He lay there looking up at a blue canvas of sky. She lay beside him. Their elbows touched. He did not speak for a while but when he did his voice was full of emotion.

"I haven't met too many people in my life that I could, well, you know, trust. People are not good, for the most part. They're out to get all they can and they really don't care who they hurt in the process."

88

She didn't say a word. She sensed he needed to go on, to spill it all.

"I saw that in college. It was 'Screw you, Jack, as long as I'm ok.' Then in graduate school it was the same way. I had a great deal of success in grad school, but the money ran out. When I tried to get scholarship help there was a line as long as this beach. Guys I knew who did not need the aid. And they knew I *did* need it."

He toyed with the idea of telling her it was med school, but he just could not trust her all the way. He had to be careful. Nothing could stand in the way of a plan he had dreamed of for years.

"What will you do in the fall?"

"Maybe work and save enough and go back."

"What do you want to do? Teach?"

"No, maybe diplomatic service. With an M.A. in poly-sci, maybe I could make it in government." The lie came easily.

He smiled to himself thinking how he could wreak havoc on small principalities by wielding his scalpel. For a moment he felt himself slipping out of reality, and the sky seemed to turn over. He lay on his stomach, rubbing his neck.

"What's the matter? You ok?"

"Yeah, I just had a sharp pain in my neck and head. It's ok, it's gone now."

She reached over and rubbed his neck while sitting up on her right elbow. He lowered his head and kissed her. She responded softly while he extended his tongue.

The sky whirled as they twisted passionately on the blanket. His hands found her breasts and she rose to his touch.

His hands found her body. All of it. And he rubbed and caressed until she whispered into his ear, "Let's go to the van."

He led her across the sand to the rear of the van.

"Wait, it's locked." He retrieved the key from under the front seat and opened the back.

They climbed into the semidark. It was cool because it was out of the sun. She hesitated at first, wanting him to be the aggressor. He leaned over and flipped two catches on each wall and a wide white-sheeted bed, more like a table, came out of the center panel. She half turned, but he brought her head around while his hands found her thighs.

"This looks like an operating room. Are you planning on operating on me, doctor?" Her breath came quickly and her heart pounded. Her words sounded glib and phony. She was trying to break that first barrier. If she could, then everything would be all right. She knew he wanted it. She hoped she could be good for him.

"It depends on what you call an operation. Maybe a little exploratory work," he whispered as he undid the blue string around her neck and brought the suit down to her navel. Her breasts needed no support. They were firm and round and he cupped them as she came into him.

As he stood bringing her into him, he could feel her pulling the suit off until she lay back on the table naked. The barrier was removed because she could tell from his blazing eyes that he liked her body.

"I'm sorry I'm not more tanned. It's all those daylight hours waitressing."

"You look just perfect to me," he said as he guided her hand along the zipper of his Levi's.

Her rocking motion was controlled but continual. She brought him to the edge twice and then slowed down, and then finally she brought him over in a great shaking thrust. He had never had it better.

They lay side by side periodically kissing until she said, "I think it's about time we got along."

"Just a few more minutes, Mary, it's so peaceful here."

90

Suddenly, there was a harsh banging on the back panel.

Doug shot up and grabbed his Levi's. Mary snapped a towel from a hook and threw it over her.

"Stay here. Some wise guy probably."

As he opened the door into daylight his eyes squinted, blurring his vision. All he could discern at first was a figure with flashes coming from his chest. As his eyes cleared, he realized he was looking directly into a badge.

"Excuse me," the figure was saying, "but you don't have a beach sticker. Are you a resident?"

"Well, not exactly, officer. Just here for a vacation."

"I suggest you try the town beach unless you're renting a house and you can get a tax bill or some verification of rental and bring it to town hall. Ok?"

"Oh, thank you, officer. I'll move right away. Thank you."

He jumped out onto the sand, and locked the door. He left Mary lying on the table. There was no other way to the cab because a large refrigerator blocked the access. Three miles down the street he stopped and helped her out.

"Well, that was quite a surprise. Do you often get visits from the police?"

"Not often."

"Say," she was saying as she looked up at him. At five foot eleven he was four or five inches taller. "What do you have in that refrigerator?"

"Why?" he demanded in a quick, stabbing voice.

"Don't get excited. I just thought you might have a beer in there, but it's locked up like a chastity belt, for God's sake."

He feigned laughter. "Oh, I just keep it locked in case some dude breaks in. He would still have to break the lock. I've got a little stuff in there. Grass and stuff. You know."

"You're not a junkie are you?" And she pretended extreme naïvete.

That took the edge off and he broke into uncontrollable laughter. He sat down in the marsh grass at the side of the road and rolled over laughing. It was infectious and in moments she was giggling without control as he pulled her down on top of him and they rolled and kissed together through the high waving grass.

When he dropped Mary off at the seawall near her home, he had already decided he would repaint the panels of the van. They were too easily spotted and identified, and Mary's friend Liz Thorne had seen him. She may not be able to identify him, but she could easily identify the van. Liz Thorne. He would not forget that name.

Mary . . . She was becoming so important in so short a time. He couldn't allow that—not yet, but he was so peaceful with her, it was so good. He couldn't just stop seeing her. Women, they always fucked you up one way or another; even when they tried to help they fucked you up. It was too bad about Mary because he could love her if he knew how, if he could let her in. He had never been this close to someone before—how strange that he should grow so close to her in the middle of his mission, and she a part of the town. Mary . . . It really was too bad.

The town beach was packed, even though it was nearing sundown. It was two miles from The Hill, so it did not attract the college kids or the bikes. The only vans in sight had no panels, all windows. Half-naked and naked babies were dipped into the blue surf for their salty baptism while the spreading fleshy bodies of their mothers and the bulging middles of their fathers laughed and joked under the hot orange sun.

One middle-aged father flapped his way to the water's edge, his sale-reduced snorkle cupped in his hand. As he flapped his duck feet into the water, one of the fins came loose and he had to sit in the surf to adjust it. His back

92

was russet from his first day in the sun. His night would not be comfortable.

The world was blue green and daylight clear in a depth of seven feet. Tiny fish appeared and darted in speckled schools below and around him. It was a silent world and the cool water soothed his back. He did not wish to go any deeper or any farther out. *Jaws* had frightened the hell out of him. Me, he thought. An ex frogman. He surfaced and treaded water. The beach was mobbed. "Two weeks. Two sweet weeks with the wife and kids in the sun." His back smarted a bit and he made a mental note to cover up when he got in. There was plenty of time for a tan before he got back to the telephone company.

Harry adjusted the gear and slipped below the surface and was mesmerized by that quiet and golden ray of sunlight that cut through the water turning the blue green to an amber, giving a scrim effect to the bottom. He let himself be carried parallel to the shore. He parted the tiny fish with his hands. The booze from the night before was leaving his body and he felt good. He was glad Madge had pushed him. He thought of Madge. Tonight they would have a few drinks after the kids were in bed. She gave him that look when she was putting that suntan oil on her thighs. He thought her thighs had already turned brown. He explored the pebbles and stones of the ocean bottom —all seven or eight feet of it—and he scooped at the sand with a shell. The scooping disturbed the tranquillity, and smoky clouds appeared in front of him. He waited for the clouds to vanish as he kicked casually along. Suddenly, his outstretched hands touched something. His thrust-out hands inadvertently closed around it as the mud clouds disappeared. His head tightened and his temples boomed, his eyes shot up into his head and he opened his mouth in horror. He tried to blow the water out, but instead he became disoriented and swallowed more. His lungs shrieked for air and he sprang off the sand and exploded into the surface coughing, gagging, and floundering. He sucked in the air and violently sniffed the mucus from his nostrils.

Madge yelled from her blanket. "Be careful, honey, that's the worst place to lay if you don't want a burn."

He did not answer.

She rolled over on her stomach and humped the sand and then lay quiet.

(What the hell did I see? he thought. Worse, what did I touch? I can't tell them. Either they'll think I'm nuts or they'll panic. I gotta do something. He sat up and slowly turned toward the beach. Kids were everywhere. What if some kid? he thought. The lifeguard. I'll tell the lifeguard. He'll know what to do.)

He kicked off the fins and waddled over to the lifeguard's chair. He looked up at the kid. Only a kid, what does he know? The kid looked down and smiled that YMCA smile. He was blond and lithe—very tanned with white cream on his nose. He would be picked out of a New Year's celebration in Times Square as a lifeguard.

"May I help you, sir?"

"Yeah, could I talk to you?"

"Sure." And he swung himself out of the tall chair and dropped catlike to the sand.

Harry felt foolish. How could he convince the kid? And he studied his hands and rubbed them on his swim trunks.

Madge turned around to see Harry gesturing and pointing. The lifeguard, with hands on hips, listened politely while scanning his beach zone. Then she noticed the guard turning from the beach and gesturing back at Harry.

Harry was raising his right hand.

"What the hell is he doing, getting sworn in to the guard? She giggled into her hands. The guard grabbed for a long bamboo pole with a net on it and he and Harry headed for the shoreline.

The kid grabbed the pole and waded in up to his shoulders. He turned back to Harry, who was standing in ankle-deep water, and then he surface dived.

Kids lined the shore in little huddles, cued in by the lifeguard and the long, netted pole, scanning the water for a jellyfish.

The kid crashed to the surface, the pole trailing in his right hand. His tan was gone. He turned on his side and puked his guts into the waves.

"Hey, look at the guard. Afraid of the little fishes?" yelled a bony kid from shore.

"Yeah, watch out for *Jaws*." They laughed and punched each other.

"You kids knock it off," Harry spat out at them.

The kid stroked his way into shore with his right hand while keeping the pole at a distance. When he felt the sand in his hand, he rose up and pulled the pole in. He was ashen, not just his face, but his entire body.

"Get me a towel, please." He looked at Harry pleadingly. The net was dragging in a foot of water, its contents unseen.

Harry pushed his way through the curiosity seekers.

Kids started crowding in.

"You guys take off, will you?" he said softly, his breath coming in gasps.

"What are *you*, some kind of cop or sumthin? We just want to see the savage fish that gave you such a fight out there in the deep."

This broke them up. One grabbed the pole to steady it while the other went around to the net.

"I said, get out of here. Split."

They crowded in on him closer as the blankets emptied and more of the curious came over to the circle.

There was bumping and shoving and one of the group

—the bony kid—started wrestling the lifeguard for the pole. The jostling continued as the adults laughed and gently chided the teenagers to stop it and allow the lifeguard to do his job.

The pole came free from the guard's hands.

The bony kid lifted the pole from the water and shook the net free. He juggled it and handled the pole like a lacrosse stick curling, and twisting it as he ran, stopped, ran, stopped, and scooped. "Hey, Chuckie, grab the pass. And he whirled and shovelled a pass to the other boy who had wrestled the pole free.

"Let's see the fish," a gray-haired man from the edge of the crowd said. "C'mon, what the hell is it, a stingray."

With a flick of the wrists, the net stayed and the contents flew into the air. The crowd's attention froze on the flying object and followed its descent to the sand, where it rolled over several times before it came to a stop. The crowd inched forward. "Be careful, Karen, don't go too close, those things can sting," a mother warned. As the crowd now closed in, a penetrating scream pierced the afternoon. One man gasped and a middle-aged woman fainted quietly into the sand. The crowd stepped back easily at first, and then the ranks broke. Screeching and screaming echoed up and down the beach bringing more numbers to arrive and shrink back in horror.

Harry wiped his face in the towels while beneath his feet a large, purple-gray head lay in grotesque silence staring up at him through watery, dirty eyes.

Five

"You can't keep the lid on anymore, *Mister* Patterson," Boyd was saying to the lank figure before him as Chief Medina walked into the oak-paneled selectmen's conference room. "The entire beach was in panic. God knows how many kids will be screaming their asses off for weeks —years, maybe. The Buckley kid's head! It's too crazy. Too incredible. I can't believe it happened. I've seen some shit in my life, but Christ knows I have never seen anything like this. I couldn't even imagine something like this. That head was not just floating. It was put there. Put there to be found."

"The head is only the least of our problems now," Medina was saying. "I just came from the trailer camp. The dead woman's husband and children are in shock. Every camper in the place knows it and a hell of a lot of 'em are already pulling out. I heard it on a Boston station. At least they had the common decency not to mention the head. They simply mentioned a pathological killer was loose in Quonsett. Specialty: dismembering."

Patterson dug his right fingernails deeply into the palm of his left hand. Generally, he became coldly calm when there was an emergency. That was basically the reason he was able to hold the selectman's job longer than anyone else had. Twenty-one years. He was irascible and disliked in several quarters, but he had the machine and he got the job done. Not always cleanly, but done. He studied the nail marks on his hand. He had never had this kind of an emergency and his usual calm was forced. He was beginning to tense up.

"Who gives a shit about campers? What do they spend? Five bucks for the camper, and a couple of bucks for bread and milk?"

"Is that all you can think about? The money? The tourists? I can't believe I just heard that. I can't believe the chairman of the board of selectmen can sit there in the face of two violent and depraved murders and tally up the financial books."

"Easy, Wayne, easy. What Frank is saying is—"

"I know what he's saying. Well, I say we call in the DA's office now."

"No, goddamn it. No. That's final." Patterson was not even looking at Boyd. He was directing his outburst to Medina. "No outside interference, or so help me, Joe—"

"Ok, ok, take it easy, Frank, take it easy. We can handle it." He paused. "The only thing is—"

"The only thing is what?"

"Well, the DA just may not wait for us. This isn't a usual situation."

"We'll just have to stall. I'll see what I can do with the *Log*. We've got to get this bastard or the town will panic. I tell you if panic takes over, the next thing will be mob rule. And if that happens there will be looting, vandalism, and destruction. This town will never recover. We've got to batten down the hatches."

Boyd stood by the window. The sweat was rolling down the back of the pleated blue uniform shirt. Patterson was right about that much. The town was in trouble. Boyd wasn't sure as he looked out on to Main Street, but there seemed to be less pedestrian traffic today than usual.

The phone rang them back so they faced each other again. Patterson grabbed it. "Yeah, yeah. Ok. There's a phone call for you." And he gave a quick jerk of the thumb to Boyd. "Take it in the other office." Boyd left the room. His hand was still shaking with anger when he reached for the phone.

"Yeah. Ok. I'll be back as soon as I can. If he calls back tell him I'll get in touch with him at that number. Right. Oh, captain, shall I pick up some clams? Ok, and onion rings. Yeah, I know, and plenty of tartar sauce. Your gut must be like sea bottom." He hung up. He considered telling Medina but then thought better of it.

It was an hour before he was able to get back to the station and make the call.

"Hello, yeah, when it's dark. The jetty at the harbor channel. Right. Between nine and nine-thirty. See you then."

At 9:10, Boyd slipped out the side door of the station to his own car. He was in mufti. He always kept civies in his closet in case the situation called for an inconspicuous meeting. He was wearing khaki's, a garish Hawaiian shirt, and loafers. A baseball cap was stuffed in his back pocket.

As he drove to the harbor, a vague and ironic smile crossed his lips when he recalled checking out Pete Cormier of *The Molly O'* only to find out the kid was a narc with the state cops. He laughed remembering how the kid almost shit when Boyd had questioned him. There had been nothing Cormier could do except identify himself. Boyd had been reassured, not that he really had to be, that in Chester he had a very valuable piece of property.

He approached the harbor entrance and pulled slowly into the gravel driveway of the old Sea Scouts Building, now a day-care center. The building was in darkness. He got out and walked slowly along the beach. There was action from The Hill behind him. Freddie's was breaking the anti-noise law again. He would tell Patterson, that would be good for laughs. He pulled the cap out of his pocket and put it on.

He stood along the edge of the shore. The tide licked at his shoes. He looked over to the jetty, where he could make out a solitary figure lit by the moon. The figure was holding what looked like a fishing pole.

Boyd sauntered along the beach, bending occasionally to pick up a flat stone to scale along the tips of the black waves.

When he reached the jetty he spoke. "Nice night. Catch anything?"

The figure continued dangling the line. His back was turned to Boyd.

"Not yet. Come on up." Boyd climbed the slick mossy rocks and stood beside Cormier. The night air was full of salt. A Boston whaler putted by.

"What did you want?"

"Sergeant, I don't know if you realize it or not, but there's more drug traffic on that hill than in all of Boston."

"Is that it? Is that all you have for me?"

"My point is this. I've been doing narcotics for a few years now and I would be willing to bet your killer is heavy into drugs."

"Why?"

"Because these killings are bizzare, and I've met any number of dudes on that hill who would be capable of wasting someone like your man did."

"Look, Cormier, I don't want theories. I want facts. And as for telling me we got drug traffic! Are you putting me on? Did you think I thought these people were on ice cream, for Christ's sake. I'd like to help you bust the whole hill, but frankly, at this time, I don't give a shit if the place has more stuff than Istanbul. I'm looking for one thing and one thing alone: a fucker who likes to cut people up."

"That's what I'm telling you. I'm getting in with some

100

people and I think I'm on to something. There's talk. Lots of talk when these people get into it, and some of them are playing games like Guess Who. Some of the Guess Who's are people I've met who seem very capable of doing a clean cut on somebody."

"Anybody in particular?"

"Yeah, a couple. I'm trying to stay with them."

"Ok, you do that. Don't get yourself nicked. Call me anytime. If I'm not at the station tell them to reach me at home. Say it's a 700. They'll know. It doesn't mean anything except the caller knows what he's talking about."

"Ok. I'm sorry I don't have more, but I wanted you to know I'm still around and getting acquainted."

"Oh, I know you're around."

"Chester?"

"Right, Chester."

"What did you tell him anyway?"

"I told him you were clean. You were gay, but clean."

"You told him that?"

"Sure, he hasn't bothered you has he?"

"No. Come to think of it."

"Be careful if you stay out fishing overnight. Chester gets horny."

"Remember, call me anytime. No matter how slight. See ya."

"Yeah, and by the way, sergeant, thanks for not blowing my cover."

"That's ok, kid. You scratch my back, I'll scratch yours."

Boyd adjusted the ball cap, jumped down to the sand, and sauntered off up the beach. Night lights from small craft twinkled and blinked from far out in the sound.

Usually The Marine Rex could not accommodate the crowds of backpacking, lunchpacking cyclists and walkers. There was always the rising crescendo of disappointed groans when the ticket booth closed and the thick hemp rope separated the boarders from the left-behinds.

Today, no one was left behind, and the thick hemp rope lay on the hardtop. Patterson thought of the bouquet of flowers with the usual crisp twenty one-hundred-dollar bills. The money had felt good to him. It had eased his money panic. It could have been one of his best summers. The weather was in his favor, and The Hill and the other enterprises would be so grateful.

Now, Kalmir and Moffit and other establishments in town were getting on his ass. The publicity had been disastrous. Motel, hotel, cottage cancellations. The chamber of commerce calling his office asking what he planned to do. The only thing that didn't change were the group rentals, and what the hell good were they? They drank beer, drove the cops crazy with their all-night parties, and once in a while hit the night spots. But they did not spend money. He thought of his mid-winter vacation in Jamaica and his pink stucco house which leaned out into the aquamarine bay, and the deliciously long nights with the dark-skinned beauties he had always enjoyed so much. But the house, the taxes, the women all cost a goddamned fortune and he needed this summer revenue. This one summer could change everything. He palmed the bald spot. This summer, only days old, already was spending his juices. He felt drained, and the hot sun of Main Street made him long for that Jamaican retreat.

He turned to face Medina, who was agitating again about the head they'd found at the beach. The beach committee had overreacted and closed every beach in town.

"They're the beach committee. They're autonomous. They don't have to consult anybody."

"I wonder what that committee thinks of the exodus." And he nodded to the window. "Do you think they would have closed the beaches if they knew this would happen?

Everyone of those bastards has a piece of the action. Regino has his motel, Reddy has the Dairy Queen, Forbusher has the liquor store. And look at Cole. He's got his dune buggies and bike rental. Who's going to be riding to the beaches now? Tell me that, who?"

"Nobody, you're right." Medina went to the window as though on cue. He shook his head. "There are more heading out than heading in, that's for sure." He came back to his chair.

"What about you, Frank?" The question was direct and Medina meant it to be.

"You bet your ass. I've got a couple of udders out there. I admit it, we're all losing. You don't think that landscaping business of yours won't fall apart if this town gets a reputation. Use your head, Joe, we're all in this thing up to our pockets."

They sat for a few moments each deep in his own thoughts. The air conditioner droned on monotonously.

The phone rang and Swanson was on the other end asking for Medina. Patterson passed it to him without comment.

"Go ahead, yeah, yeah, good. I'll check it out in detail, thanks, captain." He placed the phone back on the receiver.

"Well, it's not much, but it's something."

"What is?" Patterson's voice had a slight trace of emotion.

"Got another report back from the lab. They found a trace of angel dust on the murdered woman's body."

"Angel dust? What the hell is that?"

"It's PCP, a well-known horse tranquilizer. Kids smoke it mixed in their joints."

"Does that mean we don't look for anyone over thirty?"

"Make that thirty-five. It's not much, but it's more than we had."

"If only the beach committee hadn't closed that god-damned beach and given the story to the *Log*."

"I thought you had Dean in your pocket."

"Only for so long. He wanted this one for the wire services. Figures he can pick up one of those fucking Golden Quill awards."

"Everybody has a piece, Frank." And he came forward, resting the chair on all fours again. His tone was serious now. "Frank, I'm scared shitless. I don't know who is out there, but I know one thing, he's just beginning. Ever since the story broke in the Boston papers, and now ours, this town is beginning to stiffen. I didn't go near the dough-nut shop this morning. I didn't have to. I could picture them huddled over their coffee and Danish. If I walked in there, I would have been bombed with questions."

"That homebound traffic started at six A.M. It will get worse. All we need is one more."

"Joe, we need a break and you know that. Somebody has to see something. Call me no matter what, Joe. Ok? Anything that sounds even faintly important."

Tight lines formed across Patterson's forehead.

"Right. See ya." Medina left the selectman's office.

Main Street resembled the protest years, except quietly. The string of traffic was starting up again and the street corners held groups of people huddled as if in some secret conspiracy.

It wasn't too long before the word passed along the streets, through the bars and shops and trailer camps, across the stone fences, lawns and deck chairs, hissing at first in an amorphous whisper that began to take shape and form and finally personality under the firm but journalistically in-discreet hand of Cyrus Standish Dean as he knocked out a blistering attack of the Quonsett Police Department in his black-bordered corner of the *Log* entitled "It Looks From

Here." And it looked to Dean that the guys wearing the badges had better forget "dunkin their doughnuts at Pete's Coffee Shop. They had better forget their part-time, full-time businesses of motels and landscaping and school buses and get on with the job of police work" because

THERE IS A MANIAC LOOSE IN THIS
PICTUREBOOK TOWN OF CAPE COD.

When that bombshell exploded on the brick steps, sun decks, newspaper drops, and newsstands face-up the next morning, the coffee cups were slowly returned to their saucers and the children were herded to swimming lessons in packs by a cadre corps of distraught mothers. The word swept along the sun-baked beaches and filtered through the soft breezy green rooms of the Quonsett Golf Club and picked up a momentum that finally reared up and shouted over station WQON. "Emergency town meeting tonight—special warrant—eight-thirty—the old high school."

To most readers of the *Log*, Dean's sudden sensationalism came as a shock. The previous couched reporting, while not giving a sense of security, at least implied with some degree of subtlety that maybe the killer had gone on to other places and that the floating head was an indication of departure.

And that pattern of reporting would no doubt have continued if Frank Patterson had not begun to feel the pressure from the businessmen on The Hill.

It all came together two days before the town meeting. Patterson, newly refreshed from an early evening liaison with the owner of the Greek restaurant, where licenses and favors were discussed in her upstairs apartment and her milk-white thighs offered Patterson the only quorum he needed, walked into the *Log*'s office.

Dean, with white mane flying as he pecked persistently at the old Underwood typewriter, scarcely looked up at the lank figure in the office doorway.

"We've got some problems, Cy."

"Uh-uh," Dean offered through the hollow pecking in the room.

"Could you stop typing that Pulitzer Prize piece for a minute?"

Dean looked up slowly. He adjusted his glasses with thumb and index finger. His smile was slow and it cracked the corners of his mouth deliberately.

"I hope you're kidding, Frank. Don't be too cocky. You're not in town hall, you know."

"I know where I am." He picked up some advertising copy, looked at it, and returned it to the desk. "There won't be much advertising going into your paper if you don't help this town out. Fast."

"What the hell do you mean, me help the town out? I've played this murder thing down as much as I can. Boston is already moving on it. I've had 'em down here nesting like pigeons and I keep telling 'em, the police and the county are working on it. My stories are master-pieces of circumlocution."

Patterson wanted to tell him that that was par for all of his articles, but he was not up to the irony of such a re-mark. The sex he had enjoyed and felt exhilarated and ful-filled by was now deserting him. He was tired and drained. He dropped into a green leather-cushioned chair.

"I mean you have to write a phony article."

"Phony? Phony how?"

"You have to say something like: You have it on very good authority that the killer is no longer in this section of the country. That there is very good reason to believe he is being held in California or someplace, and local authorities are detaining him, etcetera, etcetera."

106

"Hey, wait a minute, Frank. I can write around corners and say nothing with a lot of garbage, but I am a journalist. I can't write phony news. I just can't make up a story like that. I've already suggested that the killer could be long gone. But that was just a suggestion. I can't deliberately lie in a story."

Patterson wanted to laugh in his face. "Of course you can, for Christ's sake. You can do anything you want. You run this rag. You're always saying what a big man you are. Now show me."

"Show you? Why you? Who the hell are you?"

"I'll tell you who I am." Patterson was standing now, looking down into the peach fuzz of Dean's face. "I run this town. I am this town. Nobody does anything unless I want them to."

Dean's steady eyes studied him, and then he broke into little fits of laughter. More like spasms. He took his glasses off and wiped his eyes.

"You really believe that, don't you? You think you're the Napoleon who runs this town. That's funny, Frank. That is one funny, goddamned joke."

He looked directly at Patterson. "You would be nothing if this paper didn't back you, didn't make every half-assed decision you've made look good in the paper. Everybody knows you're in the pockets of Kalmir, Moffit, and the rest of them who own the dives on The Hill. But they don't know to the extent that I do. You think I don't know that a station wagon drives up to your house nice and prompt every couple of weeks and drops a fat bouquet of flowers on your lap with a fat greeting card and a fat payoff inside? You think I don't know that? Not many in this town know, but the ones who have to, they know. And we let you do it. Because it's good for business. It's good revenue for the town and it keeps everything where *we*—no, check that—where *I* want it. Centrally located vice, so it's nice

107

and controlled. Right down there on the Irish Riviera, just where it should be."

Patterson's veins popped out on his forehead. He began palming the bald spot.

The anger was intense. It was rising up inside from deep down in his groin. This white-haired nothing who would dare to make him feel like a goat, like the village idiot. He could not control himself any longer and he lashed out his long leathery right hand and slapped Dean across the face, sending the wire glasses spinning across the room.

A tiny trickle of blood appeared under the right eye. Cut from the wire rim.

Dean never moved. Patterson, with clamped jaw, stood over him.

"We'll see who runs this town, Mr. Editor." And he turned and walked out.

Dean just sat in his chair for a few moments nodding slowly, then he got up, retrieved his glasses, put a clean piece of paper into his typewriter, and began pecking again.

They began arriving at the meeting early, around 7:30. They stood in fidgeting clusters in front of the stone steps of the high school. Heads turned quietly and suspiciously at new arrivals. Many of them had loitered years before in the same place as students in corduroy knickers, long dresses, string ties, tight-fitting jackets, white buckskin shoes, D.A.'s, crew cuts, long hair, and jeans. The years blended harmoniously into the groups. One purpose, one reason, transcended all artificial boundaries. The separation of station or money or age was nowhere in evidence.

Fulton Alain, owner of The Quonsett Inn, chatted in guarded tones with two of his busboys and Jack Symmington, of Symmington and Sims Auto-Body Shop. The year-round tan on Alain was an obvious contrast to Symmington's dirty gray face and the pitted blackheads under the eyes.

More cars began arriving, and when the overflow had no room between the white stripes, the drivers parked on the soccer field, the sidewalks, and sprawling softball and baseball fields. No one directed they do otherwise.

At 7:45 the clusters broke up and their numbers individually bent under the sacred shibboleth chipped out of the gray granite above the arched doorway of the Jason Clement Bryant High School: "In Study and Hard Work, There Is a Profit."

The high school auditorium was set up in ordinary town meeting fashion: that venerable and incorruptible New England institution, the town meeting.

Town meeting members sat in an overflowing crowd in the first twelve rows. Many sat on the armrests and on the floor, determined to be as close to the proceedings as possible. And maybe there was a little more security in a shoulder-to-shoulder crowd.

Two leggy high school girls came out from behind the stage curtains and dutifully checked the floor mikes that were positioned in each precinct area.

Edmund Petrie, town moderator, walked to the lectern and asked for quiet. His palms-up greeting to the crowd almost spelled out "Quiet in the auditorium." He was a tall slender man with blond hair peppered with gray. His round glasses gleamed from a recent polish and sent flashes into the hushed room.

"Ladies and gentlemen, I declare this meeting open. Let us first hear from our distinguished and respected member of the clergy, Monsignor Gillespie from St. Brendan's Roman Catholic Church. Monsignor Gillespie will bless the meeting." Cyrus Standish Dean bowed his head.

Monsignor Gillespie was an average sized man in his early sixties. He had no hair, not a strand, and his golfer's head was nut-brown and freckled. He spoke softly into the mike like someone accustomed to microphones and an audience. He sat at a long table supported by three wooden horses.

He began slowly. "Today, as I looked out over the pounding surf and watched the waves breaking and crashing against the jagged rocks, and as I noted the majestic gulls holding still in the air above the shore, with the blue sky a masterful and divine background, the day alive with God's sunshine shimmering and dancing on that magnificent ocean, and the fishermen rocking and bobbing in their doughty little boats, I could not help but reflect on how fortunate—how spiritually blessed and fortunate—we are to live in the lovely seaside village of Quonsett." He paused and looked out over the heads of the crowd and up into the filled balcony. He continued.

"And so, dear friends under God, I ask you to keep strength, optimism, and hope in your hearts that our little village will heal its wounds and become the quiet, restful harbor it has always been. Please, keep peace in your hearts and do not cast stones at this meeting tonight. Let us, dear God, try to solve our difficulties and offer constructive advice to our town officials. Let our purpose be one of peaceful restoration, and not of emotional and empty rhetoric at this emergency session this evening. Amen."

The words wafted like a cooling breeze out over the assembly.

"Thank you, monsignor. And now, are there any opening questions from town meeting members?" Edmund Petrie asked in a reverent voice.

A hand shot up from the third row.

"Alvin Bearce, precinct three."

"Yes, Mr. Bearce?"

"That was a nice little speech or prayer or whatever the

hell you want to call it. But I'm one of those fishermen bobbing up and down out there." A few nervous laughs rippled along the aisles.

At first surprised, and then with obvious delight at the response to his statement, he nodded several times to the audience.

"Yes, what is your point, Alvin?"

"The point, Mr. Moderator"—and he steamed confidently ahead—"is the fact that them boats are out there bobbin for nothin, because those tourists ain't comin to Quonsett and the price of fish is down, way down. Now, damnit, somethin's gotta be done, and I blame the cops and the board of selectmen, just like the *Log* says. They all better get off their fat asses and start ketchin that bastard who's out there." Applause and whistling were accompanied by a few scattered boos and shouts.

"That will be enough." And Edmund Petrie banged the gavel. "You've made your point, Alvin, crudely," he added softly, "but you made it. I want no more outbursts like that or I'll have the police clear this auditorium." He looked over in the direction of Wayne Boyd and Eddie, who had entered the hall a few minutes before. They leaned against the side door under the old clock.

"Do you know where you can find a cop to do it?" from the downstairs rear.

"And if you find one, who says he can handle the job?" another voice joined in from the balcony.

When order was finally restored, the moderator spoke firmly into a hand mike as he walked the apron of the stage.

"I will not put up with disrespect or any form of hooliganism from this audience or any audience. Are you forgetting where you are?" He allowed the pause just enough time to be absorbed.

"This is a town meeting," he said in a husky whisper to

his congregation. His tone was sepulchral. He allowed the quiet to take hold, to be the rule and not the exception, and then he sat back down behind the table.

"Any other questions or statements?"

A rotund and flush-faced woman rose and approached her microphone.

"My name is Ann B. Crockler, and I have been a town meeting member since before most of you were born."

"Yes, we know, Annie, what's your question?"

"I'll ask my question when I'm good and ready, Ed Petrie. You all remember my husband. The finest police chief this town ever had. He worked so hard, the job killed him." (Someone whispered to a neighbor sitting in the next seat, "Yeah, he had a heart attack digging a cesspool at one of his motels.")

"What's your question, Annie?" Petrie was slightly impatient.

"My question is that since we do not have adequate police protection, we should call in the National Guard. My husband used to say—"

"Ok, Annie. Thank you. We will take your suggestion under advisement."

A hand rose up out of precinct one, which was the heart of the downtown business district.

"Charles Mason, precinct one."

"Go ahead, Mr. Mason."

"Well, we came here tonight for some answers. Some direct answers. We would like to hear from Mr. Patterson to hear just what he and the town plan to do to ease our fears. And make no mistake about it, the people in this town are scared."

Stricken faces, some ashen and frowning with mouths drawn tightly shut, looked from seat to seat, with heads nodding in agreement.

One slender young man with crossed legs clasped his

knees and rocked back and forth in nodding agreement with the others. He did not seem to be attached to anyone in the crowd but everyone's singular purpose in being there was bond enough. It was much like the hours before a hurricane, when the eerie calm brings strangers together in conversation as though any social intercourse at all might act as a buffer to what is obviously imminent.

Frank Patterson came to the center of the stage. He had been slouched in the half dark of the stage-right exit. His eye lighted immediately on Dean.

It was the first time he had seen Dean since the night in Cy's office, and Dean's eyes penetrated the long lank body. Patterson looked away from the piercing eyes as he sat at the table beside Petrie.

"Just what is your question, Mr. Mason?"

"My question is, What do you, as the highest elected official in this town, propose to do about the killer who is stalking this town?"

"You're being a little melodramatic, aren't you, Mr. Mason? Stalking the town. You make it seem as though he is looking in the windows of this auditorium at this moment."

Several people nervously cleared their throats and reluctantly turned to the windows. The slender young man smiled.

"For Christ's sake, are you for real, Patterson? You talk about melodrama! A cop's beheaded, his head is found floating around at the town beach; a woman is abducted practically in full view of her family and some sadistic bastard cuts her leg off, for Christ's sake." The voice was Jack Symmington's and he was halfway up the aisle, pointing a greasy finger at Patterson. New sweat stains were forming under the armpits of the beige uniform with Symmington and Sims Auto-Body scrawled across the back.

"Who are you talking to?" Patterson shot back.

113

"I'm talking to the guy who is supposed to be running this town. We've had two murders in less than two weeks and all we see in the paper until two days ago is that the police are investigating. Investigating what? I say if the cops can't handle it, maybe individual citizens should be deputized."

"And what would they do, stand around all night and drink coffee?" Patterson's sarcasm was razor sharp.

"Yeah, then they would be just like real cops." Laughter spilled out of the balcony and rolled along the downstairs seats. Symmington did not laugh. His intention was not to be funny, and his red face told the crowd as much as he quickly turned and narrowed his eyes at them. The laughter died.

"Let's review it, Mr. Patterson. A cop is murdered. Instead of putting every available man on the case, the cops have to fight a Mickey Mouse operation on the eve of the Fourth. While they're trying to secure a pesthole, which should have been closed down years ago, the rest of the town has no police coverage. A woman is kidnapped and brutally murdered at the same time the cops are booking a hundred and twenty-seven punks from the city. The cops who weren't brawling or arresting were in on towing seven hundred and thirty-seven cars. From where? Again the pesthole. The rest of the town might as well be another county."

"Thank you for your critique, Mr. Symmington. I suppose you were doing some towing that night. Your shop has one of the contracts on towing, if I'm not mistaken. I believe I signed the agreement myself."

"You're not mistaken. But you can keep the contract. I'd rather have the safety of this town assured. This town is more important to me and my family than any added revenue." The anxious audience showed its appreciation in a loud burst of approval.

114

"Whoa, whoa, hold up a minute. You sound paranoid, Mr. Symmington. Your contract is not what's at issue here."

"Maybe not, but if we didn't have to contend with all the disturbances on The Hill, maybe our police officers could get on with policing. That's all I have to say." As he sat down, there was more applause. His neck turned scarlet red.

Alfred Kalmir looked across and up four rows to Ben Moffit. They exchanged quick glances. The almond eyes of Kalmir blazed. He did not enjoy the tone of the meeting. He did not appreciate Frank Patterson's handling of the matter. He did not appreciate it at all. He held his hands up in front of him and studied his fingernails. He decided he would need a manicure soon.

Patterson's hand was vigorously rubbing the bald spot. Strength was leaving him. He quickly caught the fire in Kalmir's eyes and saw the sharp glare of Moffit's stare. He had to get a grip on himself.

In the auditorium bodies began squirming and expressions became tight, taut lines across the mouth. There was the temptation to look into the crowd and wonder if he might be there. Heads turned and eyes roamed the crowd. The real specter emerged and trembled along the rows of residents in the form of clutched handbags and nervous fingers straightening out ties and shirts. The specter of fear. The auditorium began to close in on them. There was a great storm out there somewhere, but inside the old stucco hall there was some kind of security. It would not last, surely. But if only they could stay there forever, they would not be harmed.

As Chief Medina reached for the mike, Cyrus Standish Dean bounced to the stage and grabbed it from his hand. Dean had the microphone gripped in his liver-spotted hands and he directed his tirade against the Quonsett Police Department and the town selectmen, represented this evening by Frank Patterson, who stood leaning against a wall by the stage.

"Our police have uncovered nothing. There is a maniac loose and all they do is direct traffic on Main Street and give directions to tourists. As for the tourists, they're gone.

"Ladies and gentlemen, friends, this town is dying and it may never recover, and what are the police doing?"

"We're doing all we can," Chief Medina broke in.

"Like what? A personal vendetta against cop-haters? I know who you've been investigating. Fishermen! Because they carry knives. Why don't you go to the supermarkets and check all the butchers out? You call that police work?"

There was an agreement from the crowd in low but audible murmurs.

Medina, red-faced, sat down mopping his brow with a handkerchief.

Dean directed his remarks to the worn faces in the crowd. The tans and sunburns and freckled skin were gray now. The anxious fidgeting continued and the atmosphere of the room was tomblike. They were in a church waiting for the black velvet sarcophagus to be wheeled down the aisle and placed before them for display.

He studied them. He looked into the leathery face of Alvin Bearce and down the aisle to Annie Crockler. Dean had always possessed the power of the word in print, but tonight, in center stage, he had another kind of power in his verbal tirade. His words crept stealthily up the aisle and into the jammed balcony.

"Why hasn't Mr. Patterson acted sooner? My editorials called for the closing of all the beaches. Why didn't the selectman put out a direct order to do so? I made editorial suggestions. They were not adhered to. What is a town newspaper for, but to act as a counselor for the town? I have always had the interest of this town at heart."

116

Before Patterson could respond, a man in the back of the auditorium broke in.

"It seems to me your idea of closing the beaches and your editorial suggestions were only made in the last article. And as for your interest in the town, is it the whole town or just sections you're interested in?" The voice was nervous but prodding.

"I don't know what that is supposed to mean."

"It means," and the voice grew stronger through conviction, "that you and the selectmen don't give a damn about The Hill or its residents. As long as the money comes pouring in from those gin joints. You stand up there pontificating about the selectmen and the police not doing their jobs. What the hell have you and your paper ever done but abuse us because we want a little peace and quiet on summer weekends. Those dives are drawing lowlife. How do we know he doesn't hang out in one of those bars?"

"He's right," another voice broke in. "I think we should organize marshals to police those joints. I'm all for a vigilante committee."

"Wait, wait." And the gavel pounded on Edmund Petrie's table. The approving crowd was roaring now. It was the safety-in-numbers routine again and the camaraderie brought them together. The auditorium began to shake with an affirmative roar. The man who proposed the idea was besieged with handshakes and back-slapping.

Cyrus Dean shouted into the mike for quiet, and it was a full five minutes before order was restored. The crowd grabbed on to the idea of the vigilante committee. Their wounds were cured. The tidal wave rolled off the town leaving it crystal clear and blue under the summer sky.

Edmund Petrie took the mike from Dean and tried for quiet, but he was only mildly successful until he called on Joe Medina.

117

Chief Medina took the podium and made one simple statement. "Any vigilante group will be arrested. No questions asked."

His words dropped like lead. For five minutes they had been in a convention mood of jubilation. They had succeeded in convincing themselves that everything would be all right. Their town was safe. But the reality of the chief's words hosing down the flame of hope that had sparked and caught fire was accepted with no shouts. No admonitions. They knew he was right. All the vigilante groups in the world would not save them from a maniac whose only purpose was to kill at random.

Dean looked at the chief with a surprised and begrudging expression of respect. Maybe Medina knew people better than Dean had credited him for.

A hand shot out of the crowd. It was Charlie Mendoza, and his white hair was plastered across his forehead from perspiration.

"Yes, Charlie, what is it?" Petrie said.

"My idea is simple. Maybe too simple." He talked into his chest.

"Go on, Charlie. Speak out. What is it?"

"I think we should have all the oceanfront dives closed. All five of 'em." And he named them by ticking them off on his fingers. "Freddie's, Cousins, Long John's, The Lifeboat. Paddy's, too."

"How will that help? What good will that do?" It was Patterson climbing the three steps to the stage and grabbing the mike from Petrie.

"It will give us more cops, that's what it will do." Charlie was sure of himself now, and his seventy-year-old voice had fire in it.

"What do you mean, more cops?"

"Look, Mr. Patterson, everybody in town knows where cops spend all their time and energy. Policing them joints.

Three-fourths of this town go without adequate police protection so the lid can be kept on those pestholes."

"Now, wait a minute, *Mister* Mendoza."

"No, you wait a minute, Mr. Patterson. I'm not saying that creep hangs around up there, but most of the cops do."

"Look, Mendoza."

"I'm still talking, *Patterson*. This is town meeting rules, and I got the floor. Now you just let me finish." Nervous applause fluttered through the audience. "Go ahead, Charlie." "Tell 'em, Charlie."

"If we took all the cops off that detail we would have a hell of a lot more clout in the rest of this town. When are the people, the taxpayers, going to realize they are subsidizing protection for the very people who make a profit out of these places. . . . And while they're doing that, they don't have enough cops, north, south, or west of town. That's all I have to say." Charlie Mendoza sat down amidst applause and handshaking approval.

"Ok, Mendoza, you find me some violations and I'll close them down."

Residents of The Hill jumped to their feet screaming "Fornication," "Urinating," "Fighting," "Drunkenness," "Rape," "No fire exits," "Polluted sewerage systems stinking up the swimming areas."

Petrie pleaded into the mike for them to be seated, to be quiet, to be reasonable. "After all this is a town meeting," he urged. But, his stage presence was lost in the chaos. The mob had taken over and they were nasty and without purpose.

As the auditorium emptied out, the young man with the strong slender body and the Adidas T-shirt stuffed his hands into Levi pockets and hummed along the corridor. He stood in the doorway watching the pandemonium in the school parking lot. Two minor accidents were tying up

119

traffic as the tense and frightened leaned on their horns in a futile effort to clear the way in front of them so they could return to their families and the safety of their locked houses.

"Quite a mess out there," the young tanned cop was saying to the slender young man.

"Yeah, sure is."

"Well, watch out for yourself. He could be anywhere."

"Yeah, thanks, I will."

Douglas Peters sauntered down the stone steps suppressing a satisfied grin.

He recapped the meeting. Their fear, their anxiety, was more than he ever could have hoped for. He reviewed it.

The town was weakening. He knew it would crumble. There was open antagonism among its more solid members. Personal differences were surfacing, and the lack of direction was evident in the conflicting avenues of action he had seen at the meeting. Much as he detested Dean, he was thankful for the old prick's ridiculous article. It had fanned their fear.

The moment he especially enjoyed was the suggestion of vigilante groups. How absolutely perfect that could have been. Why, he could have joined such a group himself. The thought of seeking out and hunting himself shook his body with laughter.

Then there was the man. He had watched him with an intensity that the man must have felt, because on one occasion the man, as though knowing the hot eyes were on him, turned in the direction of Douglas Peters. His eyes had roamed the rows but did not fix themselves on anyone in particular. He would kill that man, and he reassembled the images of restaurants and the furtive, hunched figure huddled against the frame of the guesthouse and then darting down the backyard path to the next street.

He had seen enough that amused and fulfilled him. The

120

tourists were leaving in droves. He had done that part of it well. The businesses were hurt bad. Soon he would be through. He would slice that man. He would castrate him. He switched on the key in the ignition and drove slowly by the playing fields on his way back to the woods.

Six

"Do you have to whistle that goddamned song all night, Rick?"

"What the hell's eating you, Eddie?"

"Oh, there's too much mayo on the tuna. What the Christ do you think is bugging me? Have you been out there?" He threw the sandwich into the wastebasket as the shrill sound of the phone ripped through the room.

"Quonsett Police Department, Officer Singer.

"Yes, ma'am. What time did this happen, ma'am?

"No, ma'am, we don't.

"Yes, ma'am.

"How old, ma'am? Five? Your son?

"What beach was it?

"Woodchip? Yes, that's in West Quonsett. Yes, ma'am. I know it. Yes, go on.

"Do you live there?

"You don't. You're in a camper. I see.

"And what time did you see him last?

"Four o'clock? It's now, let's see, nine fifteen.

"All right, ma'am, now relax. Where are you now?

"At the Woodchip Trailer Park? The beachside? Just stay there. No, no. Don't worry about the Coast Guard. I know it's foggy. Please try to relax. I'll have a cruiser there in minutes."

Eddie cradled the phone and swiveled over to the radio.

"Oscar Five—272, Oscar Five. Come to the station. Sergeant, you're wanted on a 10-19 immediately."

"What is it, Eddie? You ok?" Rick stood over him biting into a sandwich.

"It's a child, Rick, a five-year-old child. He's been missing since this afternoon. His mother and father have been combing the woods and the beach."

He turned to answer the phone.

"Quonsett Police Station, Officer Singer.

"Yes, sir. A noisy party—214 Prospect. I'll send a cruiser.

"Hello, yes, police department, Officer Singer.

"A barking dog. In your front yard. Yes, there is a leash law. You know the owners? I suggest you call the owners, then. You can tell them if they don't come for the dog, you will call the police. You're welcome.

"Here I am working doubles, answering crap calls, and there's a killer out there. Goddamn it. When is Boyd going to let me out of the station?"

"Take it easy, Eddie," Rick yelled over from the teletype.

"Take it easy? There's five new summer guys jockeying all over town."

"I'll let you out, Singer, when I think you can handle it." It was Boyd standing in the doorway. His frame filled the doorjamb. He had that fresh, just-came-on-duty look, and yet, as Eddie knew, he had been on duty for fourteen hours. He held his sheriff's hat in his left hand and he smoothed back his dark hair with his right.

"What was the call all about?"

"Sergeant, a five-year-old boy is missing over in the trailer camp. Not far from the spot where that woman was grabbed."

"Shit, not a kid. Rick, take the desk, Singer's with me."

Rick's eyebrows raised slightly.

"Did you hear me?"

"Yes, sergeant."

123

"All right, then, get it. Can't you hear it ringing?"

"C'mon, Eddie."

"Yes, sir, sergeant."

"You drive, Eddie," Boyd barked as they descended the station steps two at a time.

They were out on to Main and up Cedar on the way west when Boyd said, "Hit my house on the way, Eddie."

"Yes, sergeant."

They flew through the night in silence until Eddie banged a right and hooked a quick left. He automatically grabbed for the searchlight by his window and danced it along the shingles of the house.

A sun-deck light flashed from off the kitchen in response.

"Ok, Eddie, make some time. Don't sweat it. There are no drawbridges on this run."

Eddie winced but clamped hard on his tongue.

The side road to the beach was rutted and bumpy. There was water in the ruts from an erratic tide that backlashed from the channel opposite the beach.

Several trailers lined the seawall. They were all well lighted, and a group of a dozen or so people stood in the middle of the park with the cruiser's lights spilling over them, cutting through the damp fog and mist.

A woman came running up to the cruiser before it stopped. She grabbed for Eddie's door as the cruiser still rocked in its premature halt.

"Officer, please, help us. It's my boy. Please."

Boyd was out of his side and gently guiding the woman back to the yellow cone of lights before she could continue.

"Please, someone, take care of this woman."

A man came out of the crowd and took her in his arms.

"She's my wife, officer. C'mon, honey, sit here." And he helped her to a deck chair that was next to the trailer's steps.

"Sir, can you answer some questions?"

"Yes, I think so."

"How long has the boy been gone?"

"Sometime late this afternoon—around four or so—I came back to the trailer to get some more bait. We were fishing off the jetty. I left him sitting there. Oh, Good God, how could I have been so stupid?"

The man kept cracking his knuckles and his voice quivered as he told of going back to the jetty to find the poles lying there and his son nowhere in sight. He had searched for an hour and a half before telling his wife. He dared not think of a drowning at first, but he returned to the jetty and dove off and searched until he was too exhausted to continue. The search had continued until dark, with the other campers joining in.

Boyd didn't ask the distraught man why the hell he waited so long to call the police. He shook his head and spoke quietly to the man while the woman, probably in her early thirties, pretty and blond, cried softly as she sat on the steps of the trailer. The lights of the trailer drew a yellow halo around her head in the fog.

Then someone asked the question he was afraid would be asked.

"Sergeant, you don't think it could be that murderer, do you?"

"For Christ's sake, shut up." Another voice hissed while gesturing with a thumb to the weeping woman.

"Look, no more talk, let's fan out again. Be careful of that marshland over there. The fog is like smoke over there and the water would be over your head in some places. We will have to save that for a larger search party in daylight."

"Some of you take the north beach. If anyone has a flashlight, use it. My partner and I will check the channel. There's a culvert that leads to the ocean. Did you check that, sir?"

"No, officer, I didn't."

"We'll check it out now. What is your name, sir?"

"My name?"

"Yes, in case the boy is afraid. We can say his father—"

"Oh, Joe Nolan."

"And the boy's?"

"Joey."

"Good. Try and relax. Try to be optimistic, Mr. Nolan."

"Why doesn't someone make coffee?"

"I will, sergeant."

Boyd and Eddie crouched through the stiff marsh grass playing their lights in a rotating movement. The water was black in the marshes. When they reached the channel it was high tide. The water was a strong current to the sea and it gushed at the opening of the culvert.

"I'll go in, sergeant." And Eddie unbuckled his belt and handed it to Boyd. He waded into the water, and immediately the strong current pulled him forward so that he lost his balance and was dragged along to the black, yawning entrance. He held on to the cement sides, his legs spread-eagled to keep him from being pulled into the tunnel.

He sputtered up to Boyd, who was standing on the mossy embankment.

"Hand me my flashlight, will you, sergeant?"

Boyd snapped on the light and passed it down to him.

With one hand digging into some loose rocks, Eddie held on while swinging his body closer to the opening. He played his light on the walls and far off into the tunnel. There was a space of twelve to fifteen inches from the water level to ceiling. About thirty feet in front of him something was resting against the right wall. The water was moving so rapidly he could not make out its shape. But it hung there, a darkened form.

"I see something, sergeant. I'm going in."

Boyd crouched lower. "That tunnel must be filling up fast, Eddie. Do you have breathing space?"

126

He shined the light in again. It was true the water level was rising, but if he went now he might have a chance.

"It's ok, sergeant."

"Don't forget. Let the current carry you. Once you get in there, there's only one way out. The tunnel runs about a hundred yards."

"Gottcha."

His heart went light, almost feathery. He remembered an early morning in Nam during the monsoon when he was coming back from a listening post. Charlie threw everything at that stream—automatic weapons, grenades, and rifle fire. He had stayed underwater for an eternity, letting the current carry him to the rapids. The force of the rapids swung him upside down in the water, crashed him against the rocks, and finally spit him up on a muddy sandbar a mile downstream. His two buddies were killed. One had a hole in his head from a dumdum bullet and the other had drowned.

He never had a deep affection for the water after that, even though it may have saved his life. He had puked that stream up for a week. That was a great irony in his life. Now he lived in a seaside resort town.

He took in a deep breath and ducked under the arch. The briny smell of salt and moss permeated the darkness. His flashlight extended over his head, searching out the form that was now a few yards in front of him. He prayed to God it wasn't the little boy. Then he was on it. It obstructed his passage. He put out his flashlight hand while palming the ceiling for support. The water was rising. It was above his chin, and he could barely touch bottom. At six feet, he was just able to keep above the water level by bouncing on his toes. But each time he did, he hit his head on the cement ceiling. He felt the panic setting in. His legs were cold, and beside him was the object he had thought might be the child. It was a long, narrow piece of driftwood lodged from one wall to the other. He tried to raise himself above it, but when he did, his right hand, numb and trembling, hit the overhead and knocked the light out of his hand. It sank beneath him somewhere. He tried to feel for it with his feet, but he already knew it was gone.

Boyd, seeing the tunnel suddenly darkened, the light snuffed out like a candle, yelled into him. "Eddie, Eddie. Are you ok? Eddie."

Eddie could not answer because the water was up to his mouth. If he lowered his jaw and opened his mouth to respond, the swirling water would choke him. Fear tied his stomach in knots. There was only one way out. He had to submerge and swim below the lodged driftwood and hope he could hold his breath long enough to gain the exit at the other end and the clear air of the beach. He knew he had to go now. His head was bobbing and banging against the ceiling. He wanted to spring up and smash his head through that cement to air and safety. His heart was beating so irregularly that he was not sure he could control his underwater breathing. And the more he thought of it, the faster his heart beat.

"Oh, God," he thought. One last breath. He slowly pulled his head back, his nose pressing against the wet mossy ceiling, and he sucked in the fetid air of the tunnel. Just as he did, the current swelled even more so, and he gulped in a mouthful of water. He tried to spit it out. He dared not cough. He slipped beneath the water and let it carry him. He lay like a spear, praying for the force of the water to carry him. Fear had increased his breathing in an irregular pattern. He could not hold his breath. He wanted to open his mouth and suck in all of Quonsett. He kept his hands outstretched. The tunnel seemed miles long. He felt his foot catch on to something. His shoe was wedged into a crevice of some sort in the wall. He could not free himself. He tried to turn and pull at the shoe, but he did not have to because the turning motion automatically dislodged his foot. He could not hold his breath any longer. He opened his mouth and let the water pour in.

"Ok, Eddie, easy now. Easy kid."

Boyd's face was bending over his as Eddie looked beyond it, seeing the stars stuck up there in a black sky. He inhaled and coughed but the air was sweet and beautiful and he was alive. He could feel the soft sand beneath him.

"Will he be all right, officer? Will he?"

"Yes, he's ok now. Just swallowed too much water, and he's not a water drinker, are you, Eddie?"

Eddie sat up and looked at the group that was standing around him.

"I'm sorry, officer," the woman was saying. "I'm sorry." She kept repeating it.

Boyd pulled him to his feet.

"Eddie, I want you to meet someone. This is Joey. Joey, this is Eddie."

A little boy with a Mickey Mouse sweat shirt and short pants smiled up at him.

"Joey had a great sleep for himself up the beach. Fell asleep in someone's boat. Didn't you, Joey?"

Eddie brushed back his hair with his fingers. He gagged and coughed, water trickled from the corners of his mouth. He wiped it away with the back of his hand as the little boy continued looking up at him. His body was trembling.

"I fell asleep," the little boy was saying.

Eddie cleared his throat. "I'm very happy to see you, Joey. You had us all worried." He looked around at them all and smiled. The trembling began to ease off.

"Ok, folks, I want to get Officer Singer into some dry clothes."

"How about some coffee, officers?" Joey's mother asked

129

as she hugged her son.

"Thanks, ma'am, but I think the best thing to do is get back to the station."

The group was still huddled in the glow of the camper's lights as Boyd helped Eddie back to the cruiser, guiding him by the elbow.

Pete Cormier sat half slumped on a barstool at Freddie's. The King and His Clowns held over by popular demand, rocked and bumped on a platform that was surrounded by a mass of sensually weaving hips, undulating bodies, and outstretched hands. The metallic beat bounced off the walls and met itself in the middle of the room.

Lights flashed red and blue and the tight asses of the dancers ground out the rhythm as though it were coming from their pelvises.

Cormier had heard it all before and it bored him, but he knew he had to make it look good, so he squirmed in rhythm and moved his shoulders in tempo. He could not help feeling effeminate in his movements. Maybe it was Boyd telling Chester that Cormier was gay. Son of a bitch, he thought. He did not have much to tell Boyd and the only two phone contacts were quick and meaningless. Shit, if Boyd wanted drug information Cormier could fill two volumes. But on the killer he had nothing.

He was beginning to think the guy didn't hang out with The Hill crowd—wasn't somebody he'd stumble across hanging out at Freddie's. But then again—who knows? A psycho like that could be a real regular guy face to face and then turn around and do God knows what when the urge hit him. Shit, he was getting frustrated. Maybe he should let Boyd know he had enough and go back to drugs. At least the people were predictable.

He ordered another beer and turned around as the King, a skinny, pockmarked kid with no hips and a concentration-camp face, pounded the drums.

Talk and noise subsided slowly as the King, who looked more like the queen, fingered the mike with long, fragile hands.

"Ladies and gentlemen. Ladies and gentlemen." He had a slight lisp and he kept throwing his head back to keep the long greasy hair out of his eyes.

"Ladies and gentlemen, now comes the moment we have all been waiting for: the Wet T-Shirt Championship of Quonsett, Massachusetts; United States; who knows— the World!" Cheering and whistling shot back to him.

"Now, I must warn you, no tittering during the contest." The boos and groans gave way to sporadic clapping.

"So without anymore delay, here they are. Twelve lovelies, or should I say twenty-four."

The lights dimmed and a spotlight roamed the room finding the first contestant as she was pushed into the center of the floor. She stood in the light, dressed in cutoff Levi's and a white T-shirt that said Freddie's across the back. The front of the shirt spoke for itself, as two muscular bouncers threw a bucket of water at her chest. At first she shook with the sudden chill of the soaking, but when the crowd hooted and hollered for her to stand up straight and parade around, she threw her shoulders back, with her large, round breasts expanding the shirt in a hard round melonlike contour. She reacted to the yelling and table-thumping by pulling her shirt tightly to the waist. Her two nipples peeked through the shirt. The crowd rose to greater approval as she circled the floor.

Pete Cormier downed the cold beer and pushed his way through the knots of screaming, stomping humanity. He gained the entrance and crossed the street to the beach. "Animals," he said to himself.

Inside, peering through a one-way window in Kalmir's second-floor office, Frank Patterson watched the passing parade. Kalmir sat in a leather chair studying Patterson's face. Patterson was completely hypnotized by the scene. At every thrust and bump and grind, Patterson reacted. He palmed the bald spot and fingered the glass.

"Seen enough, Mr. Patterson?" Kalmir was saying as he closed the shutters on the crowning of the evening's winner.

"That's some contest, Mr. Kalmir. Where do those girls go when it's over?"

"Go?"

"Well, you know what I mean? Are they waitresses?"

"Some are, some aren't."

"Oh, I was just curious if they come from Quonsett."

"You mean, you wondered if any one of them was available?"

Patterson smiled. "Yes, something like that."

"I can take care of it, Mr. Patterson, for a price—naturally."

"Oh, naturally. Everything costs money these days."

"Well, let's get down to business."

Kalmir at sixty-years of age had managed to remain youthful-looking. He wore tailored suits, always in dark colors, and he liked expensive shoes. He did not smoke or drink, and he swam for an hour each day—the ocean in the warm weather, and The Boston Club's pool in winter. He was unmarried and unattached. If he wanted it, he paid top dollar for it. He had owned Freddie's for twenty-five years and he had never had the threat of a losing year—until now. This year. This summer.

He was a well-respected member of the Boston business community with large investments in New Hampshire real estate. Kalmir liked it that way. He worked away from the people he socialized with. His business interests were vague to his friends but not shady, as far as they were concerned. His great interest was Freddie's, for two very different reasons. It was here that he had first made his money, and that made it a sentimental reason. The other reason was narcotics. The operation had been booming and he did not need any local interference. He did not need it, and that's where Patterson came in. Patterson could keep the townies quiet by telling them Freddie's was checked periodically and found to have committed no violations. Patterson would bullshit them all summer, and when Labor Day came, the townies had the place to themselves and forgot the summer.

But now this narc was snooping around. Better to get the narc now before he finds out too much.

He talked slowly, emphasizing certain phrases with a pause and a half smile.

"My message is really—" and he paused, "simple." He smiled. "I am losing money. And if I lose money, you lose money. You see a crowded house tonight only because of a foolish contest like the one you just witnessed. Even then the drop-off rate compared to other summers is very high. Many of tonight's clientele work for me or live at Moffit's. In either case, that is not big money. I need those Boston singles who come down here weekends to piss away their bread."

"Well, what can I do?" Patterson wanted to open the shutters, but thought better of it.

"You can put a fire under those Keystone Cops. Get the county in if you have to. The DA. You heard those bastards at the town meeting. Anything that happens in this town, they blame us—the bar owners. If they make enough noise, they could have the ABC on my back." He leaned forward. "And I have enough trouble these days."

"What do you mean?"

"I mean there's been a guy around here asking too many questions."

"What kind of questions?" Patterson felt a sudden surge of panic.

Kalmir raised his hands. "Don't sweat it, Mr. Patterson,

you're clean. It's my operation and my problem. We know who the guy is."

"How do you know?"

"We have our ways of knowing. This is a war, Mr. Patterson, and there are informers on both sides."

"What are you going to do about it?"

"Oh, he will—" and he paused again, "have a fight, and he will be roughed up. Some of my athletes will lean on him. Nothing serious, but he will find himself out of action for a few months. By that time Labor Day will be here and gone."

"Won't the cops trace it?"

"I have no control over a brawl that occurs outside my place. So there we have it. I'll take care of my problem, but we—" and he emphasized the we—"we are hoping you can hold up your end.

"So I repeat, get those cops moving. Because if you don't you can forget about your little bouquet. Next summer won't be quite so sweet for you."

"Hey, just a minute. Do you know who you're talking to? I could close you up for good. And the townspeople would love me for it."

"Don't bullshit the old bullshitter, Mr. Patterson. I could ruin you in this town and you know it. Now, you just get on it. That's all I have to say, you can leave now."

Patterson made no point in looking through the one-way mirror this time. He just turned and made his way down the dark stairway that led to the underground garages.

Pete Cormier began walking back to the harbor and *The Molly O*. Thinking Chester or one of the others might be aboard, he figured on bullshitting for a while over a cup of coffee. There was talk of a shipment of horse coming down from Boston, and Freddie's would be the connection. But that would be later on, probably 2:00 or 3:00 A.M., so he strolled casually along the boardwalk. The ocean was quiet, just a gentle lapping against the shore.

Up ahead a group approached him on the boardwalk. Two of them appeared to be drunk. There were six in all, and he decided he did not want the boardwalk, so he stepped off the curb into the street to let them pass.

"Hey, you fuckin yellow or somethin?" one of the drunks yelled in his face.

"Yeah, you're right. I'm yellow." He stepped back up on the curb and continued walking.

"Hey, come back here, man."

Cormier kept walking. He could feel the hair bristling at the back of his neck.

"Did you hear what I said?" And the drunk trotted up behind him. He knew it was coming, and knew he had to swing first. He spun around ducking under the right hand shot and buried his engineer's boot in the drunk's groin. His right hand tore at the face as the drunk hugged himself in an effort to stop the pain. As the drunk fell to the sidewalk Cormier was on his way. He raced for the harbor, but a car slammed its brakes in front of him cutting off any exit. The five came at him in a wedge, and he swung until his arms were pulled behind his back and they went to work on him. They worked on his stomach. Something snapped in his rib cage, his arm was turned around until the bone broke. The last thing he saw before nausea and unconsciousness overwhelmed him was the well-aimed foot of the drunk.

They dragged him down to the beach and left him there. Pete Cormier would be on sick leave for a long time to come.

Seven

"What kept you so long?" His jaw was twitching and there was a suggestion of hurt in his voice.

"I told you, it was a private party and the boss asked me to work overtime. Don't be mad. 'Sides, with overtime and tips, I made forty dollars tonight. I'm way ahead of schedule and it's only the middle of July."

"I'm sorry, Mary, I just missed you, that's all." He leaned over and kissed her cheek softly. "Hey, your hair's wet." And he smoothed her black satin hair with his hand.

"I just took a shower. You didn't think I was going to come directly from that steam table to you, did you?"

"That was very considerate of you. I wish I had dressed for the occasion." And he looked down at the white tank shirt and Levi's. "Where do you want to go? Are you hungry?"

"Hungry? Not me, I've been eating fried clams and onion rings all night. I hate to see all those leftovers on people's plates."

She was wearing a tight-fitting white blouse. Her breasts were large, but he couldn't tell if she was wearing a bra or not. He let his right hand slide over her back as he locked her door.

"Can't be too safe these days." He had felt the strap. That was even better. He would enjoy slipping it off. He felt the sudden flush come into his face. She was wearing tight blue jeans. He shut off the cab's light.

"I know a place," he said.

"A place?" She was coy, but not defensive.

"Yeah, we can talk there."

"And what do you want to talk about, Mr. Peters?"

"About next year. When you go back on Labor Day. I want to be able to see you. Someplace. Again."

He pulled the van out of the parking lot and headed along the ocean, then turned abruptly toward town.

"The town doesn't seem too crowded for July, does it, Mary." And he felt a burst of enormous pride inside.

"No, it's that madman. People are leaving in droves."

"Madman? Why do you think it's a man? And what makes you think he—or she—is crazy?"

People were leaving in droves. But the town was still jumping. There were not enough of them leaving. He would not be satisfied until Quonsett was on its knees. He had to do more and he had to do it quick. He had to do something even more sensational. He let her talk on as he began to fashion the plan in his head. He could feel her nearness in the cab. The feeling was ambivalent—puzzling.

"Well, it stands to reason, Doug, to do what was done would take real strength."

"What? I'm sorry. What did you say, Mary?"

"There you go again, drifting off somewhere else. You weren't even listening."

"No, I mean, yes, I was. You were talking about strength. What about it?"

"See, you weren't."

"No, really, I was. What about it?"

"Well, I don't think too many women have the strength to do what that killer did. It has to be a man."

"What about this madman stuff. Maybe he's very sane. Maybe he had good reason."

She looked at him with a slight smile. "You are kidding, of course. I mean, how many sane people go around cutting heads and legs off people?"

137

He wanted to scream it out at her. Those people meant nothing to him. It was what their deaths meant. But he added innocuously, "Of course, I'm only kidding. What the hell do you take me for—a madman?"

They both smiled at the joke.

He felt a warm, satisfying glow as he drove up Main Street and could see through the windows of the restaurants, the empty tables, and the few cars in the parking lot of The Pins bowling alley, and the movies. It was the family places that were hit. Family types panic easily, he thought. Of course, they were the ones who spent money. Most, anyway. Even if they did rent cottages for two weeks, they always shopped uptown on rainy days or went to a restaurant a few nights on their vacations.

As he cruised by The Pequod, he saw that it was still rocking. The porch was jammed with drinkers, singing and dancing in a noisy, swaying mass. Stupid sons of bitches. One of their own. That would send them hauling ass out of there goddamned quick. If he took one of them. A young single. He smiled. His plan continued to form slowly in his mind.

"The younger generation seems to be still very much in evidence. The youngies never scare too easily. Maybe they're just too goddamned dumb."

"You sound disappointed," and she faced him with her back against the door.

"No, just observant. It's just a sociological reality. Family people have something to lose. It's all very tangible. They have children. Children can be hurt or maimed or attacked or kidnapped. Family people have a built-in pessimism. It's because they've lived longer. Younger people, our age, we have immediate goals, like tips, overtime, Simmons, you know what I mean? We only have to be protective of ourselves. So, if some cop has his head taken off, then that's no skin—" and he laughed at the obvious pun—"off our nose. We don't identify. Or, at least, I don't. Do you?"

"Well, I guess you're right. Are we callous?"

"No, not callous, just preoccupied with having a good time and working. Take the party they're having tomorrow night at The Loft. Did you hear about it?"

"No, but what's so new about that? There's always a party at The Loft."

"Yes, but this one's different. Have you seen this?" And he reached over his head and pulled a sheet of paper from the shelf behind him.

"Here." And he handed it to her.

She sat up in the cab and read it while catching the lights from clubs and the passing cars. The paper, flaming red with black lettering, said:

> *Climb to the crest*
> *For the July fest*
> *Dismember an arm*
> *Or maybe a breast*
> *Don't be soft*
> *Come to The Loft.*
>
> *Wednesday Night*
> *Eight to Dawn.*

YOU MUST COME MINUS ONE APPENDAGE.
DOOR PRIZES TO BE AWARDED.

"My God, but that is really sick. Don't you think? I mean, that is sick shit."

"Hey, different strokes for different folks."

"Oh, I know, Doug, but Jesus."

"Do you want to go? We could go holding right hands while tucking our left into our jeans."

"Whose hand in whose jeans? Not me, thanks. Say,

where are we headed, anyway?"

His head began to throb. He looked at her briefly. Unfortunately, she was very lovely. But there really was no other way. Really no other way.

"You'll see. It's a little place in the quiet of the woods. Ever hear of Bryant Acres?"

"No, I don't think so."

"You'll like it. It's quiet and peaceful and very private. Nobody ever goes there."

"You really do know this town."

"I told you, I used to live here." They had passed The Pequod and the rest of the spots that bordered the outskirts of town. The van whizzed along the black stretch of macadam in a straight path until he turned it abruptly up a dirt road that had deep ruts in it. It was more like a horse trail than a road. As the van speared through the growth of scrub pine, branches slapped against the windows until he gained a higher ground and the road broke out into a clearing. There were five different roads or pathways fanning out like spokes from the circular clearing.

He switched the key off and sat for a moment. The only sound was the highway below and the continual night sounds of crickets.

"It's going to be hot tomorrow," she whispered in the stillness, "hear those crickets?"

He reached out for her and she slid over to him. She was warm and soft in his arms and he searched for her mouth with his. She returned the kiss eagerly, her mouth was open and wet. His tongue found hers. She gave it to him. Then withdrew it and gave it to him again. He felt her back with his hands, pulling at the straps through the blouse, tightening the bra around her breasts. She took his hands by the wrists and placed them on her breasts. He felt her chest swell. He opened the buttons on her blouse slowly and deliberately while kissing her far back in her throat. He pulled away the blouse and squeezed her full round breasts against each other. Her breath came quickly as she reached around and snapped the bra free.

His lips found her nipples, and she squirmed up and down in the seat.

"Take it easy, honey, take it easy. I want it as much as you do."

He rubbed his hands along the inside of her legs until she didn't think she could stand it anymore.

"I want it now, Doug. Take me now." She squirmed and wrapped her legs around him.

He buried his face in her breasts as she tore her jeans free.

His first act of penetration was slow and hard and he let her come to him. He began the rhythm, and the motion brought her tightly into him. She had no breath, and all that came from her was the whimpering of her voice asking for more.

He drove into her with full force until he thought he might drive her through the cushions, but she responded, rocking in an erotic harmony until she felt herself coming from somewhere deep inside her. He climaxed at almost the same moment, driving deeper than he ever had before. She grunted with animal satisfaction just as he reached for the needle and stuck it quickly into her right shoulder blade while her body was rising in one last thrust.

She looked at him in a puzzled frown and then slumped against the seat. He pulled free and opened the driver's door and jumped to the ground.

He looked back at her, lying in her nakedness, with the moon washing over her form. The lovely black hair was all but covering her face.

It could have been any woman. He could have picked up anyone at a bar or someone hitchhiking, but killing Mary thrilled him in a strange way precisely because he was fond of her and had a very deep affection for her. She was sincere and warm and passionate and fun to be with. He probably could have loved her if things had been different. She could have made a fine wife for a doctor. But that was another time, another life. That could never be. So to kill her was to recognize that the other life was never to be. His head began spinning as he studied her. He wondered if she would have been like all women. His head flashed strange pictures. He could still see that man and his mother lying naked on a bed in the little guesthouse.

It had been one of those quiet days at the Shack, and his father had sent him off to play. "Go for a swim, my little buddy, go off for yourself. All work and no play will make my Dougie a dull boy, and we don't want any dull doctors. There are enough of them."

His father's kindness and gentleness brought tears to his eyes as he studied the unconscious form. A stab of momentary sorrow for Mary took hold of him. Then his thoughts returned to his mother and the man lying together on that bed. After that first time he had seen them together he was always careful to look in the window to see if anyone was in the guesthouse. And that day he saw them and watched everything they did.

The thought of his mother turned his heart to stone. The gentleness and kindness of his father was forgotten.

Mary groaned and brought him back to reality.

He liked her. He really did. But to kill her would be the ultimate. When they heard about this they would haul their asses out of town. The Pequod, The Slipper, the Other Place, The Casbah on the Beach, The Loft, Cousins, too would be empty in a week. The youngies would identify this time. Kids and families meant nothing to them. But this time it was one of their own. He knew he had to do it.

He opened the rear of the van and pulled the table out

from the wall. He took a surgical gown from the closet and tied a mask around his face. In the bottom tray of drawers he found the scalpel he wanted and he placed it in a Styrofoam plate beside the table.

He went around to the cab and carried her body back to the rear of the van, laying her on the table. She smelled of sex.

He closed the door behind him and switched on the red light. She began to stir. He suddenly felt the great sorrow returning, but he pushed it from his mind. It was much too late and he knew he would have to continue. He gave her a double jab of the hypodermic needle. It was, after all, all he could do for her.

It was during the cutting on both occasions that he dwelled on and almost became lulled by Dr. Arnold Bern's remarks before a packed auditorium. He had been working on a cadaver when Bern announced to the rest of the class, "This is the best work by a student that I have ever witnessed." Dr. Bern had given him pride. Dr. Bern had treated him with dignity. The good doctor would be proud of him, he thought.

"The best work." he said to the body lying in front of him as he began the mastectomy of the left and the right breasts. "Absolutely, the best work." He raised the bloody scalpel to the light and smiled. He wiped it on the smock and continued.

Her breasts were large and round. He cut the tissue and felt her stir as the breast came free and the blood spurted and flowed onto his white smock. He smiled through the mask. She lay still on the table. She is in shock, he thought. It won't be long.

He dwelled on every slit and cut that the scalpel made. His hand was sure and steady. The enjoyment was almost too much for him to continue. He wanted to scream out. When he was finished, he tore off the smock and mask. He

143

grabbed a shovel from an overhead rack. He dabbed at the sweat on his forehead with the smock. He left the van and walked to a dense area of growth. He buried the smock two hundred yards from the van, being careful to cover the new dirt with brush and leaves. Every action was blurred now, he felt like a man walking under water.

He went back to the van and hosed down the entire rear section with the portable water-container unit. He opened the top section of the roof and brought down the sign and studied it in the red glare of the light and began laughing. The laugh was uncontrollable and it reached an absurd high while he rocked back and forth on his knees.

"This will do it. This will fucking well do it." The laugh had reached near hysteria as he held up the quarterboard sign written in a Currier and Ives script that said The Fish Shack.

He staggered back to the van and felt her pulse. The white wrist was limp and there was no more than an occasional tremor. The blood kept flowing. He knew this would demand an even more extensive cleanup. He would do that later. He felt complete exhaustion. He decided to sleep.

The activity, the pumping of his own blood, and heightened adrenaline had tired him. He had to sleep. He must sleep.

He propped himself comfortably in the cab on the same place where just an hour before he had had sex with her. He fell off to sleep.

The wind changed slightly and blew across his face. He awoke with a sudden jerking motion. He sat up and listened. There was a vague moaning coming from the rear of the van. He checked his watch. Two A.M. Good. He had slept well. All that he needed. He felt rested and composed. He went around to the back and opened the doors. She was stirring, unable to move, but her eyes were open, and

144

they responded to the light when he snapped it on.

"You're a tough one, aren't you, Mary?"

She was no longer comatose and there was a wild horror in her eyes as she looked down at her bloody chest and then back up at him. The eyes were rolling in her head. There was a bloody drool coming from her mouth, turning her white teeth to a red froth. He reached for a pillow and placed it over her face pushing down on it, pushing harder, until he was certain. She was gone. He was pleased with himself that he had been kind to her.

He drove then down the rutted trail and out on to the highway and in the direction of the harbor. The harbor was still. There were no cars and the only noise was from the hull of a Boston whaler bumping against the pilings. He drove around to the rear of the square weather-shingled structure that faced out to the harbor entrance.

He jumped out of the van and walked to the building. He climbed the circular stairs of the Shack's deck and hung out far enough to unscrew the sign that sent a piercing stab of hate through him. He dropped the sign over the side and watched the early morning tide take it out to sea—Patterson's.

He descended the stairs and drilled four holes into the side of the building that greeted all sea traffic. He then matched the holes on the quarterboard and tightened the screws in place. He went back into the van and tied nylon cord around both of her wrists. It was the same cord he had used to secure the police officer's head to the rock.

Suddenly, headlights loomed up and around the Shack. He froze and waited. The lights rolled over the van for a moment and then turned up the road and disappeared.

He dragged her body from the van and along the gravel. He propped her against the building while securing her wrists by knotting the cords to the screws.

Her body hung limp and white in the moonlight. The

blood was caked and drying on her chest. She faced the harbor entrance bloody and spread-eagled. She would be the first person to greet the ferry in the morning.

As a parting gesture, he discarded two plastic bags into the gray water.

Eight

"Incredible, insane," was all Eddie could say as he flew along Shore Road. He was alone, and what he now had to do was something every officer dreaded. He had to notify the next of kin.

Why the hell had he ever told Boyd that he had had that duty after Nam while waiting for discharge? Breaking the news to mothers and fathers about their marine sons had been worse than a year at Key Sahn. Then having to be present at the funeral homes to be stared at, and spit at, and ridiculed, that had scarred him more than any bullet ever could.

"I have such a big mouth. Why the hell did I tell Boyd?"

He found the street and house easily because he had rented a place on the next corner several years before.

A fat balding man in his mid fifties sat on a wicker rocking chair. His hands were folded across his chest and his face was red. His eyes were bloodshot and puffy. He did not move, but kept his eyes drilled to Eddie as Eddie approached the porch.

"Well," was all he said. No, Good morning. No, What can I do for you? Just, "Well?"

"I'm sorry, Mr. Flanagan, I couldn't tell you on the phone. Please, sir, what I have to tell you is not pleasant."

The man looked at him and sat back in the rocker.

"I'm terribly sorry, Mr. Flanagan, but your daughter is dead."

* * *

Main Street was funeral quiet. There was not the feeling of fear or tenseness as much as an overt stillness, as though someone had shut a door at each end of the street.

Eddie heard the report from the bridge. Traffic was backed up for ten miles.

Those who were walking or riding through town were not traveling alone. Everyone was hanging on to someone else: the young, the middle-aged, and the old.

He parked in front of the station and mounted the steps. The front desk was mobbed with cops—state, federal and local—and in the conference room Boyd was giving a statement to the Boston papers.

"It is quite obvious we are dealing with a deranged and sick person. At this moment we have no leads, new or old. We are in the process of trying to put this thing together. Now, gentlemen and ladies, I have work to do. Thank you."

The room cleared rapidly. Eddie appeared in the doorway facing Boyd.

"Well, how was it?"

"Bad, very bad. I thought he was going to have a heart attack."

"Did you tell him how?"

"Well, sort of."

"What do you mean, sort of, for Christ's sake?"

"Would you let me finish, sergeant? It was no fucking piece of cake. She was only a kid."

"Ok, ok. I'm sorry, Eddie. Everyone is jumpy. This whole thing has got all of us fucked up."

"I didn't want to go into it with all the vivid details. I thought I'd let his doctor handle it. But I thought he should know something because it would be a double shock if he heard it before his physician got there. So I told him we had every reason to believe she was the victim of the person who has been performing those atrocities."

"You did the right thing, Eddie. You used good judgment. That's why I sent you. I knew you would."

"I left him and his wife with some neighbors I called over. What's new here?"

"Nothing."

"Sergeant, Frank Patterson is in your office. You said you wanted to know as soon as he arrived."

"Thanks, Rick. Excuse me, Eddie. This should be interesting."

Patterson was pacing. The old Yankee confidence was lacking. The cigarette was shaking in his hand.

"Sit down, Mr. Patterson, you and I are going to have a long, long, talk."

Patterson shrugged and sat down.

"Why the sign? Why The Fish Shack?"

"How the Christ do I know? You're the cop."

"Look, for the time being, let's forget our personal animosities. We have the rest of our lives to fight."

"Ok, ok, get on with it."

"This is the first time that this psycho has deliberately left a calling card. Now, my guess is that he is purposely out to get you."

"Get me? You mean kill me?"

"Yes, that is exactly what I mean. So I'm going to give you police protection."

"Bullshit."

"Bullshit to you, Patterson, I'm running this show!"

"Well, then, start getting some results. Have you seen this goddamned town today? It's Tombstone City. The only tourists around are cops and reporters. And did you hear about those weirdos over at The Loft? A dismemberment party. Jesus."

"That's been called off. This Flanagan thing must have even gotten to them."

"Be thankful for small favors."

149

"Who hates you enough to have pulled off this latest number?"

"Well, let's face it. As a selectman, I have to make a lot of decisions that are not always appreciated by the voting public. I have enemies, but none this crazy."

"The Fish Shack. Why would this killer rename it? It hasn't been The Fish Shack for twelve years."

"Not since the former owner." And he reddened.

"What was his name?"

"Who?"

"The guy you bought it from?"

"Well, I bought it through the bank. It was a foreclosure."

"Yeah, I know." And Boyd's eyes narrowed into slits as he probed deeper.

"But what was the name of the owner who lost it to the bank?"

"Why? What difference does it make?"

"What difference? Do I have to draw a picture? The killer was making a point. The point was made very obvious. There was no attempt to be subtle. That killer wants us to know who he is. My guess is that he wants us to get him and he'll just go on killing until we catch him. And that could be a basketful of killings if we don't find him soon.

"Peters. Douglas Peters."

"Well, then, maybe we should look for Douglas Peters. Is he still in town?"

"No."

"Do you know where he is?"

"Yes."

"Well, where?"

"In Quonsett Memorial Cemetery. He killed himself. Look, I don't know where this is getting us."

"Why did he kill himself?"

"Look, how should I know. What the hell, am I on trial here? Christ's sake, I'm the victim, not the goddamn killer."

Patterson was standing now, leaning over the desk. His face had bluish purple veins running under the eyes and across the nose. They were more noticeable now because anger had turned his tan face to scarlet.

Boyd narrowed his eyes more.

"Now you sit the fuck down, Patterson, and let's knock off the bullshit. I wasn't in town then, but I always suspected there was something not just right about that operation. You've got your name up there on the side of the building, or at least you did. And yet, I have never seen you near the place. And it's a fucking gold mine. Now, you tell me everything. There's a killer walking the streets and beaches of this town and I want his ass—now."

Patterson threw up his hands and heaved a heavy sigh. "Peters thought we, the town, you know, gave him a bad deal. He was accused of illegal weighing procedures, and I guess he figured he would go bankrupt and he took the coward's way out. He was always a silly bastard. The idealist type."

"How do you mean?"

"Well, he'd have orphan groups and fresh-air kids working for him for the summer. They robbed him blind. Fucking niggers from New York."

"And Indians?" Boyd stuck it out there.

Patterson bit his lower lip and continued. "No, no Indians. Indians are just getting into the act. Jigs were big twelve years ago. Peters was a do-gooder. But he got it in the end."

"Did you have anything to do with this Peters guy killing himself?" The question was direct and he placed it right below the lines under Patterson's expressionless eyes.

"Now what is that supposed to mean?"

151

"You've been selectman in this town for a long time and you have some good, very good, properties. Did you have anything to do with the illegal weighing? Did you call for the inspection? Listen, Patterson, I can go to good old Dean to find out."

"Listen, you two-bit squaw man, even if I did, do you think—?" He did not get any further. Boyd reached across the desk and yanked him out of the ladderback chair that Patterson had moved to and open-handed him twice across the mouth.

Then he threw him back into the chair, sending Patterson and the chair against a file cabinet.

"No one speaks to me like that." Boyd sucked in a deep breath that further defined the high cheekbones. "Do you understand that? Do you?"

Patterson wiped his mouth clean of the welt. "Yes, uh, yes," he nodded.

"Now, tell me all you know about Douglas Peters. Did he have any brothers, uncles, sons, daughters—a wife? Tell me. And tell me now." He was bellowing and his deep bass voice bounced and rocked through the room.

There was a knock at the door.

"What is it?"

"Everything all right, sergeant?" It was Eddie.

"Everything is fine, Officer Singer, and mind your own fucking business."

"Yes sir, sergeant." Eddie responded apologetically.

Patterson wiped blood from his lip. "Ok, Boyd, when this is over, I'll have your badge."

"You may not be around to take anyone's badge. Now, what do you remember?"

"Nothing. How would I remember anything about a guy I barely knew?"

"Yeah, I suppose you're right. What would you care if a suicide had a family? But I know where I can find out—

the *Log*." Then Boyd thought of something.

"Eddie, Eddie, come in here."

Eddie stuck his head in the doorway. "Yes sir?"

"Eddie, you have a new assignment. Don't let *Mister* Patterson out of your sight. Take Oscar Seven. Sleep with him, if you can stand it."

It was not the same Frank Patterson who sat before him. He was slouched over, his shoulders drooped, and the tall lean frame looked more like a stringed puppet. The balding crown on his head seemed more noticeable, shiny with perspiration, but Patterson did not bother to rub it. He dabbed at his mouth with a linen handkerchief.

Boyd motioned for Eddie to leave the room. He could sense that Patterson wanted to talk. Boyd rose and shut the door.

"Ok, Frank, you want to talk a little?"

It was the first time Boyd had ever called him by his first name. It had a strange ring to both of them.

Patterson looked up and smiled. The tan had turned gray on his face.

"Strange bedfellows, sergeant. They say politics does that. Police work, too, I suspect."

"Yeah."

Patterson studied his dock siders and gagged on what he said, but he got it out. "I'm sorry about the remark." It was fast, but it was out. Boyd nodded.

"I'm scared, sergeant. I am not ashamed to admit it. I am scared because I saw what that maniac did. You don't have to go to the *Log*. In fact, I would appreciate it if you didn't. Dean and I are not exactly bedfellows these days." He managed a wry smile.

"What can you tell me about Peters?" Boyd was sitting on the side of the desk.

"He had a kid. A junior. He had a wife, too. I played around with her." It bothered him to say it. His face turned

153

into lines. "I think the kid knew it. Maybe—" He had trouble finding the words. "You know." He opened and closed his hands, making and unmaking fists.

"Yeah, but why would he kill the others?"

"I don't know."

"Where's the mother now?" Boyd was digging.

"I don't know. I lost track of her. She came back a couple of times, but I didn't encourage it."

"Why?"

"Well, because, I guess, I had gotten on to other things."

Boyd didn't push it. He could guess what Patterson had gotten on to.

He knew Patterson was down. What the hell was the sense of kicking a guy when he had his head in the mud? Patterson's entire body told the story. Absolute depression etched the lines firmly under his eyes. His dynasty was riddled with holes. The money may not come again. The town fucking fathers had been using him, and the most terrifying thought of all was that at this moment somewhere out there a maniac killer was planning on taking his life.

"The strange thing about this Peters woman"—he made her sound like a stranger whom he had heard about, not someone he had shared rainy afternoons with—"the strange thing is," Patterson continued, "is that at first I thought she was meeting me so she could help her husband keep his shop."

"How did she know he was in danger of losing it in the first place?"

"Well, there were some feelers. Peters wasn't coming across."

"You mean with payoffs."

"I would rather call them gratuities." There was no smile.

"Well, whatever. Go on."

"After a while she didn't even ask me for any favors. All

154

she wanted to do was screw. She couldn't get enough of it, and here the kid thinks—whatever he thinks."

"Whatever he does think, we've got to be ready for him. Now do everybody a favor and do what the officers tell you. And for Christ's sake stay with them."

Patterson rose to leave. "Don't worry, they'll get no trouble from me."

Boyd looked after him. What a joke. The guy has nobody—nobody but me.

Nine

The *Log* was having a field day—the time of its life. Dean's editorials were scathing indictments of the police and the selectmen. He brought out the Douglas Peters, Sr., suicide. He pointed a subtle finger at town officers and their abuse of power and hinted strongly at conflict of interest.

He saw Quonsett as an innocent victim lying there waiting to be slashed and cut because of what appeared to be some personal vendetta. Why should we suffer because of the sins of others? Why should our citizens hide behind locked doors? What was our chief of police doing?

Joe Medina was acting in a PR capacity, but there was little public relations to be involved in. He met with Boyd and Swanson daily and he attended the funeral of Mary Flanagan in a very official capacity. He wore his uniform.

Mary's funeral was played out before a packed house. Her friends, the waitresses from the restaurant, and her college classmates could hardly contain themselves. It could have been one of them. The awesome quiet inside the church was matched by the ominous silence of Main Street. Fear trembled inside and outside the white stucco church.

Cyrus Standish Dean reported in great detail the minutia of the funeral. Like some ancient scrivener, he detailed with monkish fervor and callous indiscretion the most private observations—the father's unnaturally bloated red face, the mother's impassivity, and even what they were wearing. The small-town demagogue did not have the sensitivity to report with taste.

Medina, holding the *Log* up to the sun that streamed through the window, asked the question more to himself than to Boyd or Swanson. "What the hell is wrong with that man? In this piece about the funeral, he comments on me wearing a uniform. What the hell does that have to do with anything? He must be crackers."

"No, he's not. He knows exactly what he's saying. He's simply saying that the Quonsett chief of police is now on the case. Ain't we lucky!" It was Swanson. "Are you going to run the show, Joe?"

"Gentlemen, I will run this department the way I always have—quietly."

The phone cut in on them. It was a lucky thing, too, because none of them were feeling too good about Joe Medina.

"Hello, yeah, he's right here.

"It's for you, Wayne."

Boyd took it and knew immediately it was Patterson. The voice was shaking.

"Yeah, ok. Sure. I'll meet you there in ten minutes.

"That was Patterson. He wants to show me something. Thinks maybe he knows where the maniac might hide out. I'll call in if there's anything worth checking."

Boyd was standing with hands on hips by the old Victorian house when Patterson pulled up in the cruiser. The two officers jumped out first and looked around the neighborhood. Two kids on bikes pedaled by, and a milk truck roared off. Patterson eased himself out of the cruiser slowly. He looked older than he had in Boyd's office.

"I think the kid knew we used to meet down there." And he pointed to the old guesthouse. "Maybe you should check it out or keep a guard on it."

The two officers stood at a respectful distance checking the street traffic.

Boyd followed Patterson down the hill to the steps of the cottage. Patterson shook his head from side to side. "It's funny, sergeant, but you never know, do you?"

"Never know what."

"What life has in store for you."

A voice from the house behind and above them on the hill cried out.

"Hey, what's the matter? What do you want?" It was the old man who owned the house.

"Sorry to bother you, sir, but we are looking for someone who used to live here. You haven't had any guests, have you?"

The old man started from the house but Boyd said, "No need to bother you, sir. Just wondered about guests."

"Guests, we don't have guests. Just my sons and their families on weekends. Provided the weekends can be kept quiet." He smiled at Boyd.

"Well, we're looking for a young guy, early twenties, who used to live here."

"Hey, wait a minute. There was a young kid one night— few nights ago. Told me he lived here once. Just wanted to see the old place. Nostalgic, you know."

"What did he look like?" Boyd rushed into the question and was sorry he had because the old man reacted quickly.

"Who was he? Is he trouble? I live here alone except for my wife. Is he dangerous?"

"No, nothing to worry about. Nothing serious. We think he stole a car."

"Well, he was driving one of those vans. One of those Niagara Falls scenes on the side. He didn't have a car. So if he stole one he didn't have it that night."

Boyd tried to keep it cool and calm. Here was someone who had seen the vehicle and could identify it. What a fucking break.

"I didn't see the van too well. Couldn't make it out, but

158

my son did. My eyes are bad. Cataracts last year. But he was the one who saw it. He commented on it when we got in the house. Is it important?"

"Yes, very. Look, if I need you or your son I'll call you. My name is Boyd. Sergeant Boyd. Ok?"

"Be glad to help you out, sergeant. Glad to."

When Patterson ducked back into the cruiser, Boyd stuck his hand out. Patterson responded. "Good thinking, Frank, you may have given us something. Now we can look for a van. At least it narrows the field."

As the days passed slowly on, Eddie took to his new assignment with a begrudging discipline. He went directly to Patterson's home on Snow Lane every morning promptly at 8:00 A.M. and left at 9:00 P.M. each evening. In the meantime, two other officers picked up the slack when Eddie was off with Sandy and Stacey.

Douglas Peters sat in the black shiny van on Breaker Lane just off Main Street. He did not have to read the editorials, he did not have to attend the funeral and see the hundreds of terror-stricken mourners. All he had to do was gaze out of the cab and look at the town from one end to the other.

He reflected on the morning that Mary's body was discovered. It gave him great joy to remember it in detail. It soothed his anger.

He had parked the van on the south side of the harbor and pulled the curtains shut, leaving just enough space to be able to see out without being seen.

Her body hung in a naked and bloody crucifixion facing the harbor entrance. The morning had been foggy and the gray mist of 6:00 A.M. blew across the jetties. The groaning, throaty echo of the ferry's foghorn reached out from the island. He had propped himself up by the window waiting for the ferry to approach. He could not see it, so he charted

159

its advance by the increasing loudness of the foghorn. The morning mist was coming closer. It cut through the mist gradually and then it was visible. A white, hulking object seemed to rise out of the deep. It approached the harbor entrance. He could see the early morning passengers, some with coffee cups to their lips, leaning over the railings. The captain stood tall and alert in the wheelhouse as the ferry slid past the pilings and on toward Patterson's.

Suddenly, from the top deck, horror gripped the passengers. He saw coffee cups drop, some people turned away, others pointed. One man vomited over the side as the captain slowly rubbed his jaw looking sideways until he had to switch his attention back to the craft. His eyes were saucer large.

Doug Peters had waited while the ferry passed by with its staring passengers, like a ghost ship gliding by. He had waited until the police arrived and two thick-necked cops cut her down. And he had waited until he saw the sign, his sign, being replaced by Patterson's again. And he had watched the gangling, tall man with the eternal tan directing the operation. At least it was a smaller sign, hastily made, he had thought. That gave him satisfaction. But it had been everything that had warmed him, had sent a flame of rejuvenation through him. He had more power than anyone in town, and he would soak this town in its own blood, and that tanned, lanky man would be next. That man who stood palming the crown of a bald spot would see and feel the flashing, slicing cut of the blade.

But he did not want to rush anything. He wanted to enjoy the moments leading up to the next murder. Like a lover, he wanted to stroke and feel the moments, to become hot with the desire to do more. To reach a point where only pleasure, only complete satisfaction, would bring full release.

That release was about to come about, he thought as he

watched a camper pull into The Dunes restaurant parking lot. It was packed with children. He had to shut this town down and there was one sure way to do it. One more murder and he would be satisfied—cleansed—ready to put an end to it.

Quonsett was dead. It was a lifeless corpse, waxen and cadaverous, lying out being bleached dry in the summer sunshine. Many shops had changed their closing hours to long before dark. The tennis courts at the Quonsett Inn were stilled except for an occasional shout from a doubles match. But the large groups that usually signed in were not signing in anymore. The bronzed tennis players were turning pale under the oak beams and artificial lighting of the Inn as they sat over canasta, or bridge, or chess.

The cranberry farmers cradled shotguns in their arms as they walked two by two through the woods to the moist bogs. Their children were kept home.

The usually jumping, rocking, stoned-out-of-its-mind Hill was subdued. The waitresses car-pooled it to their jobs. No longer did the tall and leggy blonds saunter the boardwalk. No longer could a van or a bike pick up the ass-wigglers. No longer was anyone welcome at The Loft. Everyone in that former freewheeling, sleep around, grab-a-joint, have-a-hit, was suspect.

Some of those who had made a little bread had packed it in and left for Boston or Illinois or New York or California. Back to Big Sur and the frigid surf. The jobs were just not in Quonsett. The shops, the restaurants, and the supermarkets were dying. The most common sign in town was Vacancy.

Street corners and parking lots were deserted.

And the beaches. The reason everyone came summer after golden summer. The beaches. They sat out there playing host to gulls and the tide. The swimmers did not come. The families did not splash along the kidney-shaped channels. There were no sand castles and sand statues, no screaming and chatter, no lunches, coolers, radios, and frisbees on the grassy patches overlooking the sound, or the town beach, or Woodchip, or any of the once-glorious warm-watering spots of Quonsett.

The beaches were deserted.

He had stashed the van and was walking up Breaker and down into Snow Lane. He froze when he saw the police car heading toward him. Three figures sat in the blue cruiser as it glided by. The cruiser rolled on past but not before he caught a shot of Frank Patterson in the back seat. So he's riding around with cops.

It would have to be soon, he thought. He would have to get his man soon. He turned around and headed for the woods. He would rest and think.

Boyd cradled the phone and looked at Patterson and then at Eddie.

"That should settle it. That Peters situation I was checking on. No wonder I couldn't locate that family in New Rochelle. We knew there was no record of Peters in school, or on the voting lists or at the town hall. Nothing. You know why?"

"No, sergeant. Why?" It was Patterson and he leaned forward, his tone was respectful. Life was funny. After all these years it was only Boyd that stood between Patterson and disaster.

"Because he changed his name. Or rather his grandmother did—but not legally. She just gave him her maiden name—Baker. At high school his name was Edward Baker. Edward after his grandfather."

"How did you find out?" Eddie asked.

"I called the schools with one question. Did they have anything they could give me on a Douglas Peters? There was no record. Was there any information on those who

162

had gone to med school? The local police took it from there and came up with a list as long as your arm. That's where all our doctors come from, I guess. There was no one on the list that could have fit. I told them I needed an old address. A Cape Cod address. That was about a week ago. I kept it all to myself because I didn't know how it would turn out."

"Yes, go on."

"Then it hit me. Maybe he went to a private school. So the locals checked that out. No luck until one of them remembered the old Freeman School, which closed down two years ago. The headmaster and owner died, but his widow came up with all the records. There was a kid on scholarship—excellent student, a real loner—by the name of Edward Baker. He had lived for a time in Quonsett."

"Holy shit, and he went to med school?"

"Yeah, but he dropped out. No money. His grandmother was sick and his mother died in an institution."

Boyd let it hang out there and he watched Patterson's face turn florid. Patterson studied his hands and said nothing until the color left his face again.

"Then what, sergeant?" he continued quietly.

"Since the grandmother was next of kin, she was contacted. She's not too keen and in poor health in a county nursing home. She hasn't seen or heard from her grandson in a year. All she knew was that he dropped out of school and was heading for California."

"Yeah, by way of Quonsett, Massachusetts."

"Well, we can't be sure. But it's the only lead we've had, and I'm going to jump on it."

Eddie said, "One of the guys checked out the waitress who worked with Mary Flanagan. She says Mary was very quiet about her personal life, but she did mention a young man. Liz saw them leave together. And get this—it was in a van."

163

"Well, ok, I've got some pictures of this guy, but nothing too recent. He probably has a beard and fucking earrings hanging out of his nose by now."

The pieces were adding up, but slowly, very slowly. And the biggest piece was the one that would tell them where Peters was hiding. Where, in God's name, in Quonsett could he be hiding himself?

Doug Peters did not go to the bridge anymore. He knew he did not have to. No one was coming to town. He had seen the empty streets and closed shops. Even The Hill was a tomb. He sat now in the van which was hidden by the thick brush of Bryant Acres.

The Acres was a gift to the town by the family of Jason Clement Bryant, who made his money in tea and charitably gave most of it back to Quonsett.

Douglas Peters had played here as a boy. The highway out of town had one hidden avenue to the Acres, but the actual entrance was behind the Bryant Memorial Theater.

Local walkers and bird watchers frequented the area, but tourists never did, because for one, they didn't know it existed; and two, they couldn't cook because it was too dry; or three, swim there because the ponds were all lily pads and moss.

He was virtually a solitary citizen of some thirty-five acres, and as he sat eating wild blueberries in the cab of the van, he felt an oppressive loneliness and depression. He checked his pockets and found his last five dollars in his jeans.

He knew it was coming fast. He would kill Patterson and leave town or die trying. His entire purpose for living was the driving force of revenge. He cared nothing for those he had killed. Once he had thought about getting Dean, the old fart, but Dean had done him more good than anybody. The rag he ran had really flamed the flames of panic, that was for sure. He would see. If he could get Dean—fine. If not, maybe another time. But he had to have Patterson.

He thought of Mary, but checked himself. She was gone.

He jumped from the van and followed a twisting path through the cloaked woods. He walked deliberately through the dense growth until he reached a grassy hill. The moon was bright and it guided him down the hill to a pocket-sized pond. He had swum here as a boy and had never seen anyone else in the area. As a child, he was ecstatic that he had his own pond and his own wild and primitive playground. It gave him something no one else had. Even the townies never came there. It was his. All of it. Everything had been so wonderful in those years. He had been so happy and then it had all ended so abruptly. He ripped off his shirt and jeans and stood naked in the moonlight, the yellow light washing over him. He thought about his father and then his mother. Tears formed in his eyes. He thought that he should send a postcard or a letter to his grandmother. After all, she had tried to do all she could for him.

The hell with her.

He dove into the water, knifing through it cleanly. His sadness disappeared and his mind began clicking. He would have to get rid of the cop who was with Patterson. That part of it he rather enjoyed. Getting rid of the protection.

He had been aware of Patterson's bodyguard right after the murder of Mary Flanagan. He had parked for a moment by Patterson's home the next night pretending to check a tire and he saw a cop coming down the walk.

After that he made periodic checks. He had known the sign would blow it all. They obviously knew now who he was, and that really was the best part.

He also had great confidence in his ability to pull it off. The water was soothing and chilling. It electrified him to thought and action. The stupor and depression he had been feeling was now gone. His spirits rose and he felt immense. He felt control and authority as he lay back peering into the low overhanging trees and listening to the crickets. The nipples on his chest were hard. His only problem was the van. For the cop, he had left the van near the beach so he could act as a hitchhiker. But Patterson would hardly pick up anyone, and plus the fact he would be riding in the cruiser. No, he would have to do something different. The van would be out of the question. It was too obvious. Anyway, he was running out of the gas he had stored. It was a problem. But it was a problem he enjoyed working on. He thrashed about in the water playfully, feeling tremendous joy and pleasure.

God, do I love living down here. He blinked. His mind was clear. It was going to be ok.

Ten

Snow Lane was in the wealthiest section of town. Patterson's family had bought the sprawling French country house in the twenties, and he had raised his two sons in the fourteen-room mini-estate. The house was his pride and joy, as were his sons, who were now comfortably established in a business farther down the Cape.

The house reached out in all angles in a secluded cul-de-sac backing up to Snow Pond. An enormous hedge from one end of the property line to the other obscured all but the mansard roof of the house.

Frank Patterson had one of the choicest properties in town, and now, as it sat quietly in the moonlight, nothing was out of place except the blue and black cruiser squatting in the gravel driveway.

Inside the car, Rick Pierce sat sipping the hot coffee that Sergeant Wayne Boyd had just dropped off. It was 2:35 A.M. and the lane was like a graveyard. He had relieved Eddie hours ago.

Rick shook sleep from his head, sipped his coffee, and settled in and waited for daybreak.

Behind the house, a figure rose up out of the pond. The figure, wearing boxer-type swim trunks, had a leather belt around his waist. Hanging from the belt was a leather case that held an assortment of blades and needles that flashed in the night.

The figure, careful to keep out of the lights cast by the moon, crept slowly up the manicured lawn and then darted for a large oak that shadowed the house. Adjacent to the oak was a long wooden sun deck. Above the deck was a series of windows and another smaller, more intimate, deck, more of a balcony for morning coffee and a clear uninterrupted view of the pond.

Doug Peters smiled as he felt a tiny breeze stirring, and his gaze rested on a curtain fluttering in the night air from a window above him off the balcony.

The tree would be no problem, he knew, and he began to hoist himself up just as another figure bounded across the lawn and sprang at him. The dog's teeth clamped on the bone of the inside of his right ankle, pulling him to the ground. The pain inflicted by the growling, German police dog almost caused him to scream out, but he managed to grab for the leather pouch and pull the needle free while jamming it into the dog's back almost all in one motion.

The dog yelped and twisted in the air. The animal eyes dilated for a moment and then the quivering body went still. Peters wanted to strangle the beast. The anger and frustration mounted but he had to be still. One sound would bring the cop, and he was so close to completing his plan. Nothing, absolutely nothing, could stop him now.

He gripped the thick neck fur of the dog and dragged the unconscious bulk down to the water. He held the head under, listening to the gurgling sounds until the night was still again. He allowed the body to slip away.

The pain in his ankle stung him. He placed a hand on the bitten area, and when he pulled his hand away it was soaked with blood.

He limped back behind the shrubs and listened. A car door shut somewhere and then there were footsteps on gravel and then on grass. The beam of a flashlight speared through the blackness of the backyard and then down on the pond.

Peters waited for the beam to find the dog's unconscious

form, but the dog was now lying submerged in four feet of water. The flashlight played on every object and shrub in the yard. Doug Peters lay in a wincing pain. Covered by rhododendrons, he did not breathe until the light disappeared around to the front of the house. The footsteps crunched on gravel, and then the car door opened and closed again. He lay in the shrubs for fully fifteen minutes until he was absolutely certain that he was the only living creature aware of his presence. The sweat on his forehead dropped down onto his nose. His lips were thick and parched. He was thirsty. He wished he was back at Bryant Acres swimming in his pond.

He returned to the water and waded in until the water reached his chin. He slipped beneath the water and he felt soothed. The stinging in his ankle was somewhat relieved. He swam underwater and reached shore. The dog floated by silently. Peters managed a smile as he crouched up the hill to the tree again. He felt for knives and needles. He was satisfied that he had brought as many needles as he had. The dog had taken a full injection. He felt his ankle again. There was no blood. The water had been good. He was refreshed and in control again. Fortunately, the dog had bitten most of the flesh and not much of the bone.

He thought about going after the cop but decided he'd chance breaking into the house. With the dog out of the way maybe he could sneak in.

He swung himself up on the first limb and stood in the crotch of the tree while he reached for the next limb. He pulled himself up to where he was parallel to the balcony. He did two hand-overhands, and he was onto the balcony. The window was fully open and he peered in. He pulled himself in and found the tile floor with his feet quite easily. For a moment, he stood still, wondering if this just was not too easy. Was it a trap? But if it was, they would have had him by now. They wouldn't allow a madman this

169

close to the intended victim, would they? They would have grabbed him by now. He thought briefly of Mary.

He took a towel and wiped himself dry, noting the convenience of this particular open window. He placed the towel neatly back on the rack.

The hallway was wall-to-wall shag rug. A light from the stairway landing gave just the light necessary for him to make his way along the corridor.

The door to the upstairs sitting room and library was open. The room was vacant. He continued down the corridor to an oak-paneled door. He turned the doorknob slowly and carefully. He kept the doorknob twisted in his hand as he opened the door.

He stood in the darkness and heard the breathing of a figure in a bed in the far corner of the room. He gently allowed the doorknob to return to its normal place while closing the door softly.

He approached the bed with his hypodermic needle extended. A light summer sheet partially covered the sleeping form. The form breathed normally with very little noise. He leaned over to see who it was.

It was a woman. Her breasts, like wrinkled melons, rose and fell with her breathing. He plunged the needle into her arm. She jerked up in the bed as he covered her mouth with his hand. She struggled, but as she did, she began to weaken. Her body sagged in the bed. He would not kill her. She would be like his own mother. Left to think about it all. Left alone.

Once into the corridor, he tried two other doors, and then, at the opposite end of the hallway, he heard a man cough.

Patterson. It had to be. The thrill and excitement ran up his spine. Finally he would have the absolute revenge he had lived for.

He walked softly along the thick rug and stopped in

front of the door. His hands found the doorknob and he turned it. It was locked. He tried it again. Locked.

That fucking bastard, he thought. His own wife's door is open, and this fucking yellow coward locks his door. Rage ripped through him. Blind fury almost caused him to smash his shoulder against the panel. He tried to compose himself. He took long, deep breaths. Sweat broke out on his forehead and upper lip. He wiped it away with the back of his hand. He slowly managed to control himself. He had to think.

He slumped to a deacon's bench and rubbed his eyes and face with his hands. The hands were trembling. They shouldn't be, he thought. It's not fear. It's frustration. He thought of going back to Patterson's wife. But, no, it wasn't the woman he wanted. He wanted Patterson, and Patterson was behind that thick, oak-paneled door. He looked around at the opulence. It was quiet money but very much in evidence. Wood. Wood paneling everywhere. Not your five-dollar variety from Home Handyman, Inc., but oak, like the kind in the dean's office at med school. Old and expensive. He could have lived in a home like this. He could have had this home with a doctor's shingle hanging outside and an office off the garage. Now he would have nothing, and the reason for all of it snored on the other side of that door. The frenzy and hate came full force now. He would not allow Patterson to live another day.

He listened, not even allowing a deep breath. The night was still except for crickets and the far-off sound of a car west of the house.

He walked softly along the corridor to a lead glass window. It was cut full length into the house and it faced out on the main entrance.

The police car showed no activity except the bright, red tip from a cigarette. He had to act fast now.

171

He watched the red tip flare brighter, and then the figure flicked the cigarette out of the window onto the gravel, where it sparked like a small incendiary and then slowly died.

Peters was about to turn and walk back down the corridor when the cruiser's door was pushed open. The cop stepped out and straightened up, stretching his arms and reaching out to the night sky.

The cop looked up at the house. Peters stepped back into the shadows of the draperies. He inched against the wall while the cop stood in the driveway studying the house. It seemed that the cop was zeroing in on the large window. Peters pressed even farther into the shadows. Did that goddamn cop see me? Why the hell does he keep looking here? The questions burned into him and his heart pounded. Did the cop make a periodic check of the inside of the house as well? He didn't know. How the hell could he know? The cop began to move. He kicked at the gravel with his boot, pulled up his belt. He brought out his flashlight and swept the front of the house and yard with it. The light climbed up the side of the house. Peters slowly slid to his knees and lay on the floor. His breath was coming fast. Too fast. He had to control his breathing. The driveway side of the house grew dark again. He raised himself up to the window to see where the cop was headed. He watched as the cop ascended the front steps of the house. He heard the key in the lock. It rang in his ears. The door opened and there was the sound of feet scruffling across carpet.

"If he comes up those stairs, I'm going to take him." He held the scalpel ready. He crouched in a frenzy waiting for the cop. He panicked thinking he would never have this chance again. If he took the cop but missed Patterson they would surround Patterson with an army.

He continued to listen to the sounds beneath him. They

were not heavy sounds but the careless night sounds of someone who does not know a house that well.

Then the door handle turned and the cop was back outside with the door locked behind him. The cop turned to the path leading to the pond.

Peters thought that was worse than the cop coming upstairs. Here he would have the element of surprise, but if that cop finds the dog, he could have him trapped.

Then, just as abruptly, the cop turned away from the path, lit up a cigarette and ducked back into the cruiser.

He got up and glided back down the corridor and rapped lightly on Patterson's door. There was no reaction. He rapped louder. A sudden grunt in the middle of a snore. He rapped again. The bed squeaked and shook as Patterson sat up.

"What's that? Who's there? Is that you, Doris?" The voice was full of sleep and muffled because of the thick wood of the door.

"It's me, Mr. Patterson, the officer on duty."

"Who?"

Douglas Peters made a small bugle with his hands and repeated louder, "The police officer on duty."

"What the hell do you want?" And Patterson rolled out of bed and approached the door.

"Do you know what time it is, for Christ's sake?"

"It's your dog, Mr. Patterson, I have to talk to you about your dog."

"My dog?" First one click and then another as the double lock opened and the doorknob turned slowly.

Patterson poked his sleepy head out into the corridor, and as he did he felt a cold, stinging sensation under his right ear. The sensation continued along the same route to his left ear. He clutched at his throat, which was exploding with a wet liquid that he was now aware was his own blood. He brought flesh and ooze away in his hand as he staggered back into his room. He stumbled headlong over a chair and fell, clutching his throat. He tried to swallow, to breathe, but the flowing of the blood would not stop as he groped for a sheet to soak it up.

Douglas Peters stood over him with an eight-inch scalpel poised.

"You know who I am, Patterson, and you know you are going to die, and you know why. You killed my father just as surely as if you slashed him yourself. You fucked my mother. You made her give you a payoff with her body. She's dead and my life is ruined and useless."

Patterson's eyes bugged out as he held the bloodstained sheet like a shield in front of him. He managed a gurgling sound. "Nnooo. pleesh." Blood slurred his speech.

Peters ripped the sheet away with the scalpel and jerked the head up like a fish on a hook. He held the head up in his left hand gripping Patterson's hair, crossed over the bloody neck and dug farther into the neck until the body felt limp and he released the hair. Patterson slumped to the floor like a heavy sack. The last act was calm, methodical, and ritualistic. Douglas Peters tore Patterson's shorts away with the scalpel and performed his most efficient operation. He severed each testicle cleanly and dropped them to the floor.

Earlier that evening Eddie and Sandy had enjoyed a quiet seafood platter at The Dock restaurant.

After two gin and limes Sandy loosened up. "I've been thinking, Eddie."

"I hope so, sweetheart."

"No glib stuff, Eddie, I'm serious."

"Oh-oh, here we go. You want a bigger house."

"Please, Eddie."

"Ok, honey, what is it that you have been thinking about?"

174

"I'd like another baby, Eddie."

"Sweetheart, here? I mean, we would never be able to eat at Howard Johnson's again."

"Forget the old jokes for a minute, ok? Ok?' she repeated with intense eyes.

"Ok, honey, go on. I'm sorry."

"I love you, Eddie, and I would like us to have a son—like you and for you."

Eddie toyed with the ice in the glass and then finished off the gin. "It really isn't in the plan. We really had decided against it, hadn't we?"

"I know, but I've changed my mind. I love it down here and I think it's a great place to bring up children. I like being a mother, Eddie, and a wife. Let all those liberated women do their number on Wall Street or wherever. I think I know myself fairly well. I know who I am and who we are and I love every minute of it."

"I don't want you to have a baby just for me. It's got to be for all of us, Stacey, too."

"It will be. Let's order another drink. A couple more gins might change your mind."

"Well, let's think about it. No sense being hasty."

"About the drinks?"

"You know what I mean."

Now, as he rolled over, he felt the glowing warmth of her body. It had been a late night and they had fallen asleep after talking, well into the early morning. She rubbed his back and he caressed and kissed her breasts. He was thirsty from all the gin he had. The gin helped loosen the talk. Now he had to have her.

"I love you, Eddie Singer."

"I love you, Sandy Singer." And he moved toward her.

The phone shook the night.

"Well, I'll be a son of a bitch. What timing!"

He grabbed for the phone and knocked it to the floor.

175

He snapped on the light, and when he saw her sitting up naked, her entire body brown from the sun, he wanted to forget the phone. He picked the phone off the floor.

"Yeah. I dropped the son of a bitch. What? What? Are you shittin? Jesus Christ. I'll be right there. Right."

He slammed the phone down. He could feel the sex leaving him, he softened.

"What is it, Eddie?" Her voice was almost as urgent as his.

"Frank Patterson had his throat slashed tonight. In his own house. Every available man is being called in." He saw the shock and disappointment. "We're going to have to make babies another time."

That night while Eddie and Sandy had been dining at The Dock, Wayne Boyd and Kate were grilling steaks in the backyard.

Later that night when the boys and Kate were asleep, Boyd prepared the rods for their next fishing outing.

He had thought of hitting the sack, but he knew he would not sleep. He sat on the deck blowing smoke into the dark, knowing that out there somewhere was his man. He thought of Patterson. He was gaining perspective on Patterson. It couldn't be called respect by any stretch of the imagination, but he was beginning to see the old bastard as a person for the first time. Alienated—a lot like himself—outside of things, used by the people with real clout.

He went into the kitchen and heated the water for coffee. When it whistled hot, he poured it into the Styrofoam cup with the instant coffee in it. He placed a cover on it and prepared more for the Thermos. He drove over to Patterson's and left the cup and Thermos with Rick. Then he drove back home to try to get some sleep.

He got the call ten minutes before Eddie got his.

* * *

Boyd had called Medina immediately. It did not take much discussion to decide on calling in the DA's office. Medina had been in bed—not alone—but the call was like a cold shower. He jumped out of bed and began the next nerve-racking hours of contacting the proper people.

"Ok, quiet down. Quiet down."

They were crowded and packed into the conference room. Yawning and blinking, they rubbed at their eyes and drank coffee. Every cop, summer or full-time, was there. The chief stood red-eyed and mute, drinking from a large brown mug.

"Now, as you know, Frank Patterson is dead. He succumbed at around three fifteen. His wife discovered him. Her scream brought Officer Pierce. She said she was jabbed by a hypodermic needle. She remembers a man bending over her. It was dark, but she thought the man was young —twenties or thirties. She got some light from the moon. He got in and out through a bathroom window, and a trail of blood led to the pond."

The morning was beginning to pink through the station windows and the night lights and dawn streaks gave the dismal tone of loneliness to the station.

"I want every available unit out until I personally relieve you. This fucker has got to be caught before he turns this town into a cemetery.

"Be close-mouthed. Just do your jobs. Don't listen to those bastards in town if they try to put you down, and they will with that murderer-running-loose, and police-do-nothing bullshit. This prick is crazy, so don't hesitate, but use your heads. Be ready, but don't be trigger-happy. Ok, that's all. Get out there. Eddie, you're my driver."

The approach to Snow Lane was virtually cut off from the mainstream of town. High hedges and shrubs turned it into a green fortress. It was the kind of privacy only the wealthy could afford. Before the cruiser was halfway down the lane, Boyd noticed the three cruisers and the unmarked car in a kind of wagontrain semicircle at the bottom of the lane.

"What the hell are those bastards doing, waiting for John Wayne?"

"Well, maybe—" Eddie didn't finish.

"Well, maybe bullshit, too."

"What the fuck are you guys waiting for—the U.S. Cavalry? Move those vehicles out of here before the whole neighborhood is breathing down our necks." He looked up at the sky. It was peaking daylight now. No haze, but a definite burn-through sun.

"Who was on duty when it happened? New duty officer or Pierce? Dispatcher thought it was Pierce but he wasn't sure."

The six cops huddling around one of the cruisers looked down, then one jerked his head over to Rick sitting alone in the unmarked car dragging heavily on a cigarette.

"Ok, move your asses out of here."

"Yes, sir." The cop cleared his throat.

"I want you hitting the entire north side of this town. I want you seen—understand? I want the people of this town to think we have one thousand cruisers and five thousand cops."

They broke up and descended on their vehicles as he turned and headed for Pierce. Eddie followed at a quiet distance. The gravel crunched under Boyd's feet. The gravel was eggshells to Eddie.

Boyd leaned into the cruiser. The driver's door was open. He took the cigarette from Pierce's mouth and dropped it on the driveway.

"What happened, Rick? I'd like to hear how it all happened. Come on, get out and walk me through it."

Pierce, normally dark from his part-time swimming instructor's job, now had a gray look. He had trouble speaking and his first words were a stammer.

"W—w—well, it, ah—"

"Knock that shit off right now, *Officer* Pierce."

Pierce swallowed hard and pointed to the front door of the house.

"She—she was standing in the door, making, making a funny whimp—whimpering noise, you know what I mean, sergeant?"

"Who was?" Boyd's voice was modulated and quiet.

"Mrs. Patterson."

"Yeah, go on."

"She made this noise and as soon as I heard her, I jumped from the cruiser. I could see right then and there something terrible had happened."

"Something terrible, huh? Why?"

"Her face looked wild and her nightgown had blood all over it. At first she couldn't stop this whimpering. I tried to talk with her, but I couldn't get anything out of her. Then I thought of Mr. Patterson and I sat her down on the steps and ran into the house. I yelled his name and there was nothing. Then I hit the second floor, and his bedroom door was open. He was on the floor, blood all over him. That's when I came down and called the station. The woman was in shock so the backup on the beach took her to the county hospital. That's about it."

They were at the front door now and Boyd tapped it open with the jump boot and turned to Pierce.

"And you never heard anything all night? Nothing out of the ordinary?"

"Well, yeah, earlier I heard the dog barking around back."

"What?"

"The dog was barking."

"What time was that?"

"I don't know exactly. Maybe a few minutes—ten minutes after you brought me the coffee."

179

"What did you do?" Boyd's voice was getting a rasp to it.

"I went out back and searched the whole place with my light. There was nothing. Shit, sergeant, I'm not deaf. I would have heard something if there had been anything out there." He was shorter than Boyd and he had to look up at him.

"Did you find the dog?"

"No."

"Where the hell did it go? It must have been Patterson's. He told me he had a better guard than the entire Quonsett Police Department. Eddie, look around back." He threw the words over his shoulder.

"All right, let's go in."

They mounted the carpeted stairs, oriental runner from foyer to top step. On the way up the stairs, Boyd saw Patterson's life flash by him in pictures. Elementary school, prep school crew, college golf team, two sons, one under each arm smiling in front of a sailboat, Patterson and his wife cutting the ribbon at the entrance to—he couldn't make out—hell of a lot of trees, he thought. No scrub pine, must be Maine. Yacht club function, Quonsett summer theater shaking hands with Van Johnson, others with Edward Mulhare, Donald O'Connor, Howard Duff, and an interesting one where Patterson's tawny face was wrinkled in a leering smile at Betsy Palmer. It had been a good life, but one fucking death, Boyd thought as he stood in the doorway.

Boyd stepped into the room and gave windows and ceiling a quick glance. Then he knelt at the body. Most of the neck had poured out onto the floor. Some pieces of flesh were already sticking to the sheet that Patterson's long arms held out before him. The brown liver spots on the backs of his hands were now a dirty gray.

"You poor son of a bitch, that fucker really went to

work on you. He must have hated your guts."

Patterson lay on his stomach. Boyd saw the testicles, and had a momentary urge to vomit.

"C'mon, let's get out of here." And he closed the paneled door softly beside him.

He straightened up and studied Pierce. "How long have you been a cop, Pierce?"

"Six years, sergeant. Two permanent."

"Two permanent? More like one year and five months."

"Yeah, I guess so. Something like that."

"You're not very good at facts are you, Pierce?"

"Huh?"

"I mean putting things together." Pierce moved to sit on the deacon's bench.

"You stand the fuck up, understand?"

Pierce braced, waiting for the onslaught he knew was coming. He had seen it before. Once it started, there was no backing away. The oak-paneled wall was behind him. He tried to lean casually against it.

"I want you standing up straight when I talk to you." And he grabbed Pierce by the shirt and shoved him up against the wall, his hard knuckles driving into the shoulders.

"Now stand there nice and easy and answer me. Number one: What did you do when you heard the dog bark? Did you respond immediately?"

"Yes."

"When you searched the area, did it occur to you to look for the dog?"

"No, I guess not."

"It was almost three o'clock in the morning, a man is under police guard, his dog barks, the officer searches the yard and does not find fucking canine, so he goes to the door and knocks because protected party must be still awake if that party, moments before, let the animal into

181

the house. Why didn't you do that?"

"Because Mr. Patterson requested that all of his guards do their jobs quietly and not disturb him. Especially at night."

"Number two: What if it was a strange dog? Did you ever wonder what the dog might be barking at? Did you ever stop and think, just for a minute, that the dog might be barking at a man?"

"Hey, sergeant, sergeant." It was Eddie from the foot of the stairs.

"I'm coming." This time he did not look at Patterson's framed life.

"Cut back, sergeant, down by the pond. I found traces of blood near this tree. See there. I followed them to here, then lost them for a few feet and picked them up again there on these rocks. I spotted the dog floating against that dinghy. Figured it must be Patterson's. I spent enough time with both of them. So I pulled it out and it was his mutt."

They stood looking down at what appeared to be a drowned giant rat. All fur was curled tight and kinky to the body, and the tail was like a brown stick. The eyes were rolled far back in the skull.

"There's your watchdog, Pierce. He found his man. But the man found him, too. Ok. Put him in a sack and throw him in the trunk of my cruiser. That dog bit that killer sure as shit." The dog's teeth were clamped tight. Boyd held the flashlight close to the mouth—a large layer of human skin was wedged between the teeth.

"I'd bet it was his foot or leg. The dog caught him climbing that tree to the open window. What window is that, Eddie?"

"The bathroom. Next to Patterson's room."

"Let's check it out." And they headed back to the house.

Two burly figures were standing in the black and white tiled foyer. The one who spoke was big, two or three inches over six feet and two hundred and twenty or thirty pounds.

"Well, well, Quonsett's gift to the FBI Academy." He smiled and continued. "This is a real messy one, Boyd. I mean, when you guys screw up, you go right to the top. Shit, I know you want to be chief, but knocking off Patterson. Hell, that's what I call ambition."

"Fuck you, Durgin."

"Oh, no, no, naughty, naughty, sergeant. Benson, this is Quonsett's one-man police force, Sergeant Wayne Boyd. He's very good if he can keep his cool."

"Howareya, sergeant?"

"How are you! Shall we go on up, gentlemen?"

The bathroom did not disappoint them. Back downstairs and out to the sidewalk, Boyd traded obscenities with Durgin.

"See, Durgin, you county guys never see the real world. Or if you do, it's all pubic hairs under a microscope. See you around." And he slammed Durgin's door as the county car slid away from the curb.

So—the DA was in on it. He had ambivalent feelings about that. Yet, it was Patterson who had wanted no county interference, and, ironically, he was responsible for the DA's entrance into the case.

Life was stirring on the lawns and sun decks of Snow Lane when Oscar Four glided by the sprinklers, the morning papers, and the Bloody Marys.

"Direct to the County Investigator's Office, Eddie, all horses."

It was Friday morning, and at 8:00 A.M. Route 6 Mid-Cape was still carrying moderate traffic, mostly local, hitting the exits to town and the beaches. Eddie drew the straight line in the speed lane and watched the locals veer off to their Friday morning appointments.

The morning was turning gray and rain was predicted for the afternoon and evening.

"How did you meet that guy Durgin, sergeant?"

"We were in the same training unit for a three-month stint a couple of years ago. We were on the range and I was up on him with pistol and automatic weapons. We were going into the last frame and he leaned over and said to me, 'Boyd, maybe you'd be better if you went back to a bow and arrow. It would be more natural-like.' I almost put a thirty-eight slug right through him. I couldn't see straight. I was so goddamned mad, I barely touched the target."

Boyd began to laugh and cough because the cigarette smoke got caught in on the laugh. He continued laughing and choking until Eddie said,

"Are you ok, sergeant?"

"Sure, Eddie." And the tears rolled down Boyd's cheeks. "That son of a bitch Durgin is one hell of a cop." And he wiped the tears away as he continued to chuckle, quietly now, to himself.

They rolled on until Boyd pushed the sheriff's hat up from his eyes with the palm of his hand. "This is it, Eddie. Pull off here and hang a left and then the first right. Once inside, watch for the sign that says Lab. Fine, yeah, ok, here we go. There's the sign."

The building was functional like all state buildings. It was square and sandstone surrounded by scrub pine and wood-chips landscaping. It seemed more of a utility building for snow-removal gear and rakes and lawnmowers.

Eddie pulled around to the platform behind the lab.

"Ok, Eddie, grab the dog."

The bag was heavy with the soaked, dead weight of the dog, so Boyd gave him a hand up the steps and into the lab.

184

Two white-coated middle-aged technicians sipped their morning coffee as the body was dumped unceremoniously on the lab floor.

"And good morning to you, too, Sergeant Boyd. Anybody we know?"

"Good morning, Jenks. Look, I need blood and skin tests on this dog—immediately."

"Oh, Christ, sergeant, we're having coffee, and we have a busy day ahead. Give us a break."

"Guys, we have always been friends. Don't let me down. I need this report yesterday. Understand. Quonsett. You guys know the situation. This report can help us. What do you say? The DA is on the case now," he added.

"Oh, what the hell. Ok, wait outside. We'll do what we can as fast as we can. We'll call you."

Boyd and Singer went out for coffee. When they came back the lab door was opening. "How's that for timing?" The two white coats appeared.

"Sergeant, you are looking for a white male, approximate age twenty to thirty years, blood-type O. The dog died of drowning, but had been shot with a large dosage of Sodium Pentothal."

"The same thing he used on the victims he killed."

When they left the lab and were in the cruiser, Eddie said, "Now what, sergeant?"

"A good question, Eddie, a damn good one. Let's review it." And he pulled the hat down over his face and mumbled, "Know his name, blood type, and that he was bitten by a dog. Could alert all drugstores, outpatient—unlikely." He palmed the hat back. "The only fucking thing we don't know is where to find him—and why—oh, God why—he's killing people all over Quonsett."

Eddie felt Boyd's tension, felt he needed some support —and ear. "We know about his old man. . . ."

"You think he's killing people because his father was

accused of weighting his scales? That's a reason to mutilate four people?"

"Maybe he was more upset about his mother than his father."

"Yeah, well, Patterson won't be fucking anybody for payoffs. But that's not going to stop this weirdo—something tells me he could go on forever. We've got to find him. You know, Eddie, this guy is too smart to show up anywhere we might expect. He's self-contained. Must have his own water, his own food, a real well-stocked van, else something would have shown up."

"Where, though? The vans have to pull off the beaches at eight P.M. Where the hell does he park the thing? Where do you hide a van?"

The scudding clouds were lower in the sky, Eddie noticed. Rain was inevitable. The old Cape Cod cliché "She'll burn through" did not apply today.

"Lousy beach day, sergeant."

The day had a sudden chill and Eddie rolled up the window.

"All our beach days are going to be lousy, Eddie. You'll be able to pick your beach—your own beach—from now on. Patterson would not enjoy the future of this town. But you know, Eddie, he had quite a past. He milked every drop of enjoyment out of this town. The only other place he ever went was Jamaica. Except maybe once." He trailed off.

"Oh, yeah, when was that?" Eddie was studying the road, and his question was off-handed.

"Oh, I don't know. I was thinking about something on the walls of the staircase. He had one hell of a good time growing up. Prep school, college, fraternity shit, crew, then the cushy selectman's job, cutting ribbons, dining with movie stars and stage people from the Quonsett Playhouse—fucking vodka martinis and lobster salad at the

Quonsett Inn. Nice life. Patterson thought cops were just a hunk of meat and bone and he was the guy with the education. He wouldn't have known Thermopylae Pass from Pork Chop Hill. He was a narrow-minded bigot, and that's what happens when you stay rooted in the same place. Don't stay rooted, Eddie. Next summer go West or South, but get out of this town. Promise me that. Your job is safe, for another time. Take a summer off."

"Shit, sergeant, I plan on this job. I can use the money."

"You can use the education, too. Patterson would have been better off if he crossed the bridge once in a while. That's why I was surprised to see that picture of him cutting a ribbon at some forest in Maine. That really surprised the shit out of me. It was like seeing the Abominable Snowman in Miami."

"What picture?"

"On the wall, going upstairs."

"I saw that, when Patterson was showing me the layout. It just shows how right you are, sergeant."

"About what?"

"I'm getting to be such a townie I thought that was the naturewalk of Bryant Acres. Maybe I *should* get out of town for a summer."

"Eddie," he bellowed it, and it almost cracked the windshield.

Eddie bolted up, and as he did he momentarily lost control of the cruiser.

"Eddie, for Christ's sake. Bryant Acres!"

Eddie swerved back into the speed lane. "Holy shit, sergeant. What about it? Shit, don't do something like that."

Boyd appeared not to hear him. "Eddie," he repeated. "Eddie, I've been sending cruisers, unmarked cars, stakeouts, four-wheeled vehicles to every beach within forty square miles. I completely forgot—oh, man, I would kick my own ass if I could get my foot around. I completely forgot about Bryant Acres. How much acreage there, Eddie?"

"Oh, thirty, forty acres. We go there for picnics after Labor Day. Right now it's pretty well dried up. No one goes there in the summer."

"Bullshit! I know one guy who goes there. See, I've never been there. What a dumb shit I am. Anytime I take my sons out, it's always out of town. No busman's holiday for me. It's either the rink in Worwich or deep-sea fishing on the shoals. I have never once gone on a goddamned nature walk. That's where that fucker is hiding that van, Eddie. I'll bet my badge on it. Whip these goddamned horses. Hear me? Whip the fuckers!"

Eleven

The rain beat a heavy tattoo along the sidewalks of Quonsett. It pelted the sand of the town beaches like a barrage of gray bullets. The wind from the offshore islands drove it in a hail, sending sheets of it along the shoreline and up to The Hill. The few tourists remaining in town huddled from the rain in an unconscious—or, in some cases, conscious, attempt for protection from the anonymous caller who might be looking for shelter from this sudden summer squall.

The rain drove along the coastline and intensified as it blew inward. Main Street, already a candidate for HUD, lay in watery loneliness. A few businesses were hopefully lighted for an occasional customer, their owners staring out forlornly at the flooding wake. The sky was low and oppressive, like a great gray-black bottomless container tipped to pour all of its contents on an already beaten town. Quonsett was going down, and there was no life preserver, no Coast Guard rescue ship, and no deus ex machina to scoop and bail the water from the watery grave.

The rain pounded on the decks of the few boats that sat in the gray wet of the harbor. It winged with the gulls over the town beaches and across the highway to the cranberry bogs that lay in puddles: great trenches washing down to the steel drains.

It swirled and slanted against the yellow-slickered fishermen who tied up their trawlers and headed off for the steamy bars to forget the weather and their problems.

It blew across the tennis courts and golf courses and splashed and danced along the fieldstone patios where dancers would usually glide on starry summer evenings.

It whipped against the wide windows of the ferry as it cut through the mist of the harbor past Patterson's. The captain, peering through the rain, never looking to his right, never wanting to remember. The rain was visited upon the town like an Old Testament plague. It was not enough that a killer—a maniac—was loose and on the hunt. But nature, kind, summery, tourist-loving nature, had attacked the town. There was no place to turn.

But where Douglas Peters relaxed in an atmosphere of euphoria the rain was merely a welcomed stage-setting promoting a poetic and melancholic background for periodic dozing and sleepy contemplation.

He had done everything he had set out to do. Ever since the day he found out about his father's suicide and had been able to piece it together—the reason, and those responsible. He had longed for this day. He felt no remorse. He felt only the light butterfly flutter of joy and gaiety around his heart. He lay on the table in the van listening to the rain nailing into the roof. Sometimes it blew a feathery ruffle, other times it banged and thudded. He was naked. He felt the great and uncontrollable desire to run and jump and romp in the rain. He rose up and stepped from the van into the rubbery slick green of the woods.

The van was half buried beneath the trees and thicket that he had covered it with. It was barely discernible. And since no one came this far in, it could only be seen from the sky. He had taken care of that. He did have to rev it up to give it the momentum to carry far into the brush before it stalled. The thought had occurred to him to drive it off a pier, but that was before he decided he was going to stay on in Quonsett for a while and enjoy the fruits of his victory. So why not live in the van under the green quiet and protection of this half-submerged womb. And if things became very hot, he had the cellar, but he did not want to use the cellar unless he had to. It could be too confining. If they discovered him there, he would be like a trapped animal. From the van he could escape. He would need food, but that was all he needed. There were the berries and the water sprouts on the nature walks. He had five dollars, which could get him through three days, and who knows, he might even take a job for the remainder of the summer. Although jobs were scarce, he supposed, with this madman running loose.

His laughter split through the rain as he ran, head up and arms outstretched, along the twisted paths fingering out under the tall pines. The laugh trailed out under the tall pines. The laugh carried along behind him as he swung on low-hanging branches. He came to his pond and dove into the rain-racked waters and explored the sandy bottom. He could not be happier. The swim further exhilarated and cleansed his entire being. He swam to the mossy bank and dragged himself up. He stood, wanting to hump the day and the rain.

A sudden stab of pain reminded him of the dog. The pills were wearing off and the chill of the rain numbed him. When just seconds before he had felt in command, with a wild fury and frenzy for life teasing and urging him to a full tasting of all that was around him, he now felt nauseated. He needed more painkillers. The pain in his ankle was creeping up. It felt as though it had been stitched in leather. The leg was becoming stiff. It happened so quickly that it momentarily frightened him. That the joy of his day could dissipate so fast, that he could not be sure of things—that frightened him.

He wished he had the dog beside him. He would snap its neck. He clamped down hard on his hand because of the hatred that fired him when he thought of the dog and the shooting, burning pain that was increasing now and spreading up his leg. He blinked in an attempt to focus. The trees were weaving in front of him. The pond. He needed the pond, and he thrust headlong in a crashing surface-splitting dive. He plummeted to the cold bottom. The pain clamped on his leg and his stomach heaved to be rid of the ball of poison that was quickly making its way up through his circulatory system. He rocketed to the surface and blew his guts. It was mostly bile and it was hot, so hot it almost burned the roof of his mouth. He flailed toward shore and crawled up the muddy bank. He was feverish. He realized he was in the first stages of infection.

He hoped the dog had not been rabid. But he immediately dismissed that possibility, because if that had been true, he would feel sicker than he did.

He fell and stumbled against trees and scrub pine. Once he tumbled down a short incline only to come up, his body covered with mud and pine needles. When he rose, he was dizzy and disoriented. Panic set in because he could not remember the direction of the van. He thought he was about to faint when he grabbed on to a pine tree. Rain whipped suddenly from the northeast and blew bush and branch about in an undulating rhythm, swaying in a mesmerizing dance. His eyes rolled at the rhythm and climbed up and back into his head. He fell to the ground in a soaking heap, rain attacking his naked body.

The county sheriff, representing the DA's office, and two of his men—one a young, lithe black and the other a forty-ish red-faced Irishman—arrived in rain gear, stomping into the conference room.

The sheriff nodded and Boyd threw a hand up and

motioned them into the group of thirty officers and town officials.

"You all know Sheriff Nate Ingram, I'm sure." He looked out at them. Most of the force was present except for some night men and the few always assigned to The Hill.

"Call it a hunch, an educated guess, but I have every reason to believe our man is hiding out in Bryant Acres."

"But there's nothing there except trees, sergeant."

"That's the point. Our man is not a swinger, he's a killer. He kills, he hides, he kills. No one sees him. No clues. No witnesses. Woods, trees, ponds, bad roads. Where the fuck would you hide? I know goddamned well where I would hide." His face was flushed. He was losing his cool. He was glad Durgin wasn't in on this. Durgin had done the initial work and turned the investigation over to Boyd. Yes, it would have been bad if Durgin saw him losing his cool.

Some of the town officials turned embarrassed glances at Father Gillespie, the police chaplain, who sat in the corner. Boyd looked down at the priest.

"Continue, sergeant, you were about to say something else," Father Gillespie said.

Boyd studied the man for a moment, and then cracked a smile that broadened to a grin.

"Yeah, thanks, Father, I was about to say we have covered every area of this town, and other than a cursory patrol of that area, we have not combed those woods because I was too god—darn stupid to issue that order."

Chief Medina stood in the back of the room. He did not say anything. He was wearing a sport coat and slacks.

Boyd looked his way anticipating a remark, a sharing, and when none came he continued.

"I want to take twelve men into those woods and flush him out. I want no publicity, and I want all roads blocked off after we fan out. I want five of my men and a county sharpshooter on each team. We enter west from the highway and east from the nature walk.

"Jesus Christ, Wayne, you've got fifty men you can draw from, why go in with a handful?" It was Ambrose, the town counsel. He was fat-faced with dark, late-drinking shadows under his baggy eyes. His hangover was intense this morning and his cigarette-holding hand quivered as he bellowed his question. The voice was husky with booze and smoke. He had just returned from a Las Vegas vacation.

"Because I want this guy surprised, and I can control twelve men. Fifty I cannot."

"But if this son of a bitch slips the net, your ass will fry."

"It's my ass, counselor."

"It's your ass, sergeant," Father Gillespie quipped. "If it doesn't fry here, maybe it will in the other place."

It was enough. It broke the tension. It was said almost shyly. But it was said, and it was enough. They roared and pounded the priest on the shoulder.

"Ok, I want four vehicles—three men in a vehicle. It will be a squeeze job, but I want the least amount of notice going uptown and when we get there."

"Eddie, you're my driver, and, Rick, you have the sheriff."

Pierce looked up, then around at the other officers. He shook his head, his face gained color, and he shook his head again. He rubbed his chin, shifted from foot to foot and straightened up. He couldn't believe it. Boyd had brought him back from the boondocks. He was appreciative.

"Ok, check the board. If your name is under Team A, you're with Sheriff Ingram; Team B, you're with me. All relevant parties meet with me in my office in five minutes."

194

Boyd left the platform for a smoke. He wanted to be right. He knew in his heart the guy they were looking for was in the Acres. He wished he knew it in his head.

It was 11:15 A.M. and the day was turning darker and more dismal. Lights blazed in the station and the talk was kept at a minimum. The station had a command-bunker atmosphere. The unknown was out there. What did he look like? What was he carrying other than something to cut with? How desperate was he? How crazy was he? He must be completely insane. No man could dismember human beings with such efficiency and dispatch and still remain sane.

The shifting wind slapped a more deliberate foray of rain against the window that looked out on to Main Street. Eddie peered through the dripping and steamy glass.

"He wants us, Eddie." It was Pierce, and he threw an arm around Eddie's shoulder. "It's been quite a summer, Eddie, quite a summer."

"Summer, Rick? Do you know it's only been six weeks? We still have over three weeks to Labor Day. If we can survive that long."

Boyd had the shades drawn and the office was like a steam room. Some stood, a few sat on the floor propped against the wall, and the rest straddled chairs. The middle-aged red-faced Irishman smoked and passed cigarettes around to those who wanted them.

"Gentlemen," Boyd said as he picked tobacco from his tongue, studied it in his fingers, and flicked it into the basket. "Gentlemen, I do not know what to expect. I have no real ID on this guy except his name and IQ. He is intelligent, very intelligent. He is obviously dangerous. But I'm not sure how dangerous or effective he is in this kind of situation. He's great at killing unsuspecting individuals, but he might be an innocuous and chicken-livered fucker when he knows he is on the defensive. Be ready for anything. Oh, yes, he was bitten by a dog but we don't know if it's serious.

"Now comes the difficult part. I am no different from you. I would like to personally cut this guy's balls off. He beheaded an officer, he amputated a woman's leg, he sliced a woman's two breasts off, and he cut open and castrated your selectman. He will do the same or more to you. Try to take him alive, but do not hesitate to blow his head off if you have to."

"Sergeant, could you be a little less explicit? My office would like this killer alive."

"Why? So the DA can try him, and then run for governor?"

"Hey, Wayne, I—"

"I'm sorry, sheriff, that's not meant for you. You know that. But this will be the biggest news story in the state and a lot of guys are going to ride on it." He looked at each one of them. "The sheriff is right, to a point. Don't be trigger-happy, but don't be assholes either. I want you all back in one piece. Now, draw rain gear and weapons. I want every man carrying his piece along with what I have issued to you. Except the sharpshooters, you guys all set?" The Irishman looked at the young black man. They nodded. The Irishman smiled at Boyd. "The dude and I are ready."

Doug did not know how long he had been lying in the rain. His body was shivering and shaking as he awoke. He was still dazed as he dragged himself up by holding on to the midsection of the bending pine. Once steadied, he veered off to the van. His head was clearer and he remembered the direction. He crashed through the slippery green of the wood until he staggered and crawled beneath the green covering. In the sensual and mystical darkness, he found the handle of the rear door and crawled in out of the weather. His breath came in choking gasps as he fell onto the table. His right hand reached for the sheet on the floor and he weakly wiped the mud and rain from his naked and scratched body. The warmth of the van was sensual. He squirmed in satisfaction as he listened 'to the thumping of the rain on the roof.

He remembered the rain on the wood roof of The Fish Shack when he was a boy. He would leave two, maybe three lines dangling in the spitting calm of the harbor on a gray day and run to help his father with a customer. His father would beam at him and announce to the customer, "This is my son, the fisherman, but that's only for the time being. Some day he's going to be a doctor—a surgeon." The customer would murmur some inanity like, "That's nice, huh, could you skin it please?"

When the Shack was empty of customers and he had caught something and brought it wriggling inside, his father would light a pipe and shake his head with satisfaction while the fish was unhooked and plopped into a basin of salt water. They would sit on those long rainy afternoons buzzing about the future of the business and of school and life. There was never anyone like his father, and when the father died the boy thought his heart would break in half.

He had kept his promise. From the first time he pithed a frog in high school biology, he knew he had the hands to work the knife quickly and deftly. There were moments back then, eight, nine years ago, when he took delight in cutting up animals. One of his instructors mentioned it half jokingly one day by referring to him as the "Mad Doctor." The class laughed and the name stuck. Weeks later, when the instructor realized he had inadvertently pinned a nickname on him, he stopped Doug in the corridor to apologize. Doug accepted it gracefully until the instructor added that it did seem, though, that Doug enjoyed the cutting process more than the others. He quietly

197

told the instructor what he could do to himself. For that extravagance he was suspended for two weeks. He did not care, because by that time his mother was hopelessly insane and his grandmother believed anything he told her.

Yes, he loved his father more than any other human being in the world. His father would have been proud of him in med school. The third year had been academic disaster except for his expertise in the "cutting room," as he had called it. Had his performance been consistent at all, he could have received a scholarship after his money ran out, but the dean and his advisors felt he was not doctor material. It was nothing they could point to. They mentioned, in vague terms, his attitude.

His dream had been to move to Quonsett as an M.D. so he could enjoy a slow revenge and yet become a respected citizen of the town. That, of course, had been ruled out by the fates, and here he was burning with fever in a half-buried van, in the woods of his youth, which at one time in his life was his playground.

He scooped a handful of pills from the bottle and popped them into his mouth. He wished he had some antibiotics. He sucked on an orange for energy and brought his leg up from its dangling position. The leg was hot and throbbing, the dog's teeth marks were still visible, and now it was turning a bluish purple. He wet the sheet from the cooler and applied the sheet to the wound while grabbing for a blanket. He would sleep now. He thought of his father before he fell off. The thought of his father did not bring tears to his eyes. He would never again cry for his father. The rain gusted against the roof.

Four cruisers left within ten minutes of each other, each going in different directions, but each heading for Bryant Acres. Two would terminate at the nature walk and two at the wooded entrance from the highway. They would park a quarter of a mile from the respective entrances. Five men in each team carried pump-action shotguns able to blow a man apart from three hundred yards. The sharp-shooters had range to burn with their thirty-ought-sixes.

Boyd's vehicle was the last to glide out of the garage. Eddie tooled past the football field, came to a deliberate stop, looked both ways, and picked up speed on Main Street.

"Keep it steady, don't call any attention to us, Eddie. Take a left on Beach Street. We'll cruise the shore road and double back by the Old Salt Motel, up behind the hospital, and down the back way through the playground and along the service road. That will bring us just below the nature walk. Get to it, Eddie."

The islands were invisible in the rain. A white specter of a ferry slugged its way through the misty gloom of midday. Boyd thought of what it would be like sitting at the bar of the ferry, piping down a straight bourbon and chasing it with a beer. It would be nice, he thought. He and Kate on their way to the island and a motel room, to good cuisine, and a long, long weekend. Oh, how sweet it was. His hand trailed along the long blue steel of the shotgun barrel that separated him from Eddie. There was more than the gun that separated them. Eddie was doing it for a summer gig. Break the routine of the chalk and the rank book. Playing cops and robbers. Good at it, but playing it. But me, he mused, me chasing people into a rain forest and then getting abused by the town and the press. Must be male menopause, next will be hot flashes and an affair with a high school senior. When that's over, a wood-working course in the high school night program. Then out to pasture. God, but he was depressed.

He caught himself. He was actually feeling sorry for himself. He wanted to laugh. It was always this stream of crazy irrelevancies when he was on to something that was less than pleasant. It always threw the job into three-dimensional perspective on a wide screen.

He could almost sit back and study it objectively. He thought of his sons. This would be one wild and productive day out in the whaler. Well, they would just have to wait with the bait.

"The service road." Eddie broke into his thoughts.

"What? What did you say, Eddie?"

"I said, here's the service road."

"Right." Boyd swung around and spoke to the man sitting behind him.

"You ok, Ben?"

"Raring to go, sergeant."

Ben Anderson had been on the force twenty-five years. He had been at the Chosan Reservoir and force-marched his way with the third marines through half the Chinese army. He had made his mark in Korea. He was not a quitter and everyone in Quonsett knew it. He sat with the shotgun resting almost affectionately in the crook of his arm, smoke billowing out of his hairy nostrils from the Winston king.

"Pull over here, Eddie. We walk the rest of the way," Boyd said.

Five hundred yards up, another cruiser squatted in the shadows of tall pines. The others joined them quietly and they moved up to the bridge and the entrance to the nature walk. Boyd thought of Patterson's ribbon-cutting ceremony.

"Ok, three men at a time. You guys to the left of the bridge; we'll hit the middle and then spread out to the right. Keep the sharpshooter nearer us—to our left side. There are over thirty acres out there and only two exits. The backup will be here in five minutes. If he's in there, he's in there to stay. We are in no hurry. Do you understand? We are in no hurry. Ok, let's move out."

200

The footing was poor and the three from the second cruiser dug their feet into leaves and soil for a solid hold. Boyd watched them crouch off to the left of the bridge as he led Ben and Eddie along the narrow decline to the right of the bridge.

Under the dull red light of the van's rear interior, Douglas Peters, fully clothed, sliced an apple and ate it from the blade. It was the same blade that had severed the breasts of Mary Flannagan. The pills had a tremendous effect on him. He felt a mild high and he decided to take three more. He needed the trip because he hated the idea of the returning pain. He loathed pain and was afraid of it. He swallowed three pills and washed them down with the juice of the apple. He gagged and dislodged the last. He was gaining strength by the minute. His confidence was returning. He decided to go outside to check his cover.

He stood on a grassy knoll looking down into the van. It was almost fully covered. The Niagara Falls scene was barely visible on the panel. He had not had the chance to repaint it, but now that made little difference. He threw more brush and shrub against the side. Casual branches and small uprooted trees served to hide it further. He studied it from several angles. It was good. Unless someone was really looking for it, it would never be found.

The rain continued, but for a moment, when the wind and rain shifted, he caught hold of a sound coming from behind him—from the highway side. He froze and felt terror creep up his back. Branches and twigs snapped at the foot of the next incline. He swiftly made for the van, crawling through the brush, easing the door open and sliding into the van, quietly securing the door. He switched off the light and lay breathless in the dark. His right hand reached into one of the drawers and brought out a .38 chief's special. He rubbed his chin with the two-inch snub-nosed pistol. It had been his father's. He composed himself and smiled, thinking of the poetry of using his father's gun in the final act of his life. He knew they were coming after him. He knew it and it did not matter. He would take as many with him as he could. He put the gun between his legs and continued slicing the apple.

He could not hear anything because of the blowing rain, so he leaned ever so carefully with one eye barely touching the front side window. He felt a sudden thump at his heart as he saw a man in orange rain gear standing on the hill where he himself had just been. The man was cradling a shotgun in his arms. He caught the boots and then the legs of two others. All three were no more than fifty yards away from him. They gestured and talked and finally moved on. The van was well protected. He quietly applauded his craftsmanship and sliced more of the apple. He would have to wait until dark to secure himself in the cellar he had prepared weeks before. If they were out there, he would have to use the cellar.

The pills were urging him and pushing him to a new and giddier high. He peered out again and saw only rain and blowing leaves. He would wait until dark, and maybe then he could gain the hideout he had organized so well. He could feel no pain in the ankle even though it was puffed up with a purple sack, like a barnacle protruding from the side.

He fingered the .38 and placed it by his side. He finished the apple and wrapped an army blanket around himself. He would try to get sleep when he could. He would travel by dark. He would have to chance it. Secretly, back there in the recesses of his skull, he wondered if he really did want to be caught.

The three crept sluggishly along in the sliding mud and grass of the woods until Rick spotted Boyd's short yellow slicker. They were far enough away not to be triggered

202

into an impetuous move, and by the time they came upon each other their guns were pointing skyward.

"Nothing, huh?" Boyd said as they approached.

"No, nothing, sergeant. But there's a lot of woods out there. He could have buried himself in a hole. I read about a Nam vet who buried himself in clay and sucked air through a reed. Not a swamp like the movies, but clay."

"I can believe it," Boyd answered. "If a man is desperate, he'd climb into a nest of snakes."

"Not me," Eddie shivered. "I could never be that desperate."

"You'd be surprised, Eddie. Ok, let's head west and try to cover it. This weather is more of a help to him than it is to us."

"*If* he's here." Ben spit tobacco juice into the mud.

"Yeah, that's right, Ben. If he's here. But you know something, I've played hunches before and some have paid off and some have been bummers. I almost feel this hunch so bad I would stake my job on it."

"You just might be doing that, sergeant."

Boyd looked at Ben and shook his head. He didn't say anything else. He did not have to. They began moving out.

"You three wait here and make secondary contact. Then scatter southeast and southwest and send three more a few degrees north of us. C'mon, let's move it."

Thunder banged and roared and lightning electrified the trees turning everything into a shimmering, nerve-pattern discotheque.

The day slid by in a crude, rude shower of mud and wet branches slapping and stinging them in the face and hands. They traversed ponds and idyllic and romantic bridges, always checking from the ground or underpinnings up.

At 5:00 P.M., Boyd called a halt and ordered everyone back to the nature-walk entrance, where there was steaming coffee and ham and cheese sandwiches.

"Hey, Irish," Boyd called to the plump red-faced man sitting on a tree stump chewing ravenously on the sandwich and chasing it down with the coffee. "I'll bet a double shot of bourbon would warm the ole gut right about now."

"Is that an ethnic joke, sergeant? Don't stereotype me, ok?" His face was solemn. "And besides, I'm a rye man with beer chasers." And the blue eyes sparkled and laughed as he broke up while slapping his fleshy knees.

Nothing turned up, it was always the same. A lone rabbit, swans, burned-out cars, some kids' tree huts, skunks, nothing.

"Ok, you guys, get into those cruisers and dry off. It will be darker soon. Ordinarily, we would have two and a half more hours of daylight, but that sky is going to open up again and we'll be lucky if we can see much of anything in another hour."

"We'll move out again around six thirty. Irish, you, Rick, and Cleary head back to the highway entrance. Just give it one more shot. Check the high ground and then sit in a cruiser and dry off. Get some coffee, some rest, and move out promptly at six thirty, but head back here in a southwesterly direction. That way we won't be covering the same ground. By the time you reach us back here, it will be too dark to continue. If we don't find anything, we'll sack out in the cruiser and begin again at dawn."

Twelve

The intense heat of the van forced him out of a sound sleep. He checked his watch. It was 6:35. He could not believe he had slept all afternoon. His ankle was stiff and his forehead was a sweat band. Pain shot up his leg and panicked him. He wolfed down more pills.

It would be getting dark soon, and he might have a chance of getting through to the cellar if he wanted to. That was a conflict at the moment. Did he want to get away? It would only be a matter of time. Holed up for how long? What was left? He had done just what he wanted to do. He had done what had been on his mind and in his very being for twelve years. All those nights of waking and lying in the stillness of his bedroom, swelling on a revenge that sometimes staggered his imagination. He had accomplished it with such ease and such ecstatic satisfaction. It had been what he had hoped. None of it disappointed him. Except Dean. He would have enjoyed finishing off Dean, but Dean more than compensated for the disgusting things he printed about his father—yes, Dean had outdone himself. He had a lot to thank Dean for.

His soul was washed clean and pure. His purgation was over and his being soared. He popped two more pills and checked the pistol. He buckled his belt. He would die, of course, and that was no big thing. But he would go extravagantly—and there would be people coming with him.

He lay by the window, peering through the cracked and rain-blurred glass, and smiled as he saw the three figures coming across open wood. They turned left for a moment, avoiding the steep incline of the hill. "They must be getting tired." They would call it off for tonight and he could roam the woods feeling the great exhilaration of being the hunted and then find seclusion and safety in the cellar.

He was about to turn from the window when he saw a lone figure coming over the hill. The figure carried a long thin rifle and he had a beefy red face and a rotund middle-aged body. The figure slipped and sloshed his way down the hill and stopped and gazed slowly and deliberately at the sky and the trees and finally at the brush that covered the van. If he came any closer, he would certainly find a unique shape to those trees and brush. The van was hidden, but not to the extent that it would not be detected at close range.

The figure slipped a few more yards down the hill and walked toward the green heaped-up cover. He began pulling trees and branches, grass and hay from the van. The entire panel must be exposed by now, Peters thought, that cop would be blasting that door apart. Fear choked him. The cop would wait. He would never come in. There would be no chance of cutting him. He would have to play at being unconscious or dead. It was all he had to hang on to. He ripped off his shirt and let his trousers fall to his ankles. He grabbed the empty pill bottle and curled up on the floor of the van. He placed a long square hunting knife under his stomach and lay on it with his naked buttocks facing the door.

"Come out of there with your hands over your head."

He breathed rapidly behind the door, waiting for the voice again.

It came. "I said, come out of there with your hands over your head." There was only the sound of the rain hissing into the trees. The Irishman looked to the earth and saw footprints, but they were so obscure and trackless, he could not gain a pattern. He decided the footsteps were leading away from the van. But the rain so obliterated them, it was simply a hunch he was playing. The Irishman reached for the door handle. He turned it and swung the door open and ducked off to the side. The open door slammed against the side of the van and swung back, closing again. The silence remained.

The Irishman reached for the door handle again after several minutes. This time he opened it slowly while standing off to one side. He eased cautiously in front of the door with his finger touching the trigger on his rifle.

His heart felt as though someone had given him a right-hand shot. There in front of him lay the man they were all looking for—lying in a semi-nude heap on the floor, an empty pill bottle in his right hand. He looked like an OD, but the Irishman had been in the business too long to be tricked.

"Get up. Get off the floor, you creep, or I'll blow your head off."

The rain continued like nails on the roof. A tree's branches brushed against the van.

"I'll give you three seconds to get off that floor." The body was motionless. The Irishman looked down at the bottle that was empty, and held limply.

He prodded the form with the rifle barrel. There was no movement. He slowly bent over the body while still holding onto the rifle. He grabbed at the hair in an effort to turn the body over. As the heavy weight of the body began to turn, the knife shot up into the lower abdomen. The Irishman jumped back instinctively, palming his stomach with both hands as the knife drove quickly through his hands and stomach. His intestines spilled out before him and his eyes loomed like quarters at the horror of seeing his insides wiggling and flapping out of the huge hole that had been his belly. His intestines flowed out onto the bare chest of Douglas Peters. There was the odor of a half-exposed feces.

The last thrust drove the Irishman over backward into the rain and mud. His head sank into a puddle as Douglas Peters heard the gurgling and saw the bubbles, and then there was just the rain washing the blood away. Peters scooped water from a flooded rut and washed the blood and flesh from his own chest. He ripped the foul-weather gear from the dead body and put it on. The rain hat was stuffed into the coat pocket. He pulled it down over his head. He knew he had very little time to spare as he climbed to the top of the hill.

Coming toward him were two stooping figures huddled against the blowing rain. He motioned them back. They waved in mute understanding and continued up the trail, barely turning to watch him as he slid back down the hill and returned to the van. He filled a sack with apples and berries, the .38 chief's special, a blanket, two cans of Sterno, a full bottle of pills, and the army blanket. He smiled down at the body of the Irishman and spit on the twisted gray face. He scattered the remnants of the Irishman's wallet to the wind. Family photos of children and wife sank in the mud. He hurried off to the warmth and security of the cellar.

As a boy he had swum and splashed for hours in the pond, alone with his thoughts in a sublime Eden-world. One day when a sudden cloudburst poured into his pond, he had run for cover among the trees. In his haste, he had lost his footing and twisted an ankle. He had crawled to a grove at the top of a hill and lay there until the rain had stopped. Lying under the trees, he let his eyes roam the woods. His view was interrupted by a crumbling stone chimney that must have been the remains of an old house that had burned down years before. He did not investigate that day because of his ankle, but a few days later, while walking in the woods, he discovered a buried cellar. The trap door was gone but the depression was there, and when he scooped away the dirt there was a series of stone steps leading to a circular cellar that must have dated back to Civil War days. This had become his retreat when he was not at The Fish Shack. He spent many hours alone there, dreaming of his future. He had supplied it with a metal cot his father had rescued from the dump and kerosene lamps. It was cool and moist in the bowels of this mysterious hideaway, and the only persons who knew of its existence were his father and he.

He flew to it now. It was ready for just such an emergency because it was one of the first places out of his past that he had checked out when he arrived in Quonsett. The first visit had brought tears to his eyes because he had recalled the day he brought his father to it, making his father swear an oath never to divulge its existence. It had taken some work to reinforce the stone steps to their rightful place and to dig his way into the main cellar, but he had done it while the town reacted and ran from the series of murders.

When he arrived, he immediately picked off the section of sod and the square plywood underneath. He threw his bundle down into the pit and descended the few steps. Then he turned and placed the green rugs of sod on top of the plywood with his right hand and slid the board over the opening. The dark inside world of the cellar was damp, but a solid refuge from the rain. He climbed down the steps and made his way to the lamps, which he lighted with matches that he had left wrapped in tinfoil on top of an orange crate. The light threw shadowy finger patterns on the fieldstone walls of the circular room. He sat on the cot and bit into one of the apples. He had seven apples left, and except for a few berries he had no other food.

* * *

Boyd looked into the badly gaping hole in the Irishman's stomach as the stretcher was carried past him. He lifted the rubber sheet up over the face and cursed into his hands.

"Why did he go it alone? He was too good a cop. He had been around too long to do a thing like that. Him with six kids, and now look at him." He turned to see the stretcher slide into the rear of the ambulance.

"Maybe the van looked harmless," Cleary said.

"Yeah, maybe there should be tits on a bull. C'mon, let's gather round." He barked it more to the ground. But they straggled into a tired and forlorn circle. It had been a long afternoon, and now with the Irishman's body being driven off down the hill, there was the grim reminder that whoever was out there was better in a situation like this one than they had thought. But now, for what it was worth, they knew he *was* out there.

"I've called K-Nine. I should have done it before, but I was afraid those animals would give us away. We've got the van. They can grab all the stink they need from that. This rain won't help, though. Won't help at all. You realize he also has a sniper rifle now! He could be watching us at this minute and pick us off as we stand here. So spread out and no more circle-jerks for meetings. I'll yell to you if I have to. What I want you to do now is rest. I'm going to try it with the dog tonight. We have approximately one hour before dark. After that, we do nothing but wait until morning. Nobody leaves this command post unless I give the ok. Work out your own watch, and when you're not on, go to a cruiser and sleep. Anybody who doesn't, gets an immediate suspension—two weeks without pay, and don't give me any Police Association bullshit." He was half joking because he was adamantly anti-union, but he did want to clear the air and he goddamned well wanted them to rest.

He paced while waiting for the dog, and when the K-9

truck arrived he merely motioned to Ben to escort the dog and handler to the van. He did not want to see that vehicle again. He would not be satisfied until it burned to a crisp in the town incinerator. That, of course would be after twenty-eight assistant DA's got their jollies by climbing through it and reenacting all of the atrocities by jotting down theories in that illegible script on the long yellow lawyer-bullshit flypaper. Briefs for the court. "I got your briefs," he shivered. No, it would be a long time before the van could be destroyed. It was Exhibit A. It would be like destroying Dachau before the Nuremberg Trials.

"What's that, Wayne?"

"Oh, nothing, Nate. I was just thinking of all the half-assed lawyer types who will be playing parlor games over this one. I didn't even hear you come up. Shows how screwed up I am."

"Wayne, I know you feel something—responsibility or guilt or something about the Irishman. He was my man. I've known—" He caught himself. "I knew him for fifteen years. He has a great family and they will never get over this and that's the part I hate most. Seeing them. But don't let it get under your skin. You know he had a job and he did it. Too well, maybe. I knew everything about that Irishman, and if he could speak now he would say, 'I'll be a son of a bitch, but every time I'm sober I do the damndest things.'"

"Tell me, Nate, what was the Irishman's name? I never found out."

"Jack, Jack Callahan." The sheriff's voice was steady and regular; a dull monotone of anger, slowly climbed up from somewhere deep down inside him. He said nothing else. He banged a thick knuckled fist into the open palm of his hand as he walked away into the shadows of the dripping trees.

The dog and the handler came back up the hill. The dog

stood shaking the rain from his satin coat. "He gave me a pull to the east of that hill, sergeant," the young handler said as Boyd petted the dog.

"Ok, we have a half hour. Let's just move out a little way to get the feel of things. Your job will come at daybreak."

The dog did not hold back. He pulled and strained and sniffed, and his route seemed direct and organized until they reached the pocketsized pool that appeared out of nowhere. The dog seemed frustrated and he changed directions, then came back to the original route. Once, he lunged at a fallen tree and the handler had to pull him back.

"Why did he do that?" Boyd wanted to know.

"He's highly trained, you might say on the verge of being overtrained. He is highly sensitive and emotional and his frustration level is sometimes reached very quickly. With the rain and all, his tolerance is low. But he's good, sergeant, probably the best we have."

The dog's frustration peaked again and he began yelping. The yelping and whining cut through the cellar room, where Douglas Peters sat in the glimmer of one kerosene lamp. He jumped to his feet and blew out the lamp. Very cautiously and quietly he climbed the stone steps. Lifting the plywood ever so slightly, he heard the yelping again.

The rifle lay right alongside the stairs and he reached for it. When he looked back, he could see the orange figures in the gathering dusk. He raised the rifle and slipped it under the plywood, careful not to disturb the sod. He squinted through the sight and framed a perfect picture. He saw the cop first. Then the dog and the handler. Who should he take first? He rested the rifle on the level earth and tried to think. The pills and the chase and the rain were getting to him. Gnawing at him. He felt tired again. Fatigue washed over him.

"It's getting dark, they don't know where I am, they won't chance it at night. Screw it, why should I give in? I can get out of here. If I'm not caught this town will never recover." The rationalization took over. Everything was cool. "Every tourist will think I'm under the bed." He wanted to scream out laughing, but he contained himself and pulled the rifle back in and set the plywood straight. He would break out when it became dark enough. He was not going to sit while they came for him. He would wait for dark and move.

Instead of the wind and rain letting up, it became almost gale force and it blew through the woods with such intensity that he heard trees cracking and breaking in half above him. When he climbed out of the cellar, he could smell the fresh bark of the trees that had snapped in two. The night had the balmy, after-a-hurricane smell and taste to it. He replaced the sod and headed into the biting, squalling rain. He was soaring and his ankle was like new, although pus and blood soaked the cloth that stuck to the festering sore. He could only get out two exits. Behind him led to the highway, if he eventually made it. Ahead of him was the road he used for access with the van, and the nature walk was south of it. He would strike out for the nature walk.

He carried the rifle at port arms, not so much because he was knowledgeable but because it was comfortable that way. His walk was somewhat erratic from the high he was experiencing and he stopped to gain composure. In the wind's infrequent lulls, he heard the whining of the dog, and it struck him that the dog was his most potent enemy. He must destroy the dog before it hunted and hounded him out. But he found it increasingly more difficult to maneuver. His mind was in turmoil. He would have to return to the cellar, and that would mean another full day

213

before he could chance it. His thoughts danced and his balance left him several times as he fell into trees, holding on until some kind of composure returned.

By the time he reached the cellar, he was doubled up and his vision was blurred. He covered himself with the blanket and sank into a dead sleep.

Thirteen

Ben Moffit sat with a Bloody Mary cupped in his pudgy hand. "You know, I can get these kids to tell me anything. Imagine, a fullscale police operation in effect and only the cops know about it. The cops and now *me*." He chuckled.

"That kid must be some summer cop. One of Quonsett's finest," Kalmir said, sitting back in the captain's chair.

"Oh, he's ok. He directs his traffic, gets his poon tang, and every once in a while he lets me in on something. I give him a room for the summer. But when he told me they had that maniac treed up there in the woods, I could have shit, because I was the only one who knew it. And I started figuring how we could use it." He did not look directly into the almond eyes of Gregory Kalmir when he suggested it. "The cops have him surrounded. It could be a good number for us. We get the kids involved. They do their police-work shit. They feel good. You know, down-deep good about it. He laughed in a kind of squeak while he shook more Tabasco sauce into the Bloody Mary.

"How is it good for us?" Kalmir probed with the almond eyes.

"Look, we are the only two guys on The Hill who really make money or lose it. The other joints are happy to break even. Right now, for Chrise sake, we're losing it. All the tough-guy college types are leaving this place. This town has a reputation it may never lose. I got money—big money—tied up in this berg, and, Jesus, you must have a fortune plugged into Freddie's.

"Ok, ok, you've made your point. This bastard has hurt us, I admit."

"Yeah, but we turn it around. I can get fifty or a hundred kids to jump in their vans and storm those woods, help the cops, you know—citizen-arrest shit." He finished the last of the drink and sucked on small slivers of ice.

"How will the cops take to it. You remember what Medina said at the town meeting."

"All that vigilante bullshit was before. Things were calm then compared to the way they are now, what with that chick hanging from Patterson's. And Patterson—Jesus—what happened to Patterson. His wife is a basket case, I hear. The papers will talk about the young people and how they pitched in, kind of thing. Where did they come from? Most of them are employed by Gregory Kalmir and are summer residents of Ben Moffit's Loft. Are you shittin me? We'll be cult heroes. The youth." And he squeaked off a laugh. "The fucking youth, what assholes. *The Quonsett Log* will eat it up. What d'ya say?"

"I like it. Do it."

In less than an hour a convoy of vans and cars was headed up Main Street. The children's crusade was on. Beer cans were drained. Grass was sucked, and horns shrieked as Ben Moffit and Gregory Kalmir saluted the swinging circus from the steps of Freddie's. A blue ocean curled jettyward behind them, with a hint of sun lingering momentarily in the flushed sky.

Main Street to Bryant Acres was 3.8 miles, and before one mile was covered, cars and vans began jamming up.

The few residents who still came downtown stood in terror as the finger-gesturing vigilantes swilled down beer and relieved themselves indiscriminately on the vehicle-glutted streets.

One environmentalist urinated into a beer can and

hurled it through the skin-back top of a Volks convertible.

Then the jam was broken and the convoy continued past the village green and the gull-spotted statue of the Unknown Soldier and on up to Bryant Acres.

Wayne Boyd was waiting for them. He stood squarely and resolutely on the gravel parking lot next to the nature walk. His cheekbones moved in and out. He had heard them. He had been told over the CB that they were coming and his own men had delivered the word.

When the first van arrived, he walked over to the driver's side and softly said, "Thank you for coming, but everything is cool."

"Hey, man, we ah heah, to help the po-leece."

Boyd reached in and grabbed the driver's tank shirt. "Listen, fucker, move and move now, and tell that to the rest of your Boy Scouts."

The driver pulled back in the seat and with his thumb pointed out the convoy. "You tell the Boy Scouts, policeman!"

But the vans were already descending on the parking lot. The scene was hairy and Boyd knew it better than anyone. He called to the other officers to come in from their team search, and when they arrived they found him surrounded by a mob turned wild.

A group was stalking him to the chants of "Kill the pig. Kill the pig." He stood his ground firmly, reluctant to pull the magnum from the holster. Two muscular whites held tire irons, as a black flanked him with chains wrapped around his large hands.

"I don't want anyone hurt here. Now just move out slowly and quietly. You are interfering with police work."

"Police work? Your police work is dumping drunks and stoned-out dudes out of bed. We came to help the cops, man. What do you guys say?" And the kid swung the chains around his head lariat fashion and faced the mob.

"Yeah," a big, blond yelled over the mob. "He was the big man who broke up the Fourth of July party. You don't look so cool now, pig."

Boyd felt the hand go stiff. He was trying to keep his temper. Don't pull that gun, he kept thinking. Keep that gun in the holster. He remembered the FBI school. Durgin's words came back to him. He was not going to blow his Indian cool.

"Look, sergeant, we wanna help. Give us a break. Let us help you out." The voice was sincere. The kid, about eighteen, a bosomy brunette in tight Levi's and tank shirt, broke out of the pack. "We just wanna catch him. For Christ's sake, don't you believe us? Shit." And she sat squatting on the still muddy ground, crying. "Oh, shit. It's all going wrong. We just want to help."

She was sincere. He knew it. And she was scared. Her face said that. The tears, the pinched eyes. Yeah, her face said it all. She was not psyched for the chase, but the rest were. They wanted it. They would not be denied. They all were. They had the fever of the hurt in them. They smelled the psycho. He was out there in those woods and they wanted a piece of him. They wanted all of him. They edged closer. A great ring of sweating bodies began to circle him. He had never been faced with a situation like this before. Korea, he had been in charge. Then he could have blasted any fucker who moved. Even that night on The Hill, the mob had expected him to be the take-charge guy because that was the game. Let the pig take over and then fuck the pig.

But this. They were too hyper for him to bullshit. And he did not have enough police people to hold them off.

They began a weaving snake dance. Their shouts were taunts.

"We want him."

"We want the butcher."

218

"We want the psycho."

"We want him now."

"We want that prick."

"Give him to us."

They shrieked it, bending their bodies in a primitive dance.

The circle was becoming smaller. He felt the hand going for the piece. He did not think he could control it. He rubbed his hand along the blue stripe of the uniform.

Then the girl got to her feet again. "Look, sergeant, we just want to help out."

"I understand what you want to do and I appreciate it. But I can't let you go in there."

"Hey, she was one of ours. You know what I mean? She was just like us. A kid. Jesus." She brushed her hair back. "Jesus." And she turned to the crowd. She was pleading now and her eyes had that dancing flash of fear in them. He had seen that kind of fear before. Too many times.

His hand was free of the piece. Eddie and Rick rushed through the ring and joined him in the circle.

The three exchanged glances. Boyd, with hands outstretched, reasoned with the mob as it moved closer. Eddie and Rick, knowing better, kept silent. He was the man. He could handle it.

"I can't let you go in there." The circle had almost enveloped them as more officers arrived.

The cool was leaving him. Boyd knew it. He could feel it.

"Now you listen to me. Move back. Stop crowding us. See those men. They're part of a search team. And instead of searching, they're here because you won't let us do police work. Now get back."

"We want to help."

"We want to help."

The chorus began again. The circle was smaller now and

the pushing and shoving began. Boyd felt the impact of bodies banging into him.

He whipped the piece free of the holster and backed up. He held it in two hands, steady. Police-fashion. He pointed it directly into the mob.

"You put one bullet into anyone in this crowd and you are finished, policeman." It was Ben Moffit and he pushed his way through the crowd. His bulky body waddled as he stepped into the circle.

"You're responsible for this, Moffit." Boyd kept the pistol leveled at the mob.

"These kids are trying to bring some law and order to this town. You better put that thing away before somebody gets hurt." Moffit knew he had the mob, and he played them by making a circle motion with his hands.

The silence mounted. It seemed to rise up from the gravel and sweep up into the trees. A sea gull hung overhead.

Boyd put the pistol back into the holster and as he did the mob broke through and roared, thrashing and screaming like mad wounded animals. Their bulk was too much to handle as they toppled Boyd into the dirt and charged off.

Eddie and Rick and three other cops helped him up as they watched them go.

"There's no stopping them, sergeant. I just hope nobody is killed," Rick said.

"Let's hope no one is, do you hear me, Moffit? Let's hope no one is, because if anyone is, I'll see you behind bars. I'll haunt you."

Moffit was hoisting his fat body into the jeep when he turned, "You just take care of the town, policeman. That's what we pay you to do."

They watched the jeep disappear down the road and then Boyd called for as much backup as he could get.

* * *

Douglas Peters woke quickly. The shrieking and yelling bolted him upright. He grabbed for the light and blew it out, then he carefully picked his way through the dark and pulled himself up the stone steps. He peered through a slight crack between plywood and earth. What he saw brought horror to him. He froze in the darkness. The woods were jammed with yelling, wild-eyed kids throwing each other into the brush, pushing and shoving each other into *his* pond. His breath came in short gasps. He could only figure one thing: They were coming after him.

Suddenly, a thought, starting slowly in the back of his head, began taking on tremendous possibilities. He was a kid like them. If he could get out and join them, he could get lost in the crowd. He could be free. He could actually be free. He reached under the cot for the hunting knife and left everything else behind except the .38 caliber pistol that he tucked under his belt. He was careful to let the shirt hang outside the Levi's.

He crawled back up the steps and waited for his moment. Groups were fanning out below and to the left. His heart raced and pounded. He knew he would have to join a group quickly. He could not be a straggler. He needed numbers. He watched closely. Some headed for the pond as others descended.

He pushed up the plywood and pulled himself free of the hole. He made his way to the pond and the bridge. As he groped his way through the brush, his hand, in reaching out, touched something. A lean young man stood holding the girl who had pleaded with Wayne. The girl was terrified. The kid tried to comfort her. "Look, I'll take you back," he was saying.

"No, I want to help, too," she sobbed.

As Peters came through the brush and touched her, the three of them seemed unaware at first, as though they were frozen in time and space.

Then the tension and surprise eased off. "Hey, man, do

I know you?" The tall, lean kid looked down at the infested ankle and shook his head trying to remember something. Peters eyes, wild for freedom, flashed at the two of them. "Hey man, don't get excited. What the fuck is up? You look out of it, man. Easy," the lean one said.

Peters dove at the lean kid and pounded the knife into the heart like a fist. The body fell to the ground and Peters mounted him, trip-hammering the blade. He rolled off and caught the girl as she mutely and vainly tried to grope her way through the brush. He cut her four times in the back before he let her slip to the ground. He hurled the knife into the deep brush.

The yells of an approaching group drove him to new hysteria. He ran out of the shadows of the trees and yelled at the group.

"Hey, over here. I think I found something." And they turned in his direction. He trotted over to them even though his leg was beginning the stinging throb.

"Yeah, whataya got."

"Follow me."

"Hey, take it easy, dude, you seen him? You find him? Where? Shit, slow down."

He knew he was shaking, but strangely it was working for him. They reached out to comfort him. "Here, man, take a hit." And the big blond guy handed him the joint and he sucked it in. Its effect was almost immediate. His chest expanded and he looked up and cracked a smile and passed it back. The group nodded at one another, smiling, then nodded at him.

"Now, take us to the trouble, mother." The blond threw a tanned, hairy arm over Douglas Peters's shoulders.

"Over here, I found something." And he brought them to the old ruin. "Under there." He pointed to the plywood. They stepped back furtively. "Is there somebody down there, man?"

222

"No." And he moved the plywood over, exposing the stone steps.

"How do you know that?"

"Because I checked it out." He sat down on the dirt and they circled him. There was a grim silence except for the faraway shouts of other groups. They knew. They had him. He waited until the last minute before pulling the pistol out.

"You are some dude; you mean you just went down into that hole and checked it out." It was the blond guy again and he was squatting campfire-style beside him.

"Yeah," he stammered.

"What was down there?"

"A rifle, a rack, couple other things. Go check, he's long gone."

The black guy, still holding the chains wrapped around his hands, pushed the others out of the way. He dropped the chains and backed down the stone steps. Sweat broke across his forehead in large drops as he disappeared. His muffled voice verified the report.

"He's right, man, there's a fuckin rifle down here longer than my joint."

"Goddamn it, bring it up."

He climbed back up, rifle first, and the group shrieked and whistled.

"Good, man. Let's get out of here and find him. We'll blow his balls off." And now, as the sniffing, hungry pack unleashed, they tore through the woods. Douglas Peters hung back just on the edge of that frenzied pack.

He had seen a face in that group. A face that he vowed he would not forget. It was Liz Thorne, and the doubts crowded in on him. Had she ever gotten a good look at him while he was picking Mary up at the restaurant? Had she ever parted the curtains and peered out in curiosity, wondering who this Douglas Peters was?

223

He kept his eyes on her round fleshy body as she held on to the shirt of the black dude with the chains. Shouting continued from other sections. It was a high for them. A first. A real hit and they were sucking it in. Liz Thorne looked back at him and his eyes met hers squarely. Nothing. No recognition. They continued. Two guys from another group joined them from the rear. He was hemmed in now. He would never get out of this pack if they caught on. They approached a clearing. The black seemed to be in charge as he raised the chains and signaled them to stop. He continued in a half crouch to his left as a low moaning sound rose slowly and continuously into a grating shriek. The rest of the group stood frozen in silhouetted horror as Liz Thorne's piercing scream rang through the wet, drooping woods. She pointed with a trembling finger. Below the grassy knoll where they stood like mannequins were the bloody bodies of the girl and the man.

"Call the police," somebody yelled. The storm of fear broke. "Call the police. Call the police." And the pack drew closer to one another. Some began holding hands, then others, until ultimately the mob that moments before had run in the woods now huddled like animals in a rain forest crying out, "Police, police, police. Help us. Save us."

Boyd and Eddie and five other officers found them that way. A daisy chain of sobbing, frightened children. Boyd gently guided the first few along the path leading back to the nature walk. The rest followed in a mute procession. The black dropped the chains by Boyd's feet as he climbed into a van. The slouching shoulders of the quiet crusaders gave evidence of shock as bodies ducked into vans or stumbled into cars and jeeps.

Boyd watched them go down the hill as the ambulance passed them on the way up.

Fourteen

The interior of the van was dark and silent. Douglas Peters sat on the brown shag rug, propping himself against the van's walls. Two guys sat up front and three others and a girl shared the floor with him. They passed joints. Except for the throbbing in his ankle, he felt his body expanding with joy. He had done it. He had pulled it off just the way he had planned it. The silence of the van told him what he already knew. They were in terror, and if they were—the stoned-out, freaked-out Hill mob—then what about the straights—the residents? Quonsett would have cactus brush blowing down Main Street. It will be Ghost Town, U.S.A.—the Tombstone City of the East. He suppressed a laugh by coughing. He had done it. But he had to restrain himself until he could be on his own. He looked at the others, but they paid him no attention as they stared off into nowhere.

The van crept slowly along Main Street, headlights burning in funeral fashion as the depressed convoy picked its way along the deserted streets. It was midafternoon in August in a New England tourist town and there were no tourists to greet the procession. There were no other cars. Businesses were closed. Signs hung from shops and restaurants. Closed for the Season. The season had come earlier than expected. The libraries and the parks were lifeless and The Hill was an open cemetery vault. The bodies were gone.

The driver braked the van halfway up The Hill and spoke softly.

"Well, anybody want to get out here." The girl, oblivious to faces, absently passed cookies around. Douglas Peters took some, then passed them back to her. "Keep them," she said. "I lost my appetite back there."

"Thanks for the lift," Douglas Peters said solemnly and he climbed out of the van and stared after it as it gained the hill.

This was absolutely insane. His insides wanted to explode. Before, he had accepted the fact that he would die. They would gun him down or surround him and he would have had to kill himself. That had been all right with him. He had conditioned himself to that pattern. Because under no circumstances would he have allowed himself to be taken alive.

But now he was free, and The Hill and the town had the same common denominator for once. The Hill and the town were as one. They were becoming deserted. The traffic was all going one way. To the bridge. And he had done it. He, Douglas Peters. He could go to his father's grave now and look down at that grassy plot and he would not cry. He would exhalt. He was as free as the tides, the waves, and the freewheeling gulls.

The beach summoned him. The sea smell pinched at his nostrils as he trotted over the dunes that were golden mounds. He looked up at the deserted front porch of The Loft from his place on the beach. One rocking chair moved slowly back and forth in the wind, with no one in it.

He did a kind of impromptu dance, trailing his foot in the sand that was wet and gray near the tide line. The pain was in the leg, as well as the ankle, but he felt too free to allow it to bother him. "So free," he cupped his hands to the ocean that rounded in on heavy surf. The caps of the waves were unusually white and the sun after the rain of

226

the past days glittered off the breaking curl.

He rolled up the Levi's and let the water lick the pus from his ankle. The beach was empty except for the gulls, who hung like white globes from the sky. The beach was his and the town was his.

The islands stretched out before him. Maybe he would grab a ride over to the islands and lay low for a while—recuperate and then get a job. He enjoyed the prospect of standing on one of the island's wharves and looking over at the town he had personally destroyed.

The vans were moving out above him, loaded with kids and belongings. It was full retreat, and the battlefield was his. Maybe he would stay *here* and get a job. He could have any job in town. He could have any name he wanted. He stretched back on the sand. The afternoon sun broke through the clouds and warmed his face. The gulls were lazy in their flight. The whole town would be lazy. He thought of his father and mother and the pride of revenge swelled him. He pulled some cookies from his pocket and he nibbled on them, although he had no real hunger. His real hunger was satiated.

A herring gull glided overhead and circled in a laconic arc several feet above him. It hovered for a moment and then fluttered to the wet sand. Its webbed and veined feet scratched archaic writing on the sand; a long smooth white hood lifted and turned in and out, the yellow beak seemed to peck at the salt air.

"Well, just the two of us, and I'm just as free as you are, old bird."

The gull strutted to him leaving more writing in the sand.

Douglas Peters reached out and offered the cookie to the approaching gull. The gull pecked at it and tossed the crumbs back down into its throat. The white hood roamed the sky and lurched forward for more of the crumbs.

"You liked that, didn't you, old friend? Ole Jonathan Fucking Seagull." The gull pecked at the outstretched crumbs, but this time did not toss them back. Instead, the hood came back to the hand, but the crumbs were gone. "Easy, I'll get you more." And he fed the insistent gull until he had only one cookie left.

"That's it, ole gull, man, I need this one for myself." The bird's hunger had sparked his own, and he placed the cookie in his mouth. The old eyes of the gull, like buttons pinned to the face, studied him. The beak flashed out, and pecked at his lips as he chewed the cookie.

"Hey, what the!—!" He screamed out in pain. Blood dripped from his lip.

"You son of a bitch." He scooped wet sand and threw it at the darting hood.

The gull's quick response was an immediate lifting of the wings out of the supporting feathers. The neck stretched and the head pointed downward. It thrust forward, pecking at the hand, and flew above the flailing arms and alighted on the man's chest delivering a series of wing blows. Douglas Peters rolled along the sand, covering his head with his elbows extended over the ears. The gull backed off, readying itself for flight by flattening its plumage and raising its wings while bending in its heel joints. Then the white-gray body stretched itself with the great grace and intensity for flight.

It was in the air hovering once again above him as he slowly took his hands from his head.

"Get out of here. Get out, you son of a bitch." He struggled to his feet and tried to run from the bird. It rose higher in the air and then veered off. He spit out the blood that dripped from his lips. The fear, the absolute horror, of having the thing peck at his lips repulsed him. He looked skyward while wiping the blood away with the back of his hand. The blood kept coming. Each time he brought the hand away it was smeared. He ripped off his tank shirt and shoved it to the mouth. "What is this? What's happening?" he stuttered to the red stains that ran across the shirt, making the Adidas partially indecipherable. He went to the shoreline to wet the shirt. He leaned into the water. The sun seemed to disappear as a great, black shadow fell across the water below him. A chill came over him. A sound. At first, barely audible; a *keew, kleew,* rose somewhere behind him, gaining in its sharp, eerie echo along the beach, mounting in sharpness. He straightened up and turned to a presence he felt. Six feet above him, hundreds of gulls hovered, wings touching, eyes splitting him in half.

"Oh, Jesus, no." The afternoon shadowed into blackness as they just hung there. The belly warbling, hoarse rhythmic *ha ha ha ha ha ha,* the urgent call to alarm drove them in one flapping group, smashing against his body, crashing and pounding into him, their vein-streaked legs, one extended lower than the other, banged into him, until he found himself backing into the sea. He screamed wildly as he tried to gain enough surf to submerge. As he plunged face downward, his shaking, bloodied hand reached for the .38 in his belt. The great shadow, like the color of doom, inked out the blue-green surf. He stared at the blackness below him. But he had to go up or drown. He had no breath. His chest exploded as he came to the surface, firing. Gulls bumped and cracked into one another. One fell bleeding beside him. The water was awash with his blood and the bird's. He dove back into the waves and stroked with his battered hands. The water was colder, therefore deeper, he thought. The attack had exhausted him. All breath control was gone now. He sucked in water and broke the surface for air. Still they came. Now pushing his body below the surf with the weight of *their* bodies. He rose up and was forced down, down, down, until the swirling arc of bubbles disappeared and the gulls circled once and then pointed off to the islands. The only sound now over the still waters was the mewing, plaintive sound of the brooding birds.

Wayne Boyd had seen it from the boardwalk that curved around The Hill overlooking the beach. The shots had brought him from the cruiser. As soon as he saw the figure on the beach, he knew it was Douglas Peters.

He had lifted the magnum from his holster and then he had shoved it back into the leather.

He watched the birds turn into black specks in the distance.

"When there's no tourists, there's no food. Nature has a way." And he jumped back into the cruiser and banged a right to Ben Moffit's Loft.